Renee

Jessica Eise

Paperback Edition March 22, 2018
ISBN 1537730479
© Jessica Eise. All rights reserved.

Dedicated to Laura

Renee

I wander into the kitchen and lift the tap. Indiana water gushes into my glass. It tastes terrible, but I drink it anyway.

An unusual sluggishness weighs on me. The move out here hasn't gone well. The initial job offer dazzled me, and why wouldn't it? The financial package and research program were unparalleled.

But they blinded me to other realities. Realities like work culture. And as I've discovered over the past two months, there's a reason they put together such enticing job offers to reel in talent.

But I accepted the offer. It's too late to go back.

The chime of my cell phone interrupts the dark thoughts flooding my mind. I walk across the chipped hardwood floor of my living room to the bedroom. My phone glows on the nightstand. Kathy's name blinks.

"Hey, what are you doing up? It's early in San Francisco," I say in lieu of hello.

"Morning, Renee." She is terse and annoyed. I walk back out of the bedroom and settle on a stool in the kitchen.

"What's going on? I was trying to talk myself into a run," I add.

"I woke up early to go to boxing class, that's what. They cancelled without letting anyone know. God forbid they use the incredibly futuristic technology of email to let us know. I traipsed all the way down to the gym at the crack of dawn for nothing."

I chuckle. My sister is hilarious when irritated. "That sucks. Get a coffee or something. You'll feel better."

She sighs dramatically before cutting me off. "Gotta go. Mom's on the other line. Their trip is imminent and we have to plan."

"Yeah, okay. Bye, Kathy. Tell mom I love her." The line clicks and loneliness wrenches my gut. The call was a bitter reminder of just how far away I am.

Mustering what little motivation I can find, I flop on the floor and tug on my running shoes. Every step feels like wading through mud but I walk down the stoop to the sidewalk and start jogging slowly. Stiff and sluggish, my legs stubbornly plow down the street toward the trail I discovered a couple weeks ago. The wind is cold and gusts up my sweatshirt. I jerk my leggings up and stuff the hem of my sweatshirt into the waistband.

A passing semi honks while I'm running under the bridge. The enclosed structure magnifies the sound and I jerk in surprise. Throwing a death glare as he blasts past, my nerves slowly calm and I continue toward the trailhead. The black, tarred trail winds off into the woods. Admiring the leaves, I almost step on a dead mouse. What is up with this run?

I make my way down the trail. The forest on my right gives way to harvested cornfields. Bent, old stalks from the summer's crop are all that remain. The trail continues to weave alongside the field for as far as the eye can see. Forest on the left, cornfield on the right. Dead grasshoppers line the side the pavement, reminding me unpleasantly of mowing the lawn as a kid in Minnesota, when biblical-style plagues of those nasty buggers leapt at me to escape the blades of my mower.

I run on. But something draws my attention from the periphery. What is that? I squint for a moment, straining to see. It almost looks like one of the trees sort of… melted? The leaves, so crisp and defined a moment ago, are now muddled together.

Something is up with my contacts. I blink hard but it doesn't help. The air is even more blurred than before. Momentum propels me forward as I raise a hand to rub at my eyes. Did one of my contacts fall out?

A strange feeling settles in my gut, like nerves or something. How can that be? And what is up with my eyes? Everything in my line of sight is now undulating and blurring. The trail, the trees and cornfield. They are masked in a deep haze. Dumbfounded, I slow to a walk. The air, so crisp and cool just moments ago, has warmed. It's like stepping off a plane into a muggy jungle. My stomach turns a little with unease as a bead of sweat rolls down my neck. Involuntarily, my hand raises to my forehead and, when I pull it away, it glistens with sweat from my brow.

Real fear stabs at me. Explanations flash through my mind. I didn't eat enough for breakfast so maybe I'm going to pass out. Or is it a panic attack? Could it be a seizure? They don't run in my family. Does that matter? My heart pounds against my ribcage, beating hard like it's trying to escape my chest.

The air shifts and moves around me. For the first time, I regret leaving my cell at home when I run. I've never called 911 before, but I wish I could now. Although what would I say? The air is moving? I'm hot and sweaty? They'd laugh and tell me to lay off the weed.

Yet this feels so real. I have the strangest sensation I've walked into something.

Panic is bubbling within me now. It's chasing away all rational thoughts. Frantic, I try to turn my head to survey my surroundings again but I can't. My entire body is stuck in quicksand. My arms, legs and neck are frozen. They won't move or obey my commands.

Discomfort quickly morphs into pain. The heat ratchets up. My skin feels like it's on fire. Sweat blinds me and salty water stings my eyes. Fever pains wrack my bones.

I've never been so afraid in my life.

My eyes throb and the world darkens to nothing. The heat is

unbearable. I open my mouth to cry out and air seers my lungs. Unbidden, my legs give out beneath me.

I can't breathe. A thousand needles stab me. My spine twists and contorts as pain devastates my world. Total darkness consumes me while I'm torn apart.

A stab of sadness pierces the pain. I'm dying. I want to fight, but have no strength. Darkness sweeps my mind, extinguishing thought and consciousness.

Log Entry: R 247 O 3037 ID: Cont 2 YunJon

Kar acquired this log chip for me while visiting Continent 6 on a research mission. He gave it to me as a gift. He swore it is secure and double-checked himself.

The software in the chip cloaks its presence on the logbook system. It sets up a firewall to mask the activity, preventing central control records from triggering a scan.

It is an illicit item. If it were discovered, I would be sanctioned. Yet I did not report Kar for acquiring illicit goods, even though it is my responsibility as his commanding officer. What is more, I kept it.

Now, I am using it.

It is a foolish risk, yet I feel I must. These events may alter history. Do I not have an obligation as a scientist to record what is happening? Is observation not one of our most sacred duties?

While we have not yet revealed her presence to anyone outside of our unit, we will. We will have to. When that times comes, perhaps I can redact these notes.

But in the meantime, I will keep everything in the black until we have a better understanding of what is happening. The chip shall remain securely fastened in my wristband at all times. We have reason to be cautious.

It is difficult to focus as my epinephrine and cortisol levels are high. I tested them earlier. The alarm sounded before I could rip the sensor off my wrist. I was able to deactivate it before it registered in the central database.

Even now though, my hands shake and my heart-rate exceeds 70 beats per minute, which is far above average. Yet I also refrained from entering these anomalous health stats into the station's database. I cannot afford to be put on med alert. Not now and not under these circumstances.

What has happened today is remarkable. It is nigh on inconceivable.

Our project worked. Time Window Project was a success. And we may be able keep her alive through the night!

While the results were unintended, they are no less a scientific wonder. We meant to look back in time. Instead, we succeeded in carrying a living creature across time. We managed to exceed our very own expectations, and the implications of are mind boggling.

We activated the machine at 13:00 hours. Elation rippled through the room as we watched it start to function. The elation soon turned to shock as we realized we were not just seeing something through the window, something was materializing on the platform itself.

First came the smell of burnt flesh. Then there was a sticky smack as the body struck the platform. It appeared as a pulpy mess of exposed muscle and charred flesh. We could not identify what it was at first.

Kar lunged forward, disabling the machine with the emergency power-off even as I shouted at him to do so. A mere assistant, a young female, leaped forward toward the platform. She pulled a medical scanner off her belt as she ran. Her motion was a catalyst, sparking us into action and Kar and I rushed after her. She was already scanning for biometrics and brain activity when we reached her.

The scanner beeped twice, indicating life.

"It's alive!" yelled the slight female assistant, turning to stare up at me with shockingly golden eyes.

"Get the tank," I called out to my team. "Fill it with R fluid!"

We hovered around the platform. The body's features were indistinguishable due to the severe burns. But we could see that the frame was small, like a large child. We struggled to breathe from the stench.

Kar barked out commands to his tech team. In under two minutes, the tank was there. Snapping on our med gloves, four of us lifted the body into the tank as it filled rapidly with R fluid. The body was light and sticky. An outline of burnt flesh and blood remained on the platform.

We wheeled the tank into the adjoining emergency med station and activated the advanced scanner. Three dimensional images arose on-screen. Kar and I linked eyes. My surprise was reflected back in his. This thing's anatomy was a near exact match to our own.

Oxygen levels were dropping rapidly and nearing irreparable levels. Brain activity was plummeting as well. We needed to reactivate the heart. As I scanned the 3-D imaging to search for injuries, I realized with a jolt that it was a female's bone structure. She was also fully grown, despite her small size.

Only from the three dimensional projections could we discern any details of her anatomy. The physical body in the burn tank was just a charred, bloody mess. Even the scent of burnt flesh remained overwhelming despite the air purifier on full.

"Reactivate the heart," I commanded. Kar grasped the MedX Machine. He is the best Science Lead on our station. His skill is unparalleled. I turned my attention to the assistants so he could stay focused on his task. Yet despite his skill, nothing happened. Her heart would not beat. I felt a wave of frustration.

"Forget protocol!" I yelled. Protocol was not going to save her. "Do whatever it takes, Kar!"

Gasps rippled through the team. "Focus on your tasks," I

snapped, glaring around the room.

Tense minutes passed. Her levels dropped lower and lower and dipped below irreparable. Just as I was on the brink of calling off our medical efforts, the monitors exploded with a sudden burst of activity. He got the heart beating again. We could hear it echo across the room, amplified by the machine.

Only the battle had just begun. Her heart failed six more times across the afternoon. Every failure was more painful than the last. With each passing minute, we became more hopeful she might live. Minutes stretched to hours. Sweat dripped from Kar's brow. He had to snap at an assistant to wipe it away. They stood paralyzed, staring at me nervously to see if I would relieve him of duty. Before I could speak, an assistant stepped forward, the same slight female that had dashed toward the platform earlier. She raised herself up onto her toes to gently pat the drops off his brow and stayed there, carefully monitoring Kar. Fire glinted in her unusual golden eyes.

I disregarded protocol once more and ordered the team to stay on task despite Kar's state. Sweating demonstrates an agitation that impairs decision-making. Protocol dictates I relieve him of duties. But had I followed protocol, she would be dead. Kar may have been sweating, but his hands were steady. I watched them. I knew. Although my own judgment may have been skewed from the adrenaline, I find I do not care. She is alive.

By late evening, she remained in critical condition, although heart was beating steadily. The trauma from the burns became our biggest concern. Permanent brain damage, second.

R fluid, or restoration fluid, is a recent invention originating from Continent 4. It is an extraordinarily complex blend of medications designed to repair and regenerate body cells. The single most remarkable characteristic of the fluid is that it can be inhaled into the lungs. The fluid itself is infused with oxygen. According to the trials, when an individual is completely immersed in the fluid, wounded or burned skin should fully regenerate within 15 rotations. However, it has never been tested on such a severe case as this. Can it completely rebuild an entire dermis? Will she even respond to a fluid calibrated for our biochemistry. There is no way to know. We do not even know yet from where or when she comes.

What's more, there is the matter of brain damage. There is nothing we can do to repair brain damage. Kar advised against feelings of hope. He suspects her brain has been damaged beyond repair due to oxygen deprivation. Nonetheless, he continues to measure her brain activity obsessively and reports substantial amounts of activity. The odd part is that it occurs in peculiar areas. He suspects this indicates damage, although admits to a slim possibility that this is her normal state.

It is a shame. We can regenerate everything except the brain. This is the one mystery that defies us in Science and Medicine. We can calibrate brain chemicals to a high degree of precision, but we cannot undo damage.

We conjecture that she experiences consciousness in relatively the same way that we do given her other anatomical similarities. Therefore, it would be logical to conclude her brain activity should be comparable. The unusual brain activity we are monitoring ought to be construed as an indication of damage. I ought to prepare myself for the highly likely outcome that her brain is too damaged to allow her to regain any form of functional consciousness.

Yet the hope that Kar warns against, the hope that infuses my team, is creeping into my own psyche. This is my Empathy Trait at work. Individuals with a high E-Trait are poor fits for SciMed. They are a poor fit for this very reason. Being overly empathetic can cloud the rational approach necessary for scientific pursuits.

But I desired a life in SciMed more than anything and my general exam scores were so high they were willing to overlook this one weakness. SciMed will do anything to get the best. We all know this. So I was not forthcoming about my internal emotional state on the evaluations. I cited the Genetic Test's margin of error. The Genetic Test, compulsory at birth, is never 100 percent accurate. There is a 1.2 percent anomaly rate. They suspected my dissembling, but could not prove it. Nor did they want to, what with my dossier.

I do not regret my choices. Without science, my life would be nothing.

Who is she? What is she? Even now, life clings resolutely to those small limbs and imperfect skeletal structure. What could she tell us?

RENEE

A masked man faces me and pulls out a gun. Paralyzed, I watch as he squeezes the trigger. A bullet pierces my heart. The pain is indescribable. Blood oozes from my chest. I collapse to the ground.

Back on my feet again, a man chases me down an asphalt road. No one is in sight but the man in black who wields a knife dripping in blood. I gasp for breath but am too tired to run. Stumbling to the ground, he approaches and leans down to stab me in the chest over and over. The pain is unbearable. I try and fight but I can't.

Cars stream past me on a busy highway. I'm lying in the center of the road with bound hands and feet. A car approaches but doesn't stop. The car runs over me and the wheels crush my ribs. Car after car lurches over my chest. It is an endless stream of pain.

What is this?

I grasp for something, for some kind of reality, but it streams through my fingertips like sand.

Am I awake? Asleep? In hell?

One world fades into another. All of them are full of fear and pain where inescapable horrors chase me and I die wretchedly only to be pulled back to life to die again.

Nothingness beckons me, singing a siren's call of peace and painlessness. I could fall into that void of nothing. It would be so easy.

But wait.

Kathy? She walks out of the woods. Her long dark hair streams down her back. She reaches out her hands to me as I fight my way toward her. The moment my hand touches hers, she whisks me away. We arrive at a hot spring on the top of a mountain. Steam rises from the water. "Get in," she says. "Get in, little sister, get in."

Crying, I walk into the steaming water. It burns my skin fiercely. Kathy smiles and her hands gently push me forward. The burning fades. Soft, heavy relief envelopes me. Sun filters through wisps of clouds. A valley unfolds below us. Let's stay here forever.

But she doesn't let me. "Get out," she says, getting angry. I don't understand. She stares at me with her big blue eyes and screams this time, "Get out! Get out!"

If I climb out I will feel pain. But Kathy keeps yelling. Every step up brings terrible coldness to my flesh. It pierces my bones. "Keep going!" she shouts.

Out of the water, I turn toward her, but she is gone. The spring is gone. I walk for an eternity, lost.

Log Entry: R 262 O 3037 ID: Cont 2 YunJon

Exactly 15 rotations have passed since her arrival. I roll out of my sleep pod with a vitality I have not felt since my developmental years.

She is still alive.

We have not disclosed her presence yet. We have not even informed our neighboring experimental unit. Our units are relatively isolated here in this branch of the station. We could safely disclose to Luya's Unit 31 given our isolation. But I hesitate.

I do not want to put them at risk. For now, they can still claim ignorance. This will protect them. They need the protection, particularly after what happened to them last orbit.

The Balance Committee has ordained that a small amount of risk-taking and experimentation is healthy for a society. Experimental units such as ours are thus viewed as a necessary anomaly. Our sole purpose is to push the boundaries of science. We are needed to maintain an ideal societal balance but are found irksome to most nonetheless. Units 1 through 30 do not disguise their distaste for our mission.

This forms part of my reticence to disclose our findings. Continent 2 SciMed has a notoriously low tolerance for experimental units. If it were not for the Balance Committee mandate, we would not be here.

They make this clear in many ways, such as their response to Luya's last project and the ways in which they allocate resources.

I do not need their resources. I knew my team was extraordinary before we initiated Time Window Project. How else could we design such a complex experiment?

Yet in these last rotations, they have risen above and beyond. There has been a dramatic spike in requests for educational materials. Our common area is alive with activity like never before, full of assistants pouring through medical logs. The young female assistant with the golden eyes, the one with such initiative, requested permission to lead an analysis team. Technically, I should not have sanctioned her request as assistants do not lead research. It was clear that their efforts would extend well beyond analysis.

I granted it nonetheless. And my lax attitude is extending well beyond just this. On the third rotation after her arrival, Kar informed the team he was seeing a strong and steady regeneration in her dermis and anticipated continual growth. Two female assistants clasped the others' upper arms and smiled.

They saw me watching and instantly dropped their arms to their side. There was fear in their eyes and an expectation of retribution. Yet I said nothing and looked away. They knew I saw. The whole team knew I saw. They watched me do nothing, which is in itself a sanction of their behavior.

With each passing day, I break protocol time and again. Each breach is more egregious than the last. Yet, I cannot stop. And tomorrow will be the worst.

We will revive her. We will release her from the restoration fluid and bring her back to consciousness. Even still, I will not reveal our results to Continent 2 SciMed Command. I do not trust their response. We have seen what they can do. There is too much on the line this time. Too much yet to uncover. We cannot risk a preemptive project termination order simply because they are threatened by our results.

Watching her regeneration in the tank has been the most fascinating scientific experience of my life. By her seventh rotation with us, I could see a light pink dermis spreading across her body.

Kar spent several rotations working exclusively on her eyes. They are very different from ours and were severely damaged. He managed to design a three dimensional image of what he believed they ought to look like when fully regenerated. She can see colors differently than we can. They are also blue. Her eyes! It was too fantastical to believe until he showed me the genetic code. I could not deny his work. Blue!

Her teeth were simpler. They are different from ours but easier to model and construct. She has four teeth across the front that appear normal with two peculiar teeth, one on each side, that jut down. These are mirrored on the bottom as well. They are reminiscent of what one might find in an animal.

The material of her teeth is weak and prone to decay. Kar enhanced them and filled in several odd gaps in her molars that were filled with strange metallic material.

Otherwise, he has not changed her aesthetics in the slightest. We want to keep her as close to her original form as we possible. Now, 15 rotations out, her dermis appears fully regenerated and is an opaque cream. I have never seen skin so pale. It is several shades lighter than ours. It appears entirely impractical. Such delicate and fair skin would not last long under any kind of environmental strain. I do not even see the aesthetic appeal.

Her general body structure is similar to ours except it is more petite. She also has a larger chest to waist to hip ratio than average. Her breasts and hips are large and rounded. Despite being of a lesser stature than our females, her hips and breasts are as large as the females of our population. Her waist is slightly slimmer when compared to the average measurement.

The most extraordinary part has been watching her hands, feet and face regenerate. The face is the most remarkable.

My page!
Kar sends off an unit-wide alert.

RENEE

Something is shifting. A heavy weight presses down on me.

A small burst of adrenaline shoots through my body. It bucks off some of the drowsiness but not much. I'm still so tired. What happened? Where am I? Was I asleep?

My body feels like an old car left out for a long, cold winter. Everything is revving up slowly and each limb and organ lumbers back to life unhappily. My skin is tingling. It's like when an arm or leg falls asleep; not painful, but not pleasant. Each hyperactive nerve sends signals to my foggy brain.

I feel clogged up with cobwebs.

I inhale. The air feels slick and dense. I explore my returning senses and my mind processes them bit by bit.

Can I move? I clench my fist experimentally and squeeze it hard. The tingling where my fingers touch my palm increases and shoots signals up my spine to my brain. It's intense. I lie still again. My memories feel like clouds. Delicate, intangible and out of reach.

I think I saw Kathy. Or was it a dream? No, it was real. I spoke with Kathy. She was annoyed. Her boxing was canceled. Mom called. She had to go. I was lonely. I went running.

What next? I can't remember. Go slowly. Piece by piece. I put on my new shoes. The wind was cold on my stomach. A trucker honked and scared me. There was a dead mouse on the path. Dead grasshoppers were everywhere. The sun was beautiful through the leaves. On one side of the trail, the forest gave way to cornfield.

Oh, shit. I remember.

In a burst of fear-driven energy, I sit up but my head meets resistance. The air feels heavy and thick. My eyes won't open. I want to see, but my eyelids are weak and unsteady. They won't obey my commands. But I have to get up and figure out what happened. Am I still on the trail? Oh God, am I blind?

Focusing intently, I manage to open my eyes ever so slightly. Light bursts in and sears my retinas. Gasping, I shut them again immediately. It was like staring at the sun. I don't understand. Where am I?

Why can't I hear anything either? It's like being underwater.

Fear is a catalyst. I push my eyes open again. I force myself to keep them open even though the pain from the light is excruciating. I open and close my eyes until slowly, very slowly, I adjust to the light. But they won't focus. Everything remains a green-blue haze. Only now I have a pounding headache.

I move my hands. They are lethargic and weak, like my eyelids. My heart beats rapidly in my chest. It alone seems unaffected, pounding away as strongly as ever.

My hands meet some kind of surface. I feel two right angles. One on my left side, one on my right. A sick feeling washes over me. This feels like a box.

It can't be in a box, though. That doesn't make sense.

I stretch out all my limbs. Fear-fueled adrenaline pumps through me and, at last, I cast aside the overwhelming lethargy and weakness.

It is a box! I'm trapped on all sides. Like a coffin. I'm in a coffin. Am I in a coffin? Am I dead?

Stop. Be logical. Death isn't a blue-green box.

If I were dead, my skin wouldn't tingle. Light wouldn't hurt. These are responses of someone who is alive.

My body shifts downward until my feet touch another surface. My skin and muscles pull and stretch with a weird kind of good pain. I push hard against both my hands and feet simultaneously. Feeling rushes through my nerve-endings. The bottoms of my feet and fingertips tingle, my abdomen twitches and my buttocks and thighs spasm.

I was injured. I'm in the hospital. That makes sense. I can figure this out.

Wait. What? It feels like a pressure change. I'm sinking. How bizarre. I'm being pulled down onto my back. I can feel the weight of something underneath me.

My eyes shut involuntarily. I push them open again. Yet this time, the light is stronger. It stabs my eyes like a thousand needles. I open my mouth to yell but choke instead.

Panic like I've never felt overwhelms me. I'm drowning. Coughs wrack my body. There is liquid inside my lungs and with every new inhale the choking grows worse. Get it all out! My body screams at me.

I shut my eyes and cough so hard it burns. Rolling onto my side eases the pain and eventually I can breathe unsteadily. I'm afraid and cold, lying in a puddle. Strange scents burn my nostrils.

I twitch my fingers slightly. A whimper escapes my lips.

"Hello?" My vocal cords feel limp and useless. Nothing comes out. I try again and this time, I manage to push out a soft whisper. Are those voices I hear? Oh please let it be someone. I just need one voice to explain everything.

I have to readjust my eyes again to this new, brighter light. Bracing myself, I push them open. This time, I keep them open. If I shut them, I'm afraid I will never open them again. I can't see anything but shadows. My headache worsens and pulsates across the front of my forehead and behind my eyes.

As the pain eases, I start to make out blurry figures around me. Those are definitely voices. Great salty tears fill my eyes and drip over my face. The voices are calm and soothing.

Still on my side, I reach forward with my left arm to one of the shadowy silhouettes. My arm shakes with the effort, but my craving for touch and comfort overpowers all else.

A gentle hand takes mine. The warm fingers wrap around my hand. Kathy? Mom? I must have been horribly hurt.

I squeeze the hand gently. There's a momentary pause and the hand squeezes me back. I wish Kathy would say something. Twisting my shoulder, I use gravity to flop back onto my back again. I'm cold and afraid.

A second hand, warm and soft, takes my right one. I tug at them, trying to communicate. Someone wraps their arms around me. It is soothing beyond words. I curl against the warm body that is holding me.

My fears ease. Hands gently pat my back and arms. A great weakness overtakes my limbs and body. I'm so tired. How strange, I think weakly. These softly spoken words aren't English.

But the thought slips away almost as quickly as it came.

Log Entry: R 263 O 3037 ID: Cont 2 YunJon

When Kar and I defended Time Window Project in front of the Continent 2 SciMed Board, they rejected our proposal. We presented it in the formal chamber, a pristine, white room with a half circle of raised seats running along the perimeter.

All ten of the chairs were occupied. Nine of the faces were vaguely familiar. I recognized them from Continent 2's SciMed Committee. The only unfamiliar face was the requisite Balance Committee representative. He was probably doing a mandatory, rotational stint on Earth. I suspect he was eager to return to his home station as soon as possible. I have heard rumors that they do not enjoy their duties on Earth.

I was extremely disappointed when I heard the verdict. We spent months developing the proposal. We had been meticulous in ensuring it met every requirement.

As the Station Commander read the verdict, I could sense his disdain. It was a simple read for a high E-Trait like myself.

As we prepared to leave, the Balance Committee representative stood. His uniform was white like the other members, but his pin shone with a bright cerulean blue, clearly marking his authority.

"The Balance Committee ordains that all SciMed stations devote five percent of their resources to initiatives deemed both risky and creative. This percentage of risk is the appropriate amount in order to maintain a balanced society. Time Window Project, while improbable, meets the criterion for an experimental unit initiative. The Continent 2 SciMed Station is currently underfunding risk initiatives and measures at two full percentage points below regulation. After being allotted an entire orbit to remedy this imbalance, your Station has failed to do so. Therefore, in order to ensure your compliance, I hereby invoke the authority vested in me by the Balance Committee and overturn your vote against Time Window Project. You will immediately initiate funding for Unit 32's proposed project. Funding will continue until Team Lead YunJon deems the project complete."

I was taken aback. I have never witnessed an overturned vote. They are extremely rare.

The representative sat down slowly. Waves of frustration and anger rolled off the SciMed Committee members. They were not pleased. But they had no recourse. A verdict from the Balance Committee is final and can only be overturned by our highest authority, the Regulation Committee itself.

Kar and I conferred in my quarters afterward. While we were pleased with the verdict, we also acknowledged that we had also gained strong enemies as a result. It would have been better to gain our Station's approval without interference. There are many ways to undermine a project.

This is what concerns me now. I saw what they did to Luya's last project in Unit 31. They had even been the ones to approve it in the first place. What might they do to us under these circumstances?

My concerns are heightened now that she is awake. The stakes of the game are higher.

When I ended last night's log entry at Kar's alert, I dashed out of my quarters down the hall to the Med Center. Many had arrived before me. They stepped aside as I walked forward toward the restoration tank. Kar was leaning over it and his black hair, now much longer than regulation, fell across his forehead.

I inhaled sharply with relief. It was not a medical crisis for which he called us. She was still alive. For a moment, I took stock and quickly read her vitals on the monitor. Her heart rate was up, but that wasn't what was so telling. It was the brain activity. It was flashing wildly in places I had never seen register on anyone. Additionally, all her body's functions were increasing in activity intensity.

"Kar, you did not remove the sedation, did you?" I asked incredulously.

"Of course not," he said snappishly.

"What is happening?"

"She is coming out of the induced coma naturally. I will not give her more sedation. We should not fight against her body's desire for consciousness," he answered.

I turned to the team behind me, tearing my eyes away from the tank. "Are we prepared?"

Everyone nodded. That golden-eyed female assistant spoke. I have looked up her chart. Her name is Kemi. Her assessment reports an extremely high Intuition Trait. She hales from Continent 5. She is young. There was little else in the report. It felt oddly barren. I wanted to request more background, but had no grounds for doing so and I would have been required to justify the request. It is odd enough that I would bother to know an assistant's name.

"We are ready!" she said. A smile lit up her face. Her smile is slightly asymmetrical. Odd that her birth parents did not correct such an anomaly. On Continent 2, it is mandatory. Yet I have heard Continent 5 is more lax on such issues. Although, it was not entirely unappealing, despite having little opportunity to examine it as she quickly turned away to hover near Kar.

Everyone was in their positions. I took my spot directly across from Kar. We looked into the tank. One of her thin hands with the strange, uneven fingers twitched slightly.

"Did you see that?" I asked Kar urgently.

"Yes," he responded, hints of excitement lining his tone.

She folded in half in the middle and her head raised to bump gently against the top of the tank. A collective gasp swept around the room. Her movements became steadily stronger. She pressed her hands up against the top of the tank until her feet touched the bottom.

"I think we need to let out the fluid. I believe she is confused and does not know where she is. We do not want her to become too scared or alarmed."

I looked up to see an assistant nudging Kemi to hush. It was she who had spoken yet again. She stared at me uncomfortably over Kar's shoulder. She looked very nervous, as well she should. It was an egregious breach of protocol. Yet I found myself saying, "Kar, what would the risks be?"

Minimal, he explained.

I looked back down. In light of Kemi's words, her movements did appear perhaps like the motions of a frightened being. Before I could speak, her heart-rate started to spike.

"Kar, what is the cause?" I asked tightly, intent on keeping my voice calm.

"No cause found," he responded.

I looked up at Kemi and committed another outrageous breach of protocol. "What do you think?"

Nervously, she cleared her throat and said, "She is scared and believes herself to be trapped. She cannot see nor hear and does not know where she is. She is panicking and this is the cause for accelerated heart rate."

I stared at her oddly.

"This is all conjecture, of course!" she said quickly, her eyes darting nervously to the side.

"Kar?" I said.

"Yes. That could be a viable option," he responded.

"Remove the R-fluid. Open the tank immediately. She is ready to join us. Prepare yourselves," I said.

Kar, aided by his two assistants, slid the top of the tank aside. The restoration fluid drained away.

Mouths agape, we watched in stunned silence. The details of her body were exposed to us at last. Under the gel-like fluid in the tank, she had appeared to be an ephemeral being behind a soft bluish-green veil that blurred her features. But once that was gone? What emerged was so much more remarkable and so very real. She is a true, living being. Her skin is white and delicate. It is a creamy, exquisite, snowy expanse of dermis that is thin enough to reveal blue veins running up and down her limbs.

Her fingers are impossibly thin and bizarrely uneven. The four longest taper to a point in the center. Her wrist is unbelievably delicate. Indeed, it is impractically so. Yet well-developed hips and breasts, almost grotesquely out of proportion, contrast starkly against her petite frame. Smooth curves and dips run along her body from head to toe, creating the softest outline imaginable. We were unable to pinpoint the exact year from which she hales, not yet at least, but it must certainly be before the Great Drought. No one so lacking in pigmentation could have survived those years.

Coughs wracked her body. She twitched and gasped as if drowning. Kar quickly reached out a reassuring hand. "It is to be excepted," he said, "as she must clear the fluid from her lungs."

She rolled to her side to better clear her lungs of the fluid. As the coughing subsided, we saw her face clearly for the first time. Her head is entirely bald. The hair should grow back in time, assuming she has any. Her face is practically luminescent. The features? Remarkable. Strange and alien, yet familiar all the same. They are like ours, but altered. Her chin comes down to a point rather than a square. Her nose juts out from her face further than ours yet it is slimmer. A rounded forehead slopes down to delicate eye sockets. Her lips, a soft pink, are full and bow-shaped. The most shocking feature are her eyes. Soft murmurs broke out around the room when she opened them. I did not have the presence of mind to reprimand them because I myself was so stunned. Blue. They truly are a brilliant blue as Kar had promised.

Slowly, she raised one shaking hand up to Kar's face. The hand fascinated me, so strange and so delicate.

I thought I heard her say something. I saw her lips move, but I could not be sure.

Kemi spoke again. At this point, I was too distracted to care about breaches of protocol. "YunJon, Kar, I believe she is reaching up to us. Perhaps we should speak to her and make contact."

Before I could respond, she leaned over and spoke softly.

"Hello, little one," she said softly. "Welcome. You have been through a lot. But do not worry. We are here to help you. Do not be afraid."

"I do not think she can understand you. We do not know that we speak the same language," I said. She ignored me.

"Her heart-rate is lowering," murmured Kar. "Heart-rate is steady now."

Her shaking hand stretched up towards Kar's face.

"Take her hand," Kemi urged softly. I ignored that an assistant was now issuing commands in my stead.

Kar lowered his hand until it touched hers. His motions were deliberate and gentle. A look of awe spread across his features. It was surprisingly moving to see Kar, the ultimate male of science, so touched by this encounter. He held her hand loosely in his and she squeezed softly in response. His hand dwarfed hers. Kar glanced at me nervously. I nodded. He gently reciprocated pressure on her own.

She reached up her other arm. It was quivering from the effort. Kar, with more certainty now, moved to hold her other hand.

"She is stronger than she appears," he murmured to me. "The skin looks more delicate than it is. There is a buoyancy to it. Could it be possible, YunJon, that she communicates differently that we do? That perhaps she communicates through touch? I feel that she wants physical contact."

"Do so," I said.

Kar, a larger male than most, leaned down and carefully maneuvered his arms around her. It would be no burden on him to lift her. He slid one arm under her legs, the other under her back and picked her up. In response to his gestures, she wrapped her arms tightly around his collar and nuzzled her face into his neck. We watched as her body slowly went limp and her breathing evened out.

"I believe she is sleeping," murmured an assistant. "The scanner indicates it, although we cannot say with certainty given her unique brain activity."

She is alive and responsive. It is nothing short of remarkable that her body managed to regenerate. It may be that she is more responsive to our medicines than we previously thought.

Renee

My eyelids feel glued together. My mouth is dry. Pain pounds through my skull, as if I've been run over by a dump truck. Cracking one eye open, I try to take a look around. My God, it is bright. Is this a hangover? If so, it is the mother of all hangovers.

Wait. This is not my bed.

A sick feeling settles into the pit of my stomach. Fear keeps my eyes open despite the pain of the bright light.

White material of some kind, shimmering and smooth, is spread across my body. It's almost incandescent and nearly weightless. It hugs tightly up against the curves of my legs and torso. What is this fabric? I've never felt anything like it.

I move my left hand weakly. The material shimmers and slides away effortlessly, reminding me of rippling water. Caught up in the motion of the fabric, it takes me a moment to notice my exposed hand.

Bile rushes up my throat and chokes me. What is wrong with my hand? *What is wrong with my hand?*

The skin is pale, so pale. There are no lines. None at all. The creases from bending my knuckles and joints are all gone. The only hint that the joints are even still there is a slightly rounded shape from the bones jutting out.

Nausea sweeps through me. My hands are long, skinny fingers wrapped up like bony sausages in a tight, white casing.

Shaking in fear, I muster the courage to try and lift my hand and bend my fingers. I ball up my hand hard and fast, digging the tips of my fingers hard into my palm. It hurts, but the skin doesn't tear. It's malleable, just like it's always been.

Tucking my hands back under the blankets, I breathe quickly in and out. Bits and pieces of my memory start flooding back. Going for a run, an accident of some kind…

"Jesus Christ!" I exclaim, and try to sit up. Weak and exhausted, I slump back down. The blanket slides off my body. I gag again, swallowing bile. My whole body is covered in freakish skin. All my hair, scars, freckles, lines… all are gone. Through the delicate, sheer whiteness of this new skin, I can see every blue vein crisscrossing up and down my body.

I struggle to sit up. My hands run up and down my arms, chest, stomach and legs. It doesn't feel like my skin, or any skin I've ever touched.

My fingers pinch at the flesh of my stomach. The skin gives way under the pressure and folds up, like normal skin would, but with very little to grasp. I've wasted away. My rib cage visibly protrudes and jutting hip bones stand in stark relief. There's no layer of fat under my skin. I'm a skeleton of my former self, wrapped up a pale and pliable shell.

This stomach, this bellybutton? They are not mine. The bellybutton is nothing more than an unobtrusive dimple, like what you might find on the stomach of a doll. This unnerves me the most, the vision of this bizarrely plastic bellybutton.

I can see my heart pounding and shaking in my chest. My now perfectly symmetrical breasts move slightly with each beat. I raise my hands to my face. My fingers skim the rims of my eyes, run down the sides of my nose and brush across my lips. I recognize them by touch. The skin is not mine, but at least the features are. Raising my hands to my scalp, I run my flat hand over my head. It's smooth. There is nothing there but a thin layer of fuzz. I'm bald.

What is going on? What is wrong with me?

Struggling to look around the room, everything far away appears blurry and bright, as if I'm not wearing my contacts. Yet if I concentrate, things slowly start to come into focus, like someone is turning the dial of a microscope.

Maybe I was severely burnt in a fire. Or was I in a terrible accident and lost my memory? Is this a strange experimental study? Do I have cancer? Was I in a coma?

There should be someone here. Someone should be explaining what is going on. This has to be a medical center.

As if in response to my thoughts, the door hisses open. Snatching the blanket that pooled down at my knees, I draw it back up over my naked body. I still can't see very well but it's improving. The brightness is the worst part. It creates a blur and prevents me from making out features.

"Who's there?" I say nervously. It comes out as a whisper. My vocal chords twinge uncomfortably. I clutch the shimmery blanket up against my body. As the person walks closer, I start to distinguish features, only to recoil in fear.

"What are you?" I whisper.

He is enormous; at least 6'10", not an inch shorter. His shoulders are almost twice as broad as my own and his whole body is long and lean. There is not an ounce of fat on his frame. An obscenely tight, tan jumpsuit clings to him and matching boots climb to mid-calf. I can't see a single seam or button. The material is unfamiliar. On his left shoulder, something flashes in the light.

His hair is pitch black, perfectly straight and sweeps over his forehead. His skin is the color of milky coffee, warm and brown. It is immaculate. There isn't one scar, freckle or wrinkle I can see. His eyes are also black, so black I can't distinguish between them and his irises. But the most terrifying part is that the whites of his eyes; they aren't white. They're... brown. They don't look at all like human eyes. They are like dark orbs, peering out at me between heavily shadowed lids. His forehead is flat and his eyebrows harsh, creating a strong overcast to his already dark and menacing look.

His mouth is a harsh line in his face. He has lips, but they aren't bowed like mine. They cut straight across. His chin saves my sanity. He has a dimple on his chin. It's the only thing on his face that looks truly human. I focus on it to avoid looking at his terrible and troubling eyes. What wretched illness did that to him? What horrible mutation has he suffered, such that the whites of his eyes are brown?

He leans toward me and, instinctively, I push away from his touch. My back bumps up against the wall behind me. The bed, I realize, is really a raised platform. I am only a foot or so below his eye level. My hands clench tightly around the blanket, pulling it up around my chin.

He raises a hand to my face and I cry out in fear. His hand is enormous, like boxer's hands, with thick knuckles and broad palms. The fingers don't taper down on the sides. They are all the same length except the thumb, which is normal.

In response to my cry, the man jumps back and puts his hands behind his back. I see a twitch of emotion cross his... that face. His mouth twists up slightly and his eyes widen a tad. Then his brow falls slightly, and an almost imperceptible wrinkle appears on his forehead.

Did I startle him? Did I offend him? The thought hadn't occurred to me. Yet it must be true. He's probably embarrassed by the way he looks. Maybe he's here to check my vitals or explain what's going on.

He is still standing there while I think. He's not moving. A twinge of sympathy breaks through my fear and confusion.

"Hey," I say. This time my voice is a bit louder and my throat doesn't hurt so much. I gauge his response. His head cocks slightly to the right.

"Sorry, you just startled me. Who are you? Where am I?"

He doesn't act like someone who is deformed. There's no self-consciousness in his stance. His feet are planted firmly, athletically, on the floor. His shoulders are squared confidently. Despite his massive size, he carries himself with grace.

With his dark, penetrating eyes locked on mine, he starts to speak. His voice is deep and rumbly. The cadence is bizarre, as is the intonation. I don't understand a word.

Wracking my brain, I try to identify what language he's speaking. Could this be Dutch? I don't think so. I'm vaguely familiar with Afrikaans, which has some origins in Dutch, and this sounds nothing like it. Bizarrely fascinated, I fixate on the tone. It is like nothing I have ever heard before. I let the sound wash over me. It's almost hypnotic.

He goes silent and stares at me for a moment. He raises his left hand and with his right, taps a thin, metallic band on his wrist. He speaks again, but this time his speech is much quicker, not the slow-moving cadence from earlier but rapid-fire bursts.

After a few moments, he takes a slow and gentle step towards me. We are about a foot apart now. Very slowly, he reaches out a hand and with one finger, lightly brushes my cheek. His finger startles me with its warmth.

Unhurriedly, he pulls his hand back. He smiles, revealing teeth that are perfectly white and smooth. They looked pretty normal, but have been shaved down so they are all the same length.

He points to himself and says, "Kar."

"Kar," I repeat, and point to him. I avoid looking at my hand. Keeping my eyes locked on him, I turn my hand to point at my own chest. "Re-nee."

"Rehneh," he struggles to repeat. I nod encouragingly.

"Can you tell my family where I am?" I say. I know he doesn't understand, but I can't stop myself from pressing ahead. Maybe one of their names will resonate. "Please, my sister's name is Kathy Vantel. My parents are Steven and Eileen Vantel. V-a-n-t-e-l. You have to tell them where I am. They are probably scared out of their minds."

A sudden truth hits me with the power of a freight train and leaves me gasping.

Why aren't they here with me now? They would be. They would be here no matter what. It wouldn't matter if I was on the opposite side of the world. They would find me. There's only one reason why they aren't here. And then the shadowy fingers of a dark truth claw at my heart. I can't explain why I feel it with such certainty. I can't explain why I know they're not just down the hall at the vending machine. Something happened. They're gone. I know it. I can feel their absence in my soul. Their presence is completely eradicated. They're gone, as if wiped from the face of the Earth. I can't sense them. I can't sense anyone. A strange, hideous emptiness unfolds inside me.

I slide off the bed and, rather than land on my feet, collapse from weakness onto the floor. The blanket remains clutched tightly in my hands. The man tries to help me get up and speaks in worried tones with words I can't understand. I push him away. His body is rock solid but he gives in to my pressure and backs up.

Stumbling to my feet, I wrap the blanket around my shoulders and struggle toward the sliding door. All I can think about is Kathy and Momma and Poppa.

I yell their names over and over even though I know they're gone. Tears blind me. The door doesn't open and I fall against it sobbing. A dark loneliness like I have never felt wraps its insidious arms around me, engulfing me in its suffocating embrace.

Kar is behind me and presses something gently against my arm.

Darkness overcomes me and I welcome it.

Internal Memo: Rotation 264

To:	Unit 32
From:	SciMed Command

Time Window Project was scheduled for execution on Rotation 247. Follow-up reports unsatisfactory and negligent. Full report expected by end of current rotation or punitive actions will be taken

INTERNAL MEMO: ROTATION 264

To:	SciMed Command
From:	Unit 32

Negligent reports due to faculty workload. Time Window Project results unexpected and under analysis. Request for 10 additional rotations (Rotation 274) for comprehensive report.

INTERNAL MEMO: ROTATION 264

To: Unit 32

From: SciMed Command

Additional 10 rotations granted. Committee will visit Unit 32 on Rotation 274 to assess results, analyze project merits and discuss continuation of funds.

Log Entry: R 264 O 3037 ID: Cont 2 YunJon

We will have no allies when SciMed Command arrives in ten rotations. My vague reports gave them the excuse they needed to arrange a full committee inspection.

They assume we are hiding a failure.

Yet I had no alternative but to obfuscate the truth. The situation is tenuous and unpredictable. They would not tolerate such a state of affairs.

If we attempted to present her to them now? She is weak, unintelligible and cries like an infant at birth. Her elimination would be swift and incontestable. They would not see her existence as a wonder. They would not see the potential for what we might learn. They would be disgusted.

We have witnessed their heavy-handedness. Last orbit, Luya's Unit 31 sought to develop companion assistance to raise morale amongst the elderly. Their research was exhaustive and meticulous. They sought to address the loneliness and lack of purpose prevalent in the elder population.

It is not effective for society to allot young, healthy contributors to care for the needs of non-contributors. Taking this into account, the solution they proposed was elegant and inventive.

They developed a small breed of mammal that is docile and friendly. This mammal would accompany the elderly and would require a small amount of care in order to give the elderly a purpose. They were bred to be affectionate and social, which would in turn assuage loneliness. In addition, the animals were trained to raise the alarm if their assigned elderly person experienced any medical trauma or required assistance.

What a marvelously creative solution! This problem with the elderly has proven nearly impossible to address. It has plagued our society for tens if not hundreds of orbits. It is fair to say I was quite impressed. Blinded by my excitement, I did not allow myself to consider alternative responses to their research.

When they invited SciMed Command to observe the results of their study, we were all taken aback. Unit 31 did not even finish their presentation before Chief Gan interrupted Luya.

None of us can forget his words. "This is a disgrace. We will not tolerate such a proposition nor such waste of resources and time. Humanity has evolved to the highest form. We will not allow anything to retrograde our progress, particularly interaction with a lower life form. I speak on behalf of the committee by expressing my disgust for this ill-advised folly. You debase us all by introducing contact with a lower-life species."

He looked at the lab specimens with disgust and continued, "These mammals will be destroyed immediately. The lab will be sterilized and every member of Unit 31 will undergo intensive psychological assessment to ensure they have not been corrupted by the influence of these life forms." Turning to his assistant, he snapped his fingers.

And that was it. Orbits of research, development, training and hope evaporated.

The look on Luya's face was of such devastation that it haunts me to this day. She had personally invited me to explore the lab and meet the small mammals only one rotation prior. I was quite impressed with her model, although I did express some concern about the sanitation. Yet her team had already taken that into consideration and developed a rigorous sanitation plan. The creatures were to be raised and trained before being assigned to elderly who were demonstrating morale depletion.

Yet in an instance, it was all gone.

Unit 31 was not requested, but required to observe and assist in the "deconstruction and sanitation" of their lab. Those of us in Unit 32 who were present at the research presentation were required to undergo a rigorous sanitation process.

I have attempted to visit Unit 31 since. Such a grim silence pervades the lab that it is difficult to stay. Luya, the Team Lead, is a changed person. Kar still invites her to our lab once in a while. He tries to involve her in questions concerning our research, as she has no passion for her unit's current project. They are conducting research on an existing medication for the elderly who suffer from bone density issues in order to determine if they can lower the current cost of production.

I have seen Luya with our assistant Kemi several times. Today, I checked Luya's public chart. She is also from Continent 5. Perhaps they know one another from their childhood years. Luya certainly greets Kemi with uncustomary warmth for someone so inferior in status, and I have seen Kemi spend some time with Luya and Kar before leaving them alone in the lab where they stay long past designated rest hours.

I saw Kemi walking in the passage today from the lab to her quarters. She is a shorter than the average female. Her hair is now slightly longer than regulation and she tucks the thick, black locks behind her ears to prevent them from blocking her line of vision. Her hair is not straight, but has a slight wave. Another odd abnormality that went uncorrected during her pre-birth assessment.

She smiled at me. That lopsided grin froze me in my tracks. I stood in the hallway, head cocked, fixated on her smile. She noticed. Of course, she noticed. I was anything but discreet. She also froze but, unlike me, she froze with discomfort. The smile swept off her face. Her hand rose partway to her face before she snapped it back down to her side abruptly. Then she quickly started walking past me.

I suspected I had intimidated her. She is small and low-ranking. I am not just the Team Lead but also several standard deviations above normal height. Kar and I are both of similar stature. We are the only two in the lab to reach such a size. I would have thought she would have been used to this though, what with working so closely with Kar.

I reached out a hand to block her path. I wished to apologize for making her uncomfortable. Yet rather than an apology, I found myself saying, "Why did you raise your hand just now?"

She stared down at the ground. "Please, YunJon." Her voice was pinched. "Do not draw attention to my irregularities."

"Irregularities," I said, stupidly repeating her word.

Then a rush of heat sweep through me. The half-raised hand was an aborted attempt to hide her mouth. She saw me staring at her asymmetry. She naturally interpreted my fixation to be one of disgust.

"Kemi. You misinterpret. I do not think it is a flaw. I stared only because I found it pleasing. You must forgive my breach of protocol."

Breaches of protocol, at that point.

I glanced at the temperature sensor. It blinked normally. Yet given the unusual warmth of the hallway, I made a mental note to alert maintenance.

She raised her eyes from the floor to meet mine. Her lips were slightly parted in surprise. While her pupils are as black as mine, there are gold flecks surrounding the light brown in which they sit, giving her entire eyes the golden cast I had noticed earlier.

Her gaze carried a deep poignancy that even I could not understand, despite my robust Empathy Trait.

"Excuse me, YunJon," she said, her voice carrying a slight quiver. She turned briskly to continue past me. I watched her disappear out of sight down the curved corridor.

What an odd exchange.

I must be more vigilant in my actions. If I am to have any chance with our station's Command when they visit, I will need to ensure that every single protocol is perfectly followed. This certainly precludes me from fraternizing with assistants.

But even the knowledge of the looming visit does not dull the remarkable nature of our first contact with the female of the past today.

We watched her wake through the observation wall of her room. I nodded at Kar to enter. She squinted at him with her brilliant blue eyes. They are unnerving to look at, both beautiful and eerie. Kar warned us that it might take some time for her eyes to adjust and refocus. It appeared that she could not focus on him until he was within arm's length, when the squinting of her eyes relaxed.

The exhilaration that rippled through our group was palpable. She spoke. The brain damage we feared does not appear to have manifested. She responded to Kar's presence both verbally and through her physical body language. Curiously, she pulled the cover cloth up around her body. In re-watching the interaction this afternoon, we interpreted that to be a fear response spurred by the sight of someone so unfamiliar.

After intense debate, we have conjectured that she might have the developmental capacities of today's child of five or six orbits.

She has been able to identify herself by name. She calls herself Reh-Neh. We are not certain of the exact orthography, yet I believe our historian will turn it up in due course.

This exchange between Kar and Reh-Neh was most encouraging. Kar was able to convey his identity and she was able to understand and replicate. From there, however, things deteriorated most alarmingly. She began to make sounds of extreme distress, refused contact from Kar and attempted to exit the room. We are not quite sure yet what the sounds "kah thee mah mah pah pah" mean. She repeated them over and over. We hope to turn up a meaning for them shortly.

We ran a deep language assessment off the verbal recordings. It would appear to be one of the ancient languages, dating back approximately 900 orbits to 1,450 orbits in the past. They called orbits 'years,' I discovered. How old-fashioned. Evidently this evolved from before they understood that the Earth spends 365 days on a complete orbit around the sun. Imagine not knowing that!

With a promise of strict confidentiality, we contacted one of the leading language historians on Continent Two. Through a brilliant stroke of fortune, Kar knew him distantly from a lecture he attended many orbits ago. We sent him the audio files and expect to have some basic language materials to assist us in communicating with Reh-Neh tomorrow.

On the physical front, her recuperation is going marvelously. She already has a light cover of hair on her scalp. It is growing extremely quickly. We have been pumping nutrients into her body, which may have triggered rapid hair growth. Or perhaps this is standard for her. While it is still difficult to distinguish her hair color, it would appear to be much lighter than any of ours.

I have not yet ordered any deep sequencing of her DNA nor analysis of her body functions. After the physical shock that she underwent, I suspect it will take time for everything to calibrate back to a normal level. I do not want to skew the data by being hasty.

I also want her to be able to reveal herself to us over time and at her own pace. I do not want to pigeonhole her with a Trait Assessment or assumptions based on her hormonal analysis. These may not be accurate due to her altered physiology. I want us to assess her without any data skewing how we expect her to act or based on what we project to be normal behavior.

As I alluded to earlier, we have her tentatively pegged at the intelligence level of a five-orbit child. She has demonstrated behaviors consistent with that age group. She wept tears, raised her voice, acted impulsively, pushed at Kar and acted illogically by throwing herself at a closed door. Some of these actions might be excused due to shock and trauma, which is why we are hesitant to estimate with certainty. We shall see how things unfold.

What concerns me is Command's response. They will find a babbling, unintelligible, alien and childlike creature from the past unpalatable. It will increase the risk of having our project and its finding summarily destroyed.

Therefore, we must find a way to communicate with her efficiently. We have precious little time in which to do that.

If we can communicate with her, we might make progress. She physically resembles us in nearly every way. My only concern is that the ways in which she does not resemble us are visually startling. There is absolutely nothing normal about her white skin, blue eyes with white spaces around the pupil and iris, small stature yet rounded hips and breasts, oddly curved lips, rounded forehead and pointed chin. They are very visually startling and capture much of the attention of anyone who is seeing her for the first time.

Yet the components that really matter, such as her organs and bone structure, are the same as ours apart from some insignificant and very minor variations. I must determine a course of action that will best protect her from the influence of Command. Under the best of circumstances, we would rush nothing and examine and study every interaction in detail. However, we do not have the luxury of time. I must act decisively.

EXTERNAL MEMO: ROTATION 265

To:	Balance Committee
From:	Team Lead YunJon, Unit 32, Continent 2 SciMed

I, Team Lead YunJon of Unit 32 of the Continent 2 SciMed Station, request the presence of a representative of the Balance Committee with full enforcement power of the Regulation Committee to visit Continent 2 SciMed Station on Rotation 274, Orbit 3037.

I request this visit due to the remarkable and highly noteworthy results of Time Window Project (as approved by a Balance Committee Representative for funding on Rotation 17 Orbit 3034).

The results of our project are so extraordinary we deem them worthy of the attention of the highest authority. What we have found, and uncovered, could alter both our understanding of history and challenge the reality we exist in today.

External Memo: Rotation 265

To:	Team Lead YunJon, Unit 32, Continent 2 SciMed
From:	Balance Committee

Your request has been received and is under consideration.

EXTERNAL MEMO: ROTATION 266

To:	Kar, Unit 32, Continent 2 SciMed
From:	Shee, Language History Center, Continent 2 Peace

I am leaving immediately and will arrive tomorrow, Rotation 267. We received the audio file your unit sent. I did not share the recording with anyone else on my team and erased the message from our database as you taught me. They will not find it unless they know to look for it. Do not take this as a slight upon you, my friend, but if what you have told me is true - the ramifications far exceed anything you could possibly imagine, and we must tread very carefully until we are certain. Naturally, I absolutely must be on hand for this momentous occasion. Should this be verifiable, the ramifications are life-altering. But I become too verbose, as is the tendency of a language historian. I will get to the point. The words she is speaking are, as you accurately assessed, those of a Pre-Drought language. As you know, few records remain from this time and the language has been largely lost to us. However, a colleague of mine has dedicated her career to the reconstruction of this language and has compiled a rather basic dictionary that translates these words into our modern speech. I have access to this dictionary. There are also even a few texts that remain - paper books - that miraculously survived the brutal centuries of drought and war. They are, as you can imagine, very highly prized and guarded. However, I spent the afternoon acquiring holographic copies of them. Also, I have transferred as much information on the language (including, of course, the dictionary) onto my private chip. I will bring these with me.

In my excitement, I have not even told you the language. It what they called, I believe, "American-English," from approximately the years 1900 to 2100. I cannot pinpoint the source with any more accuracy than this.

What is most important, however, are the words she was saying; "mah mah" and "pah pah." These are the affection names a child called his or her birth parents during these times. You must recall, the family structure was highly unusual during this period. The nuclear family was considered of utmost importance and its cohesion was often prized above even that of the larger social good. Imagine that! It is likely that she is calling out to them in fear or confusion if you have described the situation accurately. Although, Kar, I truly wish you and your unit would get in the habit of writing with more detail. You do leave much to the imagination. Not that mine is lacking, you should see my Genetic Assessment. Creativity is off the charts! Likely why they funneled me into ancient languages. Certainly a field where creativity is necessary, and no one gets too bothered if I stray outside the bounds of practical protocol. Yet I digress.

I am taking emergency leave to explain my absence. I will spare you the details, but I know people who can transport me expediently and with discretion. Have someone meet me at the docking gate at 0900 Earth Hours. I urge discretion, my friend. Your findings, and those who found them, may not be welcome in all quarters.

Renee

I know where I am. These domed white walls are familiar. It's so bizarre that there are no visible seams. It's one smooth, arched ceiling. How do they construct that?

The blurriness in my eyes is completely gone. I slide a hand out from under the blanket and gently probe my left eye. It hurts. There's no piece of plastic buffering my finger from my iris. I have no contacts in, even though everything is in perfect focus.

How can that be possible? I have terrible eyesight.

My room is not large, perhaps only 12 feet across. Immediately in front of me is the thin outline of a door. A piece of white fabric hangs from the top.

There is nothing else to see. No shelves, television or equipment. Nothing. The room has a hypnotic feel, almost as if I were enclosed in a warm, white womb.

My limbs and skin veritably vibrate with energy. I am so flush with health that the cells of my body feel as though they are gently pulsating with life. I raise my hand from my eye to my head and run my palm flat against my scalp.

It really is true. All my hair is gone. What's left is a soft fuzz about a half centimeter in length. I run my fingers over my eyebrows and find the same. With my eyes still locked on the ceiling, I place both my hands on my face. The skin is extraordinarily smooth. It reminds me of the texture of a flower petal that you might rub between your fingers.

Mentally bracing myself, my eyes sink down from the ceiling to focus on my hands. Flexing them, I watch as the unnaturally taut skin stretches over the bones and muscles. It's as though a machine built my skin to resemble silicon.

A feeling of dread crawls up from my belly but I swallow it down hard. There is air in my lungs. My heart is pounding steadily in my chest. All my senses are intact.

I am alive. That is what matters.

I will sort everything else out.

The facts; I suffered some health crisis while running and I've lost my memory. I don't know where my family is and I don't know where I am. I have a weird, inexplicable certainty that they're all gone. There's a gaping hole inside me where their presence should be. I can't explain it. It's an emptiness.

Maybe this is a psychotic episode. Could this vibrant aliveness I feel be a symptom of a manic episode? Hallucinations? Perhaps this is why I am in a room with so little stimuli?

It's hideous to think I may have lost my mind. Anything would be better. Anything. My mind is my identity and my livelihood. Without it, I am nothing.

But I can't panic, not again.

I must find the doctors and nurses I saw earlier. We can discover some way to communicate and piece together the facts. They must be open-minded and good people. They hired a man to work for them with a severe physical deformity.

Or was that a hallucination?

This is torture, this second-guessing.

I sit up. Grasping the thin, incandescent blanket with my right hand, I pull it tightly around my bare shoulders. It's not from cold but for modesty. I'm still naked and I can't shake the sensation that I'm being watched. There are people running their eyes over my bizarre skin. People seeing and observing my body before I have even seen it. People with more knowledge than I have about my own predicament.

Sitting now, I see I was right. There is nothing at all in the room. There's not even a chair. Everything is clean and spotless. It practically shines.

The white ought to be overwhelmingly bright, but it isn't. It's simply a gentle, warm glow.

Wait, that's strange. Where are the light fixtures? It appears as if the walls themselves have been wired to exude this soft illumination.

The seams where the walls meet the floor are not hard corners. They have been slightly rounded.

Curious, I slide off the platform that serves as my bed, walk over to the wall and crouch down. I run my fingers over the curve that melds the floor to the wall. There is not a single mar or flaw in construction.

I can't imagine the cost of constructing such a room. Is this some Nordic country with amazing health care and unusual interior decorating? They can be very minimalist, right?

No idea where I formed that impression. But maybe that could explain the bizarre and unidentifiable language I heard spoken earlier. And that man was remarkably tall. Could it be?

Rising from my crouch, I marvel at the ease with which I move. I am weak, but my knees unbend smoothly and effortlessly. There is no pain in my joints. The same piece of white cloth I saw earlier catches my eye. It's so close in color to the wall and door it's almost hard to see.

My eyes drop to the floor below it. Two white boots rest on the floor. At least, they appear to be boots of a sort. They flop over at the top.

I walk toward them and notice a slight bounce to the floor. It reminds me of the bamboo floor of a yoga studio I went to once. I only went once. The instructor's voice grated on my nerves. But the spring in the floor was the same as here. Buoyant, almost.

Reaching the door, I slide an arm out from under my blanket and run my hand across the seam where the door meets the wall.

There's no groove. Squinting, I bring my face closer. The only indication of the door's presence is a discoloration. There's a slight dimming of the soft light that emanates from the walls.

It's only cosmetic, I realize in shock. The purpose is to alert people to its presence. If it weren't for that, I might think I were trapped inside a white bubble.

Are there other doors around the room that I'm unaware of?

Nervously, I turn my attention to the item hanging off the back of the door. I grasp it and it slithers easily into my hand. It is the softest material I have felt. It ripples and streams as though water and nearly falls to the floor through my clutched fingers. Fascinated, I let my blanket drop so I can grasp it better. Ignoring the sensation of being watched, I stand naked and hold it out in both hands. It's a jumpsuit!

There are three openings. One for the head and two for my hands.

Yet it won't fit. The jumpsuit is tiny. Even with how thin I've become, I won't be able to get it on.

I've avoided looking at my body because my new skin disgusts me. Yet I can't ignore how emaciated I've become. My body is just bones and muscle with barely an ounce of fat. My breasts, normally a size C cup, would now barely fill a B. I considered myself thin before, but there was always a soft roundness to my belly, breasts and hips. That's all gone. I'm just jutting hips and visible ribs.

Jerking the material of the jumpsuit with my hands, it instantly stretches. It stretches further than possible. Incredible.

Putting my hands into the hole for the head, it opens impossibly far. I raise a leg and slip my left foot into the neck hole. The material slides smoothly and easily along my ankle, calf, knee and thigh as I shove my foot into the correct leg slot. I quickly move to push my right foot down into it.

The fabric melds to my body. My arms find their way into the sleeves. Before I know it, I'm dressed. Well, as dressed as anyone can be who is encased in a skintight, white full-body leotard.

But still. It feels so good to be clothed. The sense of empowerment is immediate and potent. I snatch the boots off the floor and step into them. They meld to my feet, only with firmer resistance.

I have an absurd urge to laugh. I could be a Cirque de Soleil performer in this outfit. Who cares, I guess? It's a thousand times better than being naked in an unknown environment. That was serious vulnerability.

Striding to the middle of my room, I stretch and explore my body. My first impressions were correct. There's a definite weakness in my muscles. It's probably because of how emaciated I am. But there's no denying the underlying feeling of health and vibrancy. All those annoying, daily little aches and pains are completely gone.

I'm tall and the lines of my body still feel the same despite how thin I've become. Even without a bra, the jumpsuit seems to support my breasts almost like a sports bra, only far more comfortably. I do a few jumps to test it.

Fascinating. How is this material constructed? Why isn't it on the commercial market?

I glance down and see my hands. They still freak me out, but I can reform calluses quickly and as soon as I'm in the sun, I'll return back to normal. Although slowly and with lots of sunscreen. A minute in the sun in my current state and I'd be a lobster.

There are no mirrors in the room. My fingers serve as a type of tactile reflection. My cheeks are more hollowed than I remember. My cheekbones themselves are subsequently more pronounced. I run my hands thoughtfully and critically over my skull. My head feels normal.

My attention returns to the walls of the room. There's someone behind those walls. I can't explain how I know it, but there's an unceasing and nagging sensation of being watched.

I walk to the wall and stand with my arms crossed and stare. After a few moments, I run my hands along the wall and bang the butt of my palm against it. A faint ripple emanates from where my hand met the wall. Startled, I jump backward. The ripple quickly fades to nothing and the surface settles into its smooth appearance.

What the hell is this? I've never read about, nor encountered, anything like this technology before.

I stare some more and smash my fist into it harder. A larger circle ripples outward. I feel uneasy, as if I'm a lab rat or something. I'm too powerless.

Taking several deep breaths, I focus on calming my thoughts. I clear my throat and speak.

"I know you're watching me. I don't know why. Please come and explain where I am and what is going on."

My voice, like my other muscles, feels weak. What I'd hoped would be a powerful statement sounded softer than intended.

A tightness worms its way up my throat. I hate being watched and studied and judged. I don't like people invading my privacy and taking away my control. It really triggers me.

This has made it hard for me professionally. It was particularly hard when it came to the government jobs. I bore the wrath of my advisor by never following through with the CIA or State Department. But how could I stand the scrutiny of those security clearances? I couldn't. It would drive me crazy.

I still remember our conversation. "With your talents, you would thrive," my advisor said gruffly and with more than a hint of impatience. "Get over the security forms. Just fill them out. Your personality is the perfect match. Skip the PhD. It will be a waste of your time."

I didn't like that he was pushing me around. I really didn't like that he thought he knew me better than I knew myself. Gritting my teeth, I said angrily, "I don't want to. It's just not who I am."

The words came out with more bite than intended. He was startled. I wasn't surprised he was startled. I'd been nothing but a compliant before.

Perhaps he did know who I was. He saw how I manipulated social situations to get what I wanted. That's probably why he thought I'd be so good in those roles. What he missed was my motivation.

He didn't get that I hate that part of life. I hate the part where I have to manipulate social situations to build connections. He also totally missed that I was doing it for survival. Not everyone was born with a silver spoon in their mouth. I had to pay my own way through life and had no family-bought social connections. I'm also not a psychopath. And you're either a psychopath or you actually buy into that jingoistic bullshit to be fine manipulating people full-time for a living.

Still nothing happens.

I keep staring at the wall. This feels too real to be a hallucination. Then again, isn't that what someone who is mentally ill would think?

I spin slowly in a circle to check if I missed anything. The bed is nothing more than a platform that extends from the wall. There isn't even a brace to support it.

Nothing is familiar. The foreignness is eerie. Odd how accustomed we are to hard corners, tech gadgets and power outlets.

A slight swishing sound catches my ear. Pivoting on my right foot, I spin around. My heart rate spikes. The door is open. The hallway outside the door is darker than my room. The figure in the doorway is almost invisible, nothing more than a shadowy outline.

Taking a breath, I step toward the shadow and smile hesitantly. There's no reason to assume this person is a harbinger of ill will.

"Hello?"

"Heh-loh."

The voice is female. The accent bizarre.

After a moment, the woman steps forward into the room slowly and cautiously. The light hits her and I gasp. What a stunning creature. She is tall, much taller than I, perhaps reaching just over 6'4". And she is slim, incredibly slim, like a lean and beautiful gazelle. She has almost no breasts to speak of and her hips are slight.

She moves with sensational grace. I don't question the peaceful intent of her movements. It is evident. She means me no harm.

It isn't until I focus on her face that I understand why she isn't on the runways of Paris and Milan making millions. She, like the other man, has some kind of deformity. Yet her mutations appear to be softer and less threatening. They even boast an odd, alien sort of beauty.

Her forehead is flatter than mine. Her chin, however, comes to a delicate, curved point. Her mouth is small but nothing like the bow-shaped lips of most. It is flat. Her cheekbones are similar to mine, high and defined.

But her eyes? I can't look away. She has no whites. Instead, they are golden. And where you'd expect to see the colored ring around the pupil? Where you would see blue, green or brown? They are jet black.

It's like the man from before, only his eyes were all black, even where the whites should be.

Is she nervous? People with deformities often are. They're afraid of being judged. A wave of compassion washes over me. I take a gentle step toward her and attempt to emulate her peaceful motions.

Her hair falls just past her chin. It is black and thick with a little bit of wave. Her skin is a golden brown that almost matches the color around her eyes. She's wearing a similar jumpsuit to my own, only in a beige that is slightly lighter in color than her skin. If you weren't looking carefully, you might think she was naked.

One booted foot steps deliberately in front of the other. Tall and slim like a beautiful creature from a fantasy film, she moves with delicate control. The meticulous movements are reminiscent of a ballerina. In contrast, I feel awkward and ungainly. Even in its emaciated state, my body is grotesquely curvy and soft in contrast to her own.

"I am Renee," I say nervously.

"Reh neh," she echoes awkwardly in a soft voice. I can see her concentration as she attempts to form words that are foreign to her. "Nahm Keh Mee."

I stare at her and tilt my head. I think she tried to say "name."

"You are Kemi?" I ask. She nods and smiles and repeats herself, "Kemi."

Tears well in my eyes at the rush of pleasure from human contact, even something so minute as a word in my own language. I look away and rub a hand under my eye. The feeling of my skin shocks me anew. I'd forgotten about it.

Kemi slowly reaches out a hand to me. Her fingers are the same length, except the thumb. The other had fingers like that too.

What's going on?

A crushing feeling of fear descends upon me and I try to hold back renewed panic. One person who looks like this is an anomaly, but two? That's not coincidence.

I'm trying to connect the dots but no picture is emerging. This incredible architecture? The foreign material? My loss of memory? The strangeness of my skin and the unknown language?

Something inexplicable and tragic has happened. But what? How?

I stare at her outstretched hand and look back into her eyes. Her gaze is poignant. She is begging me to reach out to her and to connect.

I don't want to. I'm scared now. But mustering the last dregs of my courage, I force my hand up to meet her. Trembling slightly, my fingers reach her extended hand. The skin feels warm, like mine.

External Memo: Rotation 267

To:	Hark, Unit 14, Continent 5 SciMed
From:	Kar, Unit 32, Continent 2 SciMed

My friend. Many orbits have passed since our training. My faith in you has not wavered. I write on a matter of the utmost discretion. This is the discovery we dreamed of during our late night conversations, the one that has kept our fires kindled over these slow orbits. We urgently need the best of the best in brain function to assist in the most urgent and pressing of discoveries. No one compares to you and your expertise. Your assistance is requested immediately. I must stress, my colleague and friend, that you proceed with the utmost discretion - not for our safety alone, but also yours.

External Memo: Rotation 267

To:	Kar, Unit 32, Continent 2 SciMed
From:	Hark, Unit 14, Continent 5 SciMed

I will arrive tomorrow, Rotation 268.

Renee

They are tall and sculpted, their movements grace itself. Controlled, elegant and precise.

The five of them in one room? It only serves to highlight their supernatural fluidity.

Five normal people like me milling about in this small space would be chaos. But they move smoothly. And despite their large size, they don't take up space. They don't fill the air with a messiness of sound and emotion.

I've never seen so many of them together. One of the men is unfamiliar. They all share the same odd features though. Tall and lean with black eyes and odd fingers.

The purposeful movements make me uneasy. Something is going to happen. They're organizing equipment. And even with their mind-numbing, toneless speech patterns, I can detect the slightest hint of an undercurrent of urgency.

At least I'm better now at telling differences between them. At first, they were a blur of distorted features and strange faces. Kemi is the easiest to recognize. She's become my measuring stick to the rest because she's physically more alike to me than the others. She's smaller than the rest, yet we share other features. She's the only one with wavy hair like me, for instance. All the others have stick-straight locks. Although hers, like theirs, is jet black. My light brown fuzz, sprouting with the speed and enthusiasm of a chia pet, stands in stark contrast.

Her eyes are closest to mine, which is a strange thing to feel given her whites aren't white. They are a light, sparkling, beautiful gold. The 'whites' of the eyes of the others range from brown to black, making it hard to measure their gaze. But I can read where Kemi is looking and can track her eyes on her face. She's staring up at YunJon and speaking earnestly, now she's glancing over at me.

Some of the others, like Kar, are impenetrable. It's impossible to tell where they are looking. At any moment he could be staring anywhere. I can only tell when he is very close. Then I can distinguish between the black of the center of this eyes and the dark, dark brown around it. From afar, though, the colors blur and his eyes appear like two burning black orbs that see everything and nothing.

Kemi feels tall to me, yet compared with the others, she's but a wisp of a thing. Her waist is nearly the same size as my own in diameter. Although where my hips and breasts flare out, hers scarcely do at all. She has strong, athletic shoulders when you compare them to me. But when you compare her shoulders to the others? She looks weak.

They are all towering, solid and strong. Built for survival? From what I've gathered, they average about seven feet tall with shoulders at least doubling mine in breadth. The larger they are, the darker their eyes seem to be. But I've only seen five of them. That's not much of a sample. Why do I assume there's a whole batch of people who look like them? Why would I think that?

They don't scare me as much. In the first hours of knowing them, they were a rush of foreign, alien creatures. Yet, I acclimated to their faces faster than one might expect. In hours my shock had faded and by the end of the day I was able to start reading their features. On the second day, I was picking up more details about how they move. I started recognizing gestures and I think I even know who is in charge. It's the really big one. Not

Kar, who is almost as big, but the other one.

My own feelings of self-consciousness haven't changed. I look like a child in their presence and I feel like a silly, delicate doll. An impossibly white, little and weak doll.

I don't look necessarily chubby in comparison, yet I am disproportionately curvy. Where they have lean, athletic and sinewy lines, mine are all askew. My hips flare out and the bones jut outward. Theirs don't. My ribcage is visible and each bone is easily countable through my jumpsuit. In contrast, theirs are covered in a sleek layer of muscle. I can even see the muscles ripple in their thighs and legs. Mine look like twigs wrapped up in a bit of soft flesh.

One of the men raises a hand-held device near my temple. I can hear a soft whirring and he gently presses it against my temple. We lock eyes and the sides of his mouth turn up in a tiny smile.

Shee. His name is Shee. Smaller and very wiry, he is the least graceful of the bunch. He jerks and lurches in comparison to their movements. But in contrast to any normal person like me, he'd look fine. It's like watching the world's premiere ballerinas suffer a guest member of Nebraska's ballet company.

"Hahlo Reh Neh," he says. "Hahlo. Gud."

"Hello, Shee," I say. "Yes, all is good."

Since his arrival this morning, he hasn't stopped testing out broken English words on me. Initially, I was thrilled. However, it rapidly became taxing. It isn't clear which words are gibberish and which are severe mispronunciations.

He slides his device to my other temple.

His excitement when I speak is palpable. He didn't stop recording my speech on a small digital pad until Kemi intervened. The terse exchange was sort of refreshing. It was like a blast of feeling in this desert of emotional impassivity. These people are incredibly monotone.

Shee backs away and Kemi calls to him. She asks him a question. He pulls out his pad and runs his fingers like lightening over the screen. Squinting, Kemi studies it and mouths words under her breath. She turns to me and walks closer.

"Reh Neh sahf. Wee hep. Steel plees."

Her voice is calm and soothing although she struggles to pronounce the words. Renee safe. We help. Still, please. She rests a gentle hand on my arm and gives it a very soft squeeze. Since we touched hands yesterday, this is the first physical contact I've had with anyone.

"Okay, Kemi."

I want to ask her to stay here and to keep her arm on mine. She won't understand. But even if she did, I wouldn't have the courage to ask.

They're different, these people. They sometimes feel like humans but sometimes they don't. They're foreign and strange not just in appearance but also in behavior. They are cold and impersonal. They seem to lack emotion. They don't touch. Despite the cramped quarters, not one of them has as much as brushed up against another.

The largest of the men approaches me. I think he's the one who leads them. The room gets quiet. He gently applies small pads of iridescent material across my scalp. He moves slowly and precisely. I fight the urge to fidget. I get a warm, tingly sensation on my scalp where each of the pads is placed. I focus on my breath. In and out. In and out. Stay calm. Relax. Everything is fine.

Finished, the man turns from me and speaks a word to the team behind him. A rush of fear-laced adrenaline shoots through me.

But I don't have more than a moment to be nervous.

My body jolts from a shock. It's not painful. It's a warm electrical surge.

Every thought is shoved out of my head. I hear sounds I've never heard before. Sounds that rush around, past and through the circuits of my mind. It's an audio whirlwind of vowels and consonants. It's beautiful, wild and cacophonous.

The sounds morph into words. Patterns emerge from words. I can see the patterns. Bits and pieces fit together. Then more and more, and more. I don't feel the passing of time. I don't care. I want this forever. My brain is on fire as I connect sounds and images and symbols.

I go deeper and deeper. This rapid-fire acquisition of knowledge and understanding is the most stimulating experience of my existence. Everything fits now. It fits and makes sense. I can process all the sounds, seemingly all at once, and match them to images and meanings. A more profound form of communication has embedded itself deep in my brain.

Then as soon as it began, it is gone. The warmth evaporates. An overpowering exhaustion envelops me and without warning my stomach heaves. I lean over the edge of the chair and puke my guts out. After several wretched moments, I'm able to stop, but I am shaking violently and shivering with a deep cold. My stomach empty, I wipe a hand across my mouth and without looking up, manage to croak out, "Something to rinse my mouth?"

"Here, Renee. This should help," a soft female voice answers.

My head is drooped and my eyes locked on the floor. I try to raise a hand but it's shaking too hard to grasp the extended bottle.

"Let me help you." Someone's hand holds it to my mouth and I take a small sip.

"I cannot believe it worked," I hear a low, male voice say from my left.

I roll my head to look at him. "Did what work? What did you do to me?"

Silence. The room is consumed with silence. They are staring at me in shock. I'm tired to my bones but the liquid I'm sipping revives me. It gives me just enough presence of mind to realize what happened.

My God. I can understand them. Jerking upward from my slumped position, I swallow down the nausea rising in my throat and swing my head to look around the room.

The machinery across the way? I can read it. I can read the damned thing. Hormone levels, heart-rate, brain activity. It's not written in English, nor any language I know the name of, but somehow I know how to read and understand it now.

I tear the sensors off my head, ambivalent to the pain as they catch on my short hair. I don't care. They can understand me.

"Where am I? Where is my family? What has happened to me?"

I am met with silence.

"Say something!" I yell. Their facial expressions and reticence terrifies me.

"I know you understand me now. Who are you? What have you done? What happened to me? Where is my family?"

I would rise and shake their shoulders violently if I could muster the strength to move. I can't read their expressions but the silence is telling. My heart sinks in my chest.

Kemi steps forward. She kneels and takes my shaking hands.

"Renee. You are in the future. It is 3037. You were accidentally pulled through time. I am so sorry, Renee, but your family is gone. They died many, many orbits ago, although to you it will feel like only the passing of weeks."

I don't understand. This is some kind of sick joke.

"What? What do you mean?"

Her eyes are like hypnotic golden orbs staring up at me, unblinking.

"Renee. We do not know exactly what year you come from, but you were pulled through time during an experiment. We do not know of a way to send you back. Even if it were possible, it would be too dangerous. You almost did not survive as it was. Your family is... gone. They lived out their full lives long ago. They are now a part of our history, while you have jumped forward to the future."

I stare.

This is impossible. And I don't want it to make sense. But my skin? These people? The rooms, technology, clothing, language?

Their odd behaviors and speech?

What if she's telling the truth?

Deep down I know that only something insane can explain the impossibility of my current situation. In some ways I was subconsciously preparing myself for an explanation I didn't want to hear.

But this? I wasn't ready for this. This is the world now? And my life, my world, is erased under centuries of time?

My chest feels like it's folding in on itself. A giant weight crushes the breath out of me and grinds my heart into nothing. I can't even cry. I just stare.

"Everyone I know is gone?" I whisper.

Log Entry: R 268 O 3037 ID: Cont 2 YunJon

Their survival is a paradox. She is small and weak, yet her body exudes fertility. Her waist and legs are slim and she has highly exaggerated curves in her hips and breasts. It is as though she were designed to bear children, yet her frame is so weak she might expire with even one.

I simply do not understand the practicality of it. And with the original weakness of her bones (a flaw Kar corrected with bone densifiers during her recovery), I cannot fathom how she might have safely supported the weight of a pregnancy.

Her hair, which is growing back very rapidly, lacks pigmentation as does her skin. It is a sort of burnt gold or light brown. Her eyebrows and eyelashes are several shades darker than the hair on her head, although it is yet hard to tell as they are so short. This lack of pigmentation would radically limit their sun exposure.

All her eye movements appear exaggerated. It is the easiest of tasks to track where she is looking. And her mouth is extremely expressive. The bowed lips move and twitch with her moods. They even break into smiles easily despite the strained circumstances. She smiles often and under inappropriate social circumstances.

As previously observed, her nose juts out harshly from her face. But it is not as unappealing as one might suppose. Her face has more planes and angles than ours do so it does not appear as a noticeable aberration. Her forehead is more rounded and her cheekbones more pronounced.

However, beyond the physical is the behavioral. She walks and moves as though she is tall and powerful. She does not simply step forward; she propels herself energetically toward her destination. It is a fascinating paradox to see such a weak being move so confidently.

Perhaps their adaptability was their greatest strength? After initial fear and reticence, she seems to have adjusted quickly to Shee and Kemi. Her fear-response rapidly evaporated. This, despite the fact that we must appear monstrous to her.

She does frequently touch her skin and grimace. Tomorrow, when she has awakened and I make my apology, I will inquire as to whether her skin hurts or bothers her in some way. Perhaps when we regenerated the skin we made an error in nerve reconstruction.

It astounds me that we can communicate with her so freely now. It would appear that both Kemi and Shee were right. They insisted she was not as intellectually inferior as we hypothesized.

"She is a sophisticated, sentient being with a high level of mental processing. You are carrying inherent prejudices because of her physical differences and the fact that she hales from an era past," Kemi stated boldly.

She directly contradicted me in front of the entire team. A tendril of dark hair had fallen into her face and her outer eyes sparkled golden. I managed a nod and did not reprimand her. I do not know why.

When Kar came to see me just now, I probed the issue. Our conversation was enlightening.

"YunJon, I am sorry to disturb you after a long day," he said. "However, I have an unusual request."

Kar had appeared at the door of my quarters unannounced, an act not unprecedented but highly unusual for him.

"Of course, Kar. Do not worry, my friend. Tell me what you need," I responded. While he is not my equal in terms of rank, he is my Science Lead and we have always had a very equitable and civil relationship.

He passed through the doorway and we settled comfortably on the floor.

"I would like to request that Luya from Unit 31 be briefed on our experiment tomorrow morning, and that we include her in all ongoing research until Rotation 274 when Command visits. I would ensure she will be held to strict confidentiality."

I was somewhat taken aback.

"Kar, forgive me for asking, but I am confused by this request. Why? Surely you can see that this is not an advisable move."

"She is highly intelligent and I believe she may help bring additional insights. She can also provide support for the assistant, Kemi."

"What do you mean, support for Kemi? Are we not supporting her?" I asked.

"Kemi has taken on a new role with Renee's arrival," he said thoughtfully. "This role requires a greater level of responsibility. Kemi is only an assistant. This must tax her to a certain degree. And Luya knows Kemi. They are both from Continent 5."

"Is there something I should be doing to better support Kemi? Something that I am not already doing?" I queried, feeling inexplicably uncomfortable.

"YunJon, your leadership has been and continues to be exemplary. You have demonstrated that you know when to enforce rules and when to forgo them in cases of the unexpected and unprecedented." His look was strange in that moment, and his voice more intense than usual.

"Luya is very intelligent and could surely bring insight," I responded after a few moments. But I had to make sure he knew the risk.

"She has already been severely ostracized due to Command's response to her last research project. Depending on how Command responds, exposure to this current project could put her career at further risk. It could even damage it to a level beyond repair. We have already put our entire team's careers on the line. Do we do this to her as well, simply to gain her insight? As our esteemed and respected colleague, I feel we ought to protect her from this."

"I have thought of this, YunJon," he responded. "Indeed, I have reflected on it at length. However, I am…" he paused for a moment in his speech. It was such an unusual verbal tic for him that I felt no small stab of worry.

"I am worried about her mental state," he finally said. "She appears to have lost hope in science. I understand the risk to her career but I am concerned that the risk of letting her continue as she is might be greater."

This was the first occasion I had ever heard Kar speak of another human in a personal way. I was so shocked, I did not even follow protocol and insist we refer her to the medical unit.

Instead, I swallowed deeply. This could not be a mere coincidence, could it?

"Have you noticed an increase in your desire to be in her presence over the past few rotations? Speak freely. It is… you may find me more understanding than you expect," I ended awkwardly.

"Yes," said Kar without a moment's hesitation. "Luya was always a precious and valued colleague to me. Surely you observed this given the time she and I spent together in the lab in the evenings. Yet these past several rotations have marked a noted shift in my desire to be in her presence. The injustice that was done to her at the destruction of her research has begun to burn anew. And I can see only too clearly now that she has lost her hope. She is a shell of who she once was. I must do something to help her.

"I will say now what we have tacitly understood but have

not spoken aloud. You know as well as I that this discovery will change our futures. There is no going back to how things were, ever, not for us in Unit 32. And for Luya, it would be best if things change, no matter how they change. It would have been kinder if they had repurposed her altogether. She must now work in the same lab, reminded of the same injustices done to herself, her team and the innocent creatures she bred in her lab, every single day. It is breaking her, YunJon. She is extremely sensitive. That is why she and Kemi are so close. Kemi is so intuitive she is able to sense Luya's distress and comfort her."

"She does? How do you know all this?"

"Luya told me." He gave me a strange, quizzical look, as though trying to unfold the motives behind my eager questions.

In that moment, I was struggling mightily to reform my opinion of Kar. I believed him to be solely science-focused. Not only did he rarely speak, but when he did it was exclusively related to work. But who was the person facing me now?

I had trusted him thus far. I would continue to do so, I decided.

"Your honesty is appreciated," I said at last. "As Team Lead, I grant you permission to both brief and include Luya into our research going forward. This will be under the stipulation of full confidentiality."

"Thank you. Your confidence in me will not go unnoticed," he said, somewhat cryptically.

But I did not pursue this further because a more pressing matter was weighing upon my mind.

"Before you go, Kar, there is one more issue I would like to discuss with you."

I paused. It felt strange to be admitting to these feelings, as though it indicated something dire.

"Tomorrow we need to speak about our increased emotional responses to some of the females in our immediate surroundings. If it were only me, I would attribute it to a stress-induced anomaly. Yet it is not just me. You have told me only now that you feel an increased awareness toward Luya. I have experienced a similar awareness, only not toward Luya," I added rapidly. "Perhaps the enhanced excitement due to our discovery has raised certain hormone levels to a degree that we ought to be aware of and assess."

Protocol be damned, I decided.

"Tomorrow, can you use some of the equipment, which does not report to Command's health unit, to run some tests of our levels?"

"Yes, of course, YunJon. We should do this."

We sat in silence for a few moments longer. Then with a nod, he rose and departed from my quarters.

Now thoughts, realizations and concerns flood my mind. Even yesterday, I would have said Kar was my closest peer and the one I knew best and trusted most. Yet I do not believe that I knew him as I thought I did.

For instance, those two males? The experts Hark and Shee? They dropped everything and risked their careers to join us at a single memo from Kar. They are brilliant specialists with a lot to lose if they were to get caught. How did Kar know he could trust them? How did they know they could trust him? And how do they move about with such discretion?

Hark, the brain analyst, is one of the sharpest minds I have encountered to date. His scientific expertise is on par with Kar's. If it were not for my total faith in his skills, I would never have allowed him access to Renee's brain. We simply would have dealt with the disadvantages of the language barrier and subsequent consequences we would face from Command.

Even so, even knowing Hark's brilliance, I did not make the decision lightly. I spent a sleepless night last night. It is not uncommon to stimulate the language portion of the brain for rapid language acquisition, although it is rarely necessary as we uniformly speak Standardized Earth. Since the Great Drought and the Last Wars, there has been only a single common language. Additionally, young minds absorb language quickly and we do not dare meddle with a developing child's brain. So the language stimulation is generally only used for Rangers when they need to rapidly learn a new code system. Sometimes it is even used in advanced computing in order to learn a programming language.

Unfortunately, there simply was not enough of Renee's language documented to attempt a language stimulation to teach any of us her language. On a modern human such as myself, the procedure would not have been risky. It has been honed to perfectly mesh with our brain activity and calibrated to our exact physiology. However, the activity in Renee's brain is far different from ours. Hark had to identify the language portion of her brain and make an educated assessment of how much stimulation to apply. We were also concerned that our language imparting system, a series of increasingly complex words and symbols, might be too challenging for her and could possibly backfire, causing brain damage.

Yet our fears were unfounded. I was stunned by the results, as were we all. She absorbed the language flawlessly. The only negative reaction was extreme fatigue and nausea when the process was complete. However, she demonstrated perfect language aptitude during that brief period before we sedated her. We feared for her safety due to her hysteria upon hearing what happened.

It is unusual how smoothly the language transferal process went. This process generally has a 90 percent success rate. It is impossible to say with such a brief assessment, but hers must be close to 100 percent. I cannot help but wonder if, in the polyglot period of history in which she lived, perhaps their brains were more attuned to learning and adjusting linguistically?

But far more notable was her intelligence. She is not mentally slow, she is different. The moment she could communicate with us, I was forced to reform my opinion. Confronting the biases in my judgments was uncomfortable. We interpreted her behavior and actions based on our cultural norms, not hers. We did not understand the type of society from which she haled. It was a society centered around small clans of humans. These humans were united based on birth ties, mating attractions, geographical origins and other associative reasons such as belief systems, like religion. I have learned that religion is essentially ancient world origin narratives. It is not yet all clear to me.

However, what is clear is that we did not approach her with scientific rigor and objectivity.

I also had to confront the true nature of what we have done and the female who must now pay the heavy price of our experiment.

It is so late it is likely already Rotation 269. I must stop so I can be rested for tomorrow. We are rapidly approaching Rotation 274. We have such a short time to get to know her and learn as much as we can before Command arrives. Tomorrow, I will meet with Kar, Hark and Kemi... perhaps even Luya. We must discuss how we will approach Command's visit. I would never have collaborated on such decisions before, but at this point the stakes are too high for me to make these decisions alone.

I cannot recall when I have last felt so tired. Yet a final thought lingers. What exactly did Kar mean when he said things will never be the same?

Renee

We are seated on the floor like children. I woke only fifteen minutes ago. After putting on my jumpsuit, a disembodied voice sounded.

"Permission to enter."

It wasn't really a question, more like a, "hey, I'm about to come in." It also affirmed my suspicion that I'm being watched.

I don't appreciate that.

My legs are crisscrossed, one on top of the other. YunJon is sitting in front of me, looking exactly as he always does. Deadpan.

"I am sorry," he says. His face is evenly lit from all sides. My pod-like room, with the glowing walls, illuminates everything from every direction. You don't think to miss shadows until they're gone.

He's sorry?

His impossible eyes are locked on mine. They're so bizarre. It's unnerving because I know they feel the same way toward me. Only I'm the exception. The black sheep. Well, more like the runty white sheep amidst a sea of mocha colored sheep with perfectly coiffed fleece.

Now understanding the language doesn't change the tone. It's still flat and the speech remains painfully monotone, like a robot. There's something irritating in the dead-pan cadence of their words. It sparks this urge in me to reach forward and shake them hard until I elicit some kind of emotional response. He's sorry, he says, but he doesn't sound like it. He sounds like a machine.

With long fingers he twists the top off a tube and extends it out in my direction. "Kar's team designed this nutrition to meet your body's needs. It should satisfy you until this evening. Please consume it. Your body and mind require great care after everything you have been through."

I don't want to eat. But his hand is extended now and dangles in midair. His outstretched hand clenches slightly and the fingers tighten around the tube. A nervous twitch?

I take it.

The tube is as long as my hand. It reaches from my fingertips past my wrist. The material is transparent. A whitish liquid is visible through the walls.

I know I need to eat. They're right and I do feel weak. But the sadness in my heart makes my stomach tighten and revolt at the thought of food. Yet, he's watching me expectantly. So I raise my hand.

The top of the tube touches my lip and my fingers tip it back in one go. It tastes like nothing, like my mouth is full of a tasteless kind of gel. Disgusting. I gag on it hard. Swallowing is almost impossible. Even water has flavor, I realize with surprise. But this stuff? Nothing. Gross.

"It tastes like nothing," I say, coughing slightly. "It's almost impossible to swallow."

"Taste? It is..." he stutters, which surprises me. "It is supposed to taste like nothing."

These people's lives must be so depressing.

A few hard swallows later and my stomach settles. This can't be what they sustain themselves on. My jaw yearns to clamp on something hard and flavorful.

"So what exactly are you sorry for, YunJon?" The question erupts out of me. "It's YunJon, yeah? That's your name?"

This whole encounter has a dreamlike quality. Here we are, two people sitting across from one another on the floor. Only one of them belongs a thousand years in the past.

Yet it's too raw, too vivid, to be an actual dream. I wouldn't feel the floor digging into my hip bones or the strange sensation of cool air chilling my bare scalp.

I just wish it was a dream.

The silence extends a few seconds. They do this. They often pause before they speak. While I wait, he continues staring. His eyes are radically different than Kemi's. His are all dark. The centers are black surrounded by a deep, solid brown. Kemi's eyes sparkle. They were the last things I looked at last night before I lost consciousness. The pain and confusion and shock were too fierce. Everything needed to go away. Her offer for a chance at a dark oblivion with sedation was irresistible. But this morning when reality struck, it was a fierce punch to the gut.

"Why did you say you're sorry?" I ask again. Impatience laces my tone. It's strange and wonderful being able to speak in his language now. Their technology is absolutely incredible. My English and their Earth Standard coexist alongside one another, like the new Earth Standard is perfectly overlaid on top of my English. Switching between them is seamless and easy.

Will I eventually lose my English? A pang of sadness strikes in the chest. There is no one to talk to in my English. Maybe Shee? But they told me he will have to leave soon. I already miss his annoying persistence. He's the most human of them all. Why does he have to leave? When he discussed his departure, it was clear he wanted to stay. With him, I can at least sense emotion in his voice. That's saying something for these toneless, expressionless people.

He swallows. "Yes, my name is YunJon. I am the team lead of Unit 32. Unit 32 is a part of SciMed and we are an experimental unit."

My eyes squint in confusion.

He pauses and then continues. "SciMed is the shortened

version of Science and Medicine Research. We are all scientists here at this station. We are a part of SciMed Continent 2. Each continent, except of course Continent 7, has their own SciMed Research Station."

"Continent 7?"

"Ah yes, Continent 7. Of course, you would not know. Continent 7 is autonomous. The Regulation Committee holds no authority there. It is the last wholly independent space. For the betterment of society, the Regulation Committee actively promotes moderation and tolerance. It has been deemed healthy for humanity to have a continent where those who wish to… leave our society… may go. It is considered wise for society to permit this space and to let it evolve as it will."

He sounds like those flight attendants do when they're repeating their safety speech for the thousandth time. Those aren't his words. They can't be. It was too memorized and robotic, even for him.

"Strange," I respond. "Can't people just be independent and evolve anywhere? It's not very tolerant to make them leave and go somewhere else to do something as normal as be whoever they want to be."

His head jerks back slightly. Maybe I should be more careful. I may start subconsciously trying to provoke them just to get emotional responses. And I don't really know them all that well yet. They don't seem violent. But who knows?

"Yes," he says, unsure. "I suppose it might sound that way."

His mouth opens as though he might say more. Then it snaps back shut.

"Go on," I prod him.

"Yes, of course. In Unit 32, we do purely experimental research. Kar, our Science Lead, and I were developing a project to create a window into the past. We called it the Time Window Project. The goal of the project was to create a small window into the distant past to observe where we came from and to learn more about our history. Much of what once was has been destroyed in the Great Drought and Last Wars."

He pauses for a moment, looking at me to see if I will question him. I don't and nod at him to continue. There will be time for more questioning later.

"Today is Rotation 269. On Rotation 247, we launched the project. Orbits of research came to fruition. We were terribly excited to see if our project would work, although we harbored doubts about its viability. Entering the dimension of time simply felt like an impossibility. Even though our science was, we believed, faultless." He pauses again, before continuing slowly.

"What happened exceeded anything we had imagined. We far overshot what we intended. It is for this that I apologize. We had thought that we would just create a window, but instead..."

"Instead you got me."

My voice comes out harsh.

They didn't make a window. They made a door. And there I was, at the wrong place at the wrong time. I walked right through it. The worst goddamned door in all history.

"It was an accident that we pulled you through. We did not know." A flash of humanity flickers across his face and he leans forward with intent. His hands grasp at mine. Touch. It's like an electric shock. I'm unprepared. A gesture of comfort? His large fingers envelop my thin, pale ones. Warmth transfers over from his hands to mine.

"Renee. I am sorry to have put you through this." His voice carries real emotion now. It's faint - very, very faint - but it's there. "It is our fault that you will not see your family again. It is our fault that you have had to suffer like you have. After what happened, it is a miracle that you are even alive. It is for this that I apologize."

His words infuriate me because now I can't hate him. I can't blame him. It was an accident and he feels genuine remorse for my pain. It's clear.

My eyes flood with tears. His empathy and kindness is a catalyst for my mourning and before I can take another breath,

I find that I'm weeping. The world shrinks down to nothing. Nothing but a dark, blind hole of pain.

Kathy never knew what happened to her sister. My mother and father never knew what happened to their daughter. Bereft, with questions unanswered, how did they live out their lives? Were they ruined? Did happiness ever return to them? Or were they haunted by the infinite and painful possibilities of what could happen to a young woman who disappears? A terrible accident, kidnapping, rape, murder. They never knew that I still live. There is no way they could know. They must have spent their lives questioning.

Now they are long dead. Every single person I knew, loved, laughed with, was annoyed by... every single life ended hundreds of hundreds of years ago. Their pain at my disappearance is nothing but an echo in time, long forgotten by everyone.

My tears begin to slow after some time. The weight of someone's arms are pressing into my shoulders. I would feel shame for crying like this in front of another person, but I'm spent. There is nothing left to feel. A numbness creeps into me.

I lean back slowly. My head aches. My eyes are swollen. My voice is thick and shaky. YunJon had wrapped his arms around me without me noticing. He slowly draws back and settles into a sitting position. I'm surprised he comforted me. It doesn't seem like something they do.

"I forgive you." My voice is sad and dull. "I know now that you didn't do it on purpose."

But I'm not done.

"Promise me one thing. Never conduct this experiment again. There are some things that are too powerful and too complex. Messing with time? That is one of them."

"I promise you," he says. "We have taken steps already to control the spread of our scientific findings. We will not repeat this experiment as it is."

A numb silence settles between us, stretching on and on.

Eventually he gracefully unfolds his long limbs and stands

up. He reaches down to help me to my feet. His hands, twice the size of mine, are gentle on my arms. My head tilts upward to make eye contact. I'm struck once more by his height. He's easily seven-feet tall.

"I need to speak with Kemi," I say. "And stop monitoring my room. It makes me uncomfortable."

Not a flicker of embarrassment crosses his face. "Are you certain that is wise? We are doing so for your own safety and health."

"I'm sure."

"Then we will move you to private quarters by the end of today. We did not intend to make you feel uncomfortable. Who informed you of this?"

"No one told me. It's obvious."

He keeps staring. The door is right behind him, yet he remains still. He wants something?

"In my culture," I say, the words coming out slowly, "we shake hands when we say goodbye and hello. What do you do to greet people and say goodbye?"

"We nod." He dips his head deeply. Dark locks of hair sweep down from the top of his head and brush against the skin of his forehead.

I nod back.

"And how did you shake hands?"

His use of past tense hurts.

My eyes stay locked on his face as I extend my hand. The tight, white skin of my hands and fingers is still unnerving. He mimics my motion. His fingers are slightly cupped. My four fingers slide between his thumb and palm. My thumb settles firmly on top of his fingers. I shake his hand.

"For people that we like and are close to, or who are a part of our family, we hug."

"Will you show me?"

"Sure." I pause, slightly puzzled at how to proceed. "Do you know, I was considered tall back in my time? I mean, how do you even hug someone as huge as you?"

Wait, oh my God. Is he laughing?

"No, seriously. I was really tall. Way above average. You guys are enormous. You do know that right?"

Good grief, is he going to hurt himself? Has he ever even laughed before? Each chuckle seems to be taking him by surprise, like he's straining vocal chords that haven't been used since infancy. I smile weakly in response. I'm too tired for this. His chuckles die down.

"Forgive me," he says, looking abashed. "That was inappropriate."

"Laughter isn't inappropriate," I respond. "Now lean down and wrap your arms around my shoulders. I will wrap mine around yours. No! Don't bang your head into mine. I go one direction. You go the other."

"How do you know?"

"Oh, intuition, I suppose. You just sense it. Now squeeze." He hugs so gently I feel like an invalid. I am, I guess.

"You can squeeze harder. You aren't going to break me." This time it feels normal, although he holds on too long.

"There. That's how we say hello and goodbye to friends. But we just shake hands with acquaintances and work colleagues. Though, sometimes, if we are close with certain people at work, we hug them, too."

"Thank you," he says, and nods deeply. Abruptly, he swivels on his heels toward the door. "I will get Kemi now and arrange for you to have private quarters."

The door slides shut.

I wander over to my 'bed' and run a hand over the light cover, mindlessly marveling at the slippery, sliding fabric. The crying from earlier leaves me weak and vulnerable. My body yearns to crawl back up onto the slab, pull the blanket over me and sink into oblivion.

The door swishes open again.

"Renee!" I recognize her voice without turning around. I

sense, rather than hear, her walk quickly toward me. Placing her arms around my shoulders, she squeezes me hard from behind.

"I watched your exchange with YunJon. I know about how you greet people," she explains in a calm but uplifting, pleasant kind of lilt. I guess privacy, like me, is a relic of the past here. I guess she also doesn't realize we should be facing each other.

"YunJon showed me how in the passageway. He said I should practice it with him. I like it very much."

Um, what? YunJon hugged her 'to practice'? These people don't touch each other. They don't even accidentally brush past another's shoulder.

"You are a very good hugger," I say. There will be time later to explain we should face each other.

"You assimilated our language so well yesterday! I am so happy that I can speak with you now. I have been saving up so many things to say to you over the past few days. Do you feel better today?"

She reminds me, the tiniest bit, of my sister when she's in a good mood. Words just flow out of her mouth, uninhibited and relaxed. Kathy, like Kemi, has the ability to change people's moods just with their presence. Had. Kathy had that ability. Pain stabs at my chest every time I remember.

"There certainly is a lot to talk about," I say, unsure of how to proceed.

"We do not have the leisure of time to get to know one another as slowly or methodically as I would have liked. However, I will do my best to fill you in quickly and efficiently. I am your primary point of contact with our team. Any questions or concerns you have, any at all, you may bring to me."

Her eyes are really compelling. The black spots in the middle reflect the light. The sparkling, golden orbs dance around them. It's pretty mesmerizing. No wonder YunJon wants to practice hugging.

"Shall we sit down and talk?"

We sit down on the ground again, facing one another cross-legged.

"Why do you sit on the floor like this?"

"To sit facing one another cross-legged implies the desire to speak peacefully and with harmony. It demonstrates intimacy and respect. For instance, YunJon spoke with you this morning sitting like this because he wanted to convey his respect to you and wanted to apologize. I speak like this with you now because I want you to feel comfortable and trusting in our conversation. Does that make sense? Do you do the same?"

Her face is relaxed and composed, but still more expressive than the others. It's a face of curious contrasts. Her nose almost looks Asian. It is small and doesn't extend as far from her face as does the others'. Her eyebrows jut out strongly and shadow her eyes. In direct contrast, the delicate, pointy chin feminizes her entire face. She exudes an internal energy and vivaciousness that translates into her features, making even her composed expressions appear energetic.

I like her hair. The soft waves contrast against the hardness of her lean body. There is a small badge on her left shoulder. I didn't notice that before. A thin bracelet encircles her wrist. It looks more utilitarian than decorative. She's pretty, I realize, somewhat startled.

"We don't have the same custom. Didn't. We didn't have the same custom. Sometimes we sat like this, but only as young children and rarely as adults."

She nods. "I think I should start with a brief historical overview. YunJon mentioned a few points, however you will benefit from a more comprehensive overview. Let us start in the early orbits of the 2200s, when the population of Earth began to suffer from an extreme drought. At that time, there was a vast increase in Earth's average temperature. The change was of approximately five degrees and it massively disrupted normal weather patterns and ocean currents. At first, it interrupted the food supply and initially everyone believed that would be the greatest concern.

"It soon became evident around the 2230s that the lack of

potable drinking water was the real concern. Poorer nations were struck first. People died by the millions. Soon this drought hit every nation on Earth, even the wealthiest. Many countries spiraled into anarchy. It is estimated that approximately one third to one half of Earth's population perished over the course of 200 orbits. Earth culture, as you know it, changed completely. Customs were drastically altered. Only certain peoples survived..."

Kemi pauses. I realize my jaw is quivering. This is the future of life as I knew it. I am learning the history of what happened to my people and my descendants. This is what would have happened to my great, great, great grandchildren had I stayed where I was in time.

Calm down. My family was long dead before this happened. Well, the family I knew was dead, but not my bloodline.

My bloodline? What am I doing, thinking of bloodlines? Am I some kind of medieval royalty?

I take a deep breath. "Please goes on, Kemi."

She looks at me carefully. "Around the 2450s, populations started to stabilize. Nations' boundaries had been redrawn. Some countries had completely dissolved. Others, through a miracle of governance, had managed to hold onto some semblance of the rule of law. Very little is known from this time. So much of what once was had been lost during this period of despair. There is very little recorded of the immediate aftermath or even of those terrible two centuries. We refer to these orbits as the Great Drought.

"For approximately one hundred orbits, societies kept largely to themselves in attempts to rebuild. However, many nations had developed brutal customs during the drought in order to ensure their survival. Leaders were often vicious and as populations increased, different groups began competing for resources. Around the end of the 2590s, the first of the Last Wars broke out. Bloody combat covered the majority of Earth, with only small pockets of peace remaining. Luckily, most nuclear weapons were no longer active due to neglect during the drought years, but several remained. People found a way to reactivate them and they were used. Some parts of Earth were entirely destroyed. By most historians' accounts, another half of Earth's population was decimated. It is estimated that now only approximately one tenth of Earth's pre-drought and pre-war population remains.

"Around 2700, all the wars had finally ceased. The Last Wars, as they became known, ended. Society as we know it today began to develop. Our forefathers and mothers developed a new system to govern Earth. One Regulation Committee was assembled to control governance and law. Directly underneath the Regulation Committee were set two strong counterweights - the Balance Committee and the Enforcement Committee.

"The Balance Committee ensures all regulations are neither too extreme nor too modest. We in Unit 32, an experiment unit, exist at the decree of the Balance Committee. They believe that society needs a certain element of risk and experiment in order to thrive.

"The Enforcement Committee is the hand of authority. If any mission needs to be accomplished that is in any way militaristic or martial, they are responsible for this. This branch is completely separate from the Regulation Committee. It was believed that those who create societal regulations should not be directly involved in the military. It is believed, and wisely so, that should the enforcement and regulation committees mix, their power would become corrupt and we would risk falling again into anarchy.

"Earth has been split into six continents. The seventh is left autonomous. As YunJon briefly alluded to, it was decreed that there must always be a land that is left ungoverned. It was the strongest push by the Balance Committee and is very controversial even to this day. The issue of Continent 7 is, in truth, not largely discussed. We do not know very much about it and it is more often than not ignored, particularly because it is so geographically separated from the other continents."

"Which continent is it?" I mutter under my breath.

"What did you say?" she asks.

"Maybe you can show me a map later? I would like to see which continent is Continent 7. I would also like to know where we are now."

"Oh, of course!" Kemi exclaims. "I will get one shortly. We are in Continent 2 right now. Each continent is generally kept in order by a continent-specific Earth Command. They make sure that housing is adequate, that society is working well and that citizens are peaceful and content. Each continent also has a Research and Development branch that operates independently from the Earth Command. We are a part of that here. We are SciMed Continent 2, which stands for Science and Medicine. As YunJon explained, it is one of four branches under Research and Development.

"In Research and Development, we operate slightly differently than the rest of the population as we do not report directly to Earth Command. Nonetheless, everything in today's society is designed to contribute to peace and harmony, including our work."

She stops speaking. That was a lot of information to process. But I suddenly really, really want to know where I am.

"Can you please show me the map now?"

The urge to have some point of reference suddenly feels more important than anything else.

"Yes!" She swipes her fingers across her wristband and requests that a holopad be brought to her. Not three second pass before the door opens and another female, one I don't know, quickly walks toward her and hands her a small, square pad before nodding crisply.

"Activate. Raise map of globe."

A slowly spinning Earth appears above the square pad she has set between us. She wraps her fingers around it and pulls outward. The globe expands to approximately a foot and a half in diameter.

"Highlight current location," she says. She spins the globe

and I see a blue dot.

"We are here," she says. "This is Continent 2."

There, on that beautiful three dimensional globe, is a gleaming dot on a continent I could recognize anywhere. It's North America. And there we are, almost smack in the middle of the United States.

"Indiana," I exhale softly. "I'm still in Indiana."

I feel a rush of relief, foolish though it may be. I know where I am. I am exactly where I was before. I needed some point of reference in all this insanity, something to link me to who I am and where I am from. If it can't be time, at least it can be space.

"Eendee-ahna?" Kemi says.

"Kemi, this is where I lived before, before I was pulled through time. We're in the same geographical location."

I place my hands around the globe like she did. There's a soft resistance. My arms extend outward and the globe follows suit, growing bigger and more detailed. I pull it as large as I can, scooting backward to make space. Squinting, I look for the five great lakes just north of the electric blue, glowing dot.

They're not there. They're gone. And as I look closer, I notice that Earth is not green and blue. Earth is brown, yellow and blue with only hints of green scattered here and there.

Log Entry: R 269 O 3037 ID: Cont 2 YunJon

Kar disengaged our connection with the central system so none of our results would be recorded. We ran full medical panels on every team member and compared them with their last annual results. There were no unpredicted or unexpected changes. There was, superficially at least, nothing to see.

I exhaled slowly in relief just as Luya moved to me. Having been briefed by Kar, she witnessed the entire testing. She had stood quietly near the wall, largely shielded by a piece of equipment.

By the time she stepped forward to speak with me, everyone had left and only Kar, Hart and I remained in the lab.

"Test the air," she said quietly.

"What do you mean?" I asked, confused.

"Test the air for pheromone levels," she repeated.

Kar and Hart, busy elsewhere, both turned quickly to look at her.

"Brilliant," Kar exclaimed, excitement lacing his voice. Luya's features warmed at his words, flushing to a pleasant shade. My eyes darted back and forth between the two.

"What are pheromones?" I asked.

I have never heard of these prior to today. I considered my medical training to be extremely advanced, although my expertise is more in science and particularly in the areas of time/space theory. Yet there are considerably more gaps than I had, evidently, acknowledged.

"Pheromones," said Kar. His voice was far more animated than usual. I overlooked his tone, as I had his excessive praise of Luya just moments earlier, and did not chastise him his ebullience.

"They are not studied anymore. You would not be familiar with them. They phased out its inclusion on study syllabi about 20 or 30 orbits ago. Most professionals concluded it was the stuff of folklore and no longer warranted classroom time and training. Luya, tell them."

Luya stepped forward, "I did some independent research on pheromones only recently. I heard about them when I first began my training back in 3024. It was only in passing from a fellow trainee. Yet when I started my Unit's experimental project on small mammals, we conducted additional research. Pheromones, it was hinted in certain texts, have been strongly attributed to animals. But since there are so few animals and we have such limited contact with them, there is precious little information available and data to analyze."

"Yes," I said, admittedly slightly impatiently, "but what are they?"

"Ectohormones," said Kar. "They act outside the body of the individual who is secreting them. Luya, do you still have the equipment for measuring?"

"No," she said, her voice trailing off. I felt a twinge of disappointment in my gut. Yet she continued. Her voice was oddly jilted and tight with emotion.

"But I can recreate it if you help me. Even though I destroyed my notes, I still remember all of it."

They were extremely eager and so I ordered them to get started. Within moments, Luya and Kar were absorbed in their work.

Hart took me aside and added, "Pheromones are behavior-altering agents that are released into the air. This is why they might be important in this case. They could be responsible for subtle alterations in behavior. It is a long shot and highly unlikely, but we cannot exclude it as a possibility. We know very little about how humanity has evolved over the past one thousand orbits. Renee may carry some relics of our evolutionary past that we no longer retain."

It sounded the stuff of fantasy. Hormones are personal to our own beings, affecting only ourselves as they are released within our systems. Everyone knows this. As such, I harbored a suspicion we were wasting our time on a dead-end, despite my trust in Kar and Luya. They are brilliant, but brilliance does periodically take timely detours down useless avenues. Yet we needed to exhaust our options. And after my conversation with Kar last night, I believed something was occurring to prompt us to alter our typical behaviors. I cannot deny that I feel things differently. And if my team reports similar behavior, as did Kar, then I would be an irresponsible leader to ignore such evidence.

Therefore, I swallowed my skepticism and, while they worked, busied myself. I coordinated Renee's private quarters. I sent off a perfunctory report to Command. Then, I did something very unusual. I went to the nutrition center. Typically, I take my nutrition in my quarters. As Team Lead, I am afforded this privilege.

But I wanted to see my team. I wanted to observe them.

So I went and sat and watched them chatting and interacting with one another. Were they different? Was there more touching, laughter and emotion? Having never taken the time to do this before, I have no real point of comparison. And surely everyone was altering his or her behavior slightly given my presence. This is the customary response to authority. We learn it in our training. Nothing stood out to me as exceptional, until a young female on our team, tall and athletic, smiled at me when she walked past. I nodded in response, on instinct.

That was unusual behavior. Engaging in a smile, outside the context of a conversation, is simply not done - especially with a superior.

Her smile made me think of Kemi. My thoughts spiraled to that morning and my meeting with Renee. It is clear Renee's culture tolerated, and promoted, a significant amount of affection and interpersonal contact. When I paged Kemi and met her in the hallway outside of Renee's medical quarters, I briefed her on our conversation. I described the handshake and the embrace.

"Show me," Kemi said, looking up at me.

"What?" I asked.

"Show me the hug," she said again, insistent. "I want to make sure I understand it properly."

I stared down. An unexpected twist wrenched at my stomach. A jolt of adrenaline dashed through my limbs, settling in my chest. Kemi knows the rule about interpersonal contact between an authority figure and a team member. Everyone knows the rule. I read the challenge in her eyes. She knew what she was asking, and she wanted it anyway.

I would not do it, of course. That would be irresponsible and a breach of protocol. But then I took a step toward her anyway. Those golden eyes were locked on mine, vibrating with an intensity I have never formerly observed. I believe I must have temporarily lost my grip on reality. Using my peripheral vision, I checked that the corridor was empty. Assured no one was coming, my arms moved of their own volition. Reaching forward, settling my hands on her thin upper arms, I pulled her toward me roughly and, playing off the momentum of her body, wrapped my arms around her torso as she fell against me. She felt slight but powerful, soft but strong. It was a mess of contradictions, and it was exquisite and overwhelming.

What would I have done had I not heard voices from down the passageway? Even knowing someone was coming, I could barely force myself away, as though my limbs and body were moving by their own will. It took all of my mental strength to break away, just before they turned the corner and we were in view.

Kemi's eyes, as she stared up at me for a moment, were confused and alight with emotions. But then, without a word, she was gone, darting into the room to meet Renee. I stared after her, at the closing door, suppressing my desire to chase her. I might have, had the assistant not spoken to me.

"Are you well, YunJon?" asked one of the males who had rounded the corner. He stared curiously.

"Yes, yes, of course. Thank you for asking. I was reflecting for a moment." I nodded courteously, and turned to hurry down the hallway.

I have mated before, opting in when slots came open and I felt the primal desire. I have not chosen to be a birth father yet, though. Does Kemi participate in the mating cycles? Many choose not to. I could never ask, it is forbidden. But I want to, I realized, sitting there in the cafeteria.

As I was thinking, the sounds of conversation in the cafeteria had muted, dimming to almost nothing, while I replayed the memory in my head. The vibrating alert of my wristband startled me, harshly snapping me back to reality. I leapt from my spot, surprised to see the eyes of the female, the one who smiled at me, locked upon mine. With another brisk nod, I turned and walked rapidly out of the nutrition center and back to the lab.

I entered to find Hart, Kar and Luya speaking excitedly in the corner.

"It is operational!" Luya exclaimed.

"Brief me," I said, keeping my voice calm. She would not be so excited if they had not found something, I thought with fearful certainty.

Despite my nerves, I was intrigued to see the animation and excitement running across Luya's features. It was transformative. It had been well over an orbit, since the destruction of her team's project, that I had seen her exhibit her customary passion. I had forgotten who she had once been, and how magnetic and lovely and brilliant she was when excited and engaged. Shame for my neglect of our friendship, and for having ceased visiting her over the past orbit, rippled through me. I thanked Kar silently for having reached out to her, for being a better friend than I.

"We have tested a sample of the air from the lab," Kar said. "It tested positive for releaser pheromones, primer pheromones and modulator pheromones. Come with us now to Renee's medical quarters. We want to test near her to see if there is a change in the levels. It will establish whether our theory is accurate."

Curiosity was biting at me. What did this mean? What were the implications? But I stifled my questions. They would explain in due course.

"Of course, let us go. Kemi is with her now, but for the time being, until we know more, we keep this confidential."

"Yes," they murmured.

Luya conducted the test alone in the room. I did not want to overwhelm Renee with too many people. When Luya exited, and met us in the passageway where we waited, she was positively glowing.

My stomach dropped. I instantly hushed her. "All of you, come to my private quarters. No more discussion in the open like this."

Once in my quarters, Luya tested the air in my room. Staring down distractedly at her holopad, she said, "Kar, explain it to him while I finish this chart."

I beckoned them to sit. Kar launched into speech before we even settled on the floor.

"Pheromones, in normal working and living quarters, are almost negligible. A scant amount exists, but the levels are so insignificant that they hardly, if ever, even register for measurement. Most people are entirely unaware of them, and given that they have been removed from training, in another generation the memory of them will likely be entirely lost. I find it suspicious that there is so very little publicly available research on it. I can only suspect there is more that is restricted, but," he coughed slightly, "I did not have the time to," here he coughed again, "go exploring some of the restricted areas, um, independently."

"I did not hear that," I said, raising a hand to my forehead in exasperation.

"Yes, of course, yes. As I mentioned, pheromones were monitored carefully for some time. This is in the records. But regular monitoring was phased out, without any reason listed, and I could not find any supplemental explanation for why testing was curtailed some decades ago. The natural deduction is, of course, that levels were so low for such an extended period of time that it simply made no sense to continue. Yet it is all rather vague, without much explanation as to why such little data remains, why instruction ceased and so on.

"No blueprint, patterns or even instructions on how to conduct the test are available. We could recreate the measuring device so quickly only because Luya had already created one during her team's former experiment. It is quite simple, actually, as it is not a sophisticated test. You simply have to know what you are looking for. That is why we were able to do it so rapidly. The trick is in the calibration and determining what, exactly, you are measuring. Luya was able to rapidly reconstruct those elements and how we needed to program the system to do so.

"We first tested the devices in Unit 31 to ensure it was calibrated. Levels registered at near zero, which is what we expected. Then we returned to Unit 32. What we discovered were substantial increases in, as I mentioned earlier, three pheromones. The first are releaser pheromones. These elicit an immediate response that is rapid and reliable, and usually linked to sexual attraction.

"The second, primer pheromones, work over a longer period of time. They influence development and reproduction physiology, including puberty. The third and final we registered were signaler pheromones. These can alter or synchronize bodily functions. For instance, they can enhance tension or relaxation. These can affect a woman's fertility cycle."

I stared in startled shock. I was grappling with my ability to believe what they were saying, and to process the mammoth implications.

Kar nodded at Luya. Luya has long, thin hands and fingers. They danced gracefully over her holopad as she began to speak and enlarge the graph she had designed.

"What we confirmed, when I went into Renee's quarters, was that the closer to her body, the higher the levels of pheromones in the air. Allow me to demonstrate," she quickly indicated the data points on the graphic that she placed on the table between us.

Looking at me, she said nervously, "You do, of course, know what this means."

I did know.

"Renee is the one emitting the pheromones," she said slowly. "The only reason we knew to look for this was, due to the continued exposure of your team to her over the past orbits while in closed quarters, your behaviors have changed. Even I was able to notice," she paused, and I saw her eyes dart toward Kar, then continued, "changes in Kar's regular behavioral patterns.

"When Kar told me yesterday evening that you," Luya paused again now, this time faltering, as though uncertain she might be betraying a confidence. I nodded anemically at her to go on. "He mentioned he may not be alone in these changes and that you encouraged us to research more. That was, YunJon, a very enlightened decision. I am impressed. Thank you for allowing us to pursue this path of research freely."

Praise is rare. It is frowned upon. Yet I think of those words now, and the accompanying nod of agreement from both Kar and Hart, and I feel a great swelling of joy in my chest. It is unproductive for society to applaud an individual for doing what they should do for the betterment of all. Yet, how oddly satisfying and encouraging it is. Heat even rose to my cheeks at Luya's words. Perhaps she may even share her praise with Kemi.

After thanking Luya for her words, I sat back and requested

a moment for reflection. Scenarios flitted through my mind. Pieces of the puzzle fell into place. My heightened emotions, my awareness of females, the magnetism of Renee, the team's united desire to protect her, the interruption of routine and the lack of desire to return to our regular, pre-Renee lives.

Does the existence of these pheromones imply we have no autonomy? That we convert to mindless creatures, responding to external stimuli, with no control over ourselves and our choices?

I dismissed the questions as soon as they came to mind.

While we may be catalyzed to behave in certain ways, the behaviors they provoke are ones that are latent within us. We are still ourselves. I am the same person, only provoked, or perhaps awakened.

I will not deny the truth. I enjoy it. It is exciting, exhilarating, thrilling. Never before have I felt so fully the sensation of being alive.

We have set off down a path to which there is no return. We can panic in the face of the unknown, such as these pheromones, and retreat away from the possible implications of what they mean, or we can boldly confront them head on with the open spirit of science and research.

Cont. 2 SciMed Command will not approve. They will not approve of even her presence.

But the Balance Committee? We had a shot of persuading them to tolerate her so long as she was not disruptive to society. This changes things. Behavior-altering pheromones will be seen as intolerable - a radical, dangerous threat to the balance and peace of society. They will practice no restraint in eliminating her.

"Luya, Hart, Kar," I said, leaning forward. "This information must absolutely remain confidential. I want you to destroy any trace of the tests you ran today. Any proof of what you have found - the search history on the database today, anything that can even hint at what we have discovered - wipe it clean."

They nodded, muttering their agreement.

"When I say the utmost confidentiality," I said slowly, myself only processing the weight of what I was saying, "I mean from everyone, keeping it even from the Regulation Committee, until I deem it safe to disclose, which may never come to pass. Can you do this?"

Renee

I jerk awake. Where am I? Was it just a dream?

Of course it was.

I squeeze my eyes shut tightly, as though the act alone could lock the images into my head. Maybe it will keep them from flying away like dreams do.

Kathy and I are home for Christmas. The sun streams through the sliding doors. She complains about bad cell reception at the house. Dad is on his computer playing an obnoxious Christmas carol spoof. Mom wipes down the counter.

I'm at the table with a paintbrush in hand and a blank canvas in front of me. I hesitate to set the bristles down because I'm unsure of what to create. Everything is warm, soft and gentle. But then my family's faces slip away like sand through my fingers before I can stop them.

My heart breaks all over again.

It's like this every morning. I think I won't be able to survive the agony of remembering and the realization that everything is gone.

And every evening, I think I will die of sadness.

Mornings and evenings are the hardest. The pain and loneliness slam down on me with unforgiving brutality.

During the day, distractions keep me occupied. I can push

aside the pain until it's a dull and manageable ache. There are periodic and unexpected flare-ups, but they subside quickly.

I didn't know humans could survive this kind of heartbreak. It's like a heavy rock crushing my chest. There is real, physical pain.

Get out of bed, Renee.

I don't move.

Get out of bed.

I scoot one hand to the edge of the blanket. I push it down. I want the cold to make me uncomfortable. If I'm uncomfortable enough, I'll get up.

Not until goosebumps cover my skin do I manage to crawl out of bed.

My jumpsuit is hanging by the door. It's blue. I asked for it. I don't really know why. I guess I'm just tired of looking at their mundane tans, whites and grays. It's dismal. With their technology, I knew they could create some gorgeous colors. I was right.

Although now that I see it, I wonder why I had to ask for something that would make me stand out more.

But Kemi and Luya acquiesced readily so I didn't think much about it. They looked at me with their heads tilted slightly. I've noticed they often mimic each other's behavior and are seemingly unaware of it.

Luya had a curious smile dancing about her lips. I couldn't help but ask her why she was smiling.

"Because I finally have something worthwhile for my unit to work on," she said. Then she and Kemi broke into laughter, which I found oddly charming. They do it so rarely. Their laughter always sounds a bit startled, as though it took them by surprise.

I asked Luya what she meant by that comment, but she didn't explain.

Whatever she meant by it, her team must be talented because the suit is stunning. The blue is pure and multifaceted. It is truly radiant. With the technology to create such beauty, I don't understand why they wear the colors they do. I shimmy into it and it molds deliciously to my skin.

It would be nice to have a mirror.

My hair is growing back quickly. It's a soft fuzz already. Maybe I've got an edgy, high fashion look. Or not.

It's stupid to think about that anyway. I'm a freak here, no matter how my hair looks. With my pale skin, eyes, height and body shape, my hair could be two feet long and it would be the least exciting thing about me.

Exciting? That's the wrong word. I'm not exciting. I'm alarming. I'm going to look perpetually and unendingly alarming to every single person I meet for the rest of my life.

But I'll have a healthy back. I stand straighter than a tree. My posture is utter perfection. The irony is not lost on me. Back in middle school when I was taller than all the boys, what I wouldn't have given to be shorter. Now it's like someone let loose a gymnast at the NBA's summer camp.

They're all hulking.

But their heights vary somewhat. Kemi is smaller. YunJon and Kar are particularly big. That's basically where the differences end though.

Everyone is tall, slim, athletic and well-muscled with clean, trim lines. They're all a bit androgynous.

I run my hands self-consciously over my breasts and hips. The fabric clings to every curve on a person's body. There's no hiding my shape. Even as emaciated as I've become from my medical travails, I don't fit in.

Everyone goes to some kind of cafeteria to get their food. But for me, the lab tailor-makes my nutrition. They say it's matched to my unique biological needs. I don't doubt it. I'm flush with a health I've never before experienced. My skin is clear and smooth. My muscles are strong and limber.

And like any young woman at the peak of health, my libido is strong and raging.

That's a bitter pill to swallow. It's almost enough for me to rue my good health. I'm never going to have sex again.

Who would find me attractive?

And that could be beside the point. Do they even have sex anymore?

I could ask. It's been on the tip of my tongue. But I'm afraid of the answer. Either no one is doing it or it's going to be weird. Sex is probably measured, controlled, rational and overseen by a committee.

That's not really sex then, is it.

And so I'll spend the rest of my life drinking from tubes and staring at androgynous-looking asexual giants who are incredibly intelligent but artless, humorless and sexless.

Right.

That's a rabbit hole I don't want to go down.

I need to focus.

Important people are coming today. It's rotation 274. Luya, Kemi, Kar and YunJon sat down with me yesterday to explain. We had a long talk. They didn't say it outright, but I could read between the lines. Their bosses are coming to check in on the experiment's results. In other words, they're checking on me.

I got the alarming sense that they don't actually know about my existence. Even a week ago I could never could have discerned that from their voices and expressions. But I've picked up a lot. Even their expressionless faces carry shadows and hints of feeling and tension if you look carefully enough.

With a nervous sigh, I propel my legs forward. My quarters are sparse. There's a bathroom in the corner with a toilet-like contraption and a shower that doesn't clean you with water. It uses some substance that sprays on and dries within a minute. It leaves my skin smooth, soft and fresh.

With my index finger applied firmly to the small pad by the door, it slides open. The passageway is empty, which elicits a mild sense of relief. Even a false sense of autonomy is something. No one is actively hovering by my door to see if I made it through another night anymore.

I turn left. The second right takes me to the lab. Kar is there because Kar is always in the lab. I like him. His presence is soothing. He reminds me of some of my mathematician friends who pretended to be antisocial because interpersonal relationships were hard for them. But they weren't. Underneath it they craved company like everyone else. They were also, like Kar, completely brilliant.

He's in the far corner creating some kind of 3-D model on one of their holopads.

"When do you sleep, Kar?" I ask him.

He turns to look at me. The corner of his mouth twitches with the hint of a smile. A tiny bit of joy creeps around the greyness of my grief.

"Do not tell anyone, but I also tailor my nutrition like yours. I have designed it so that I need less rest than is average," he says.

"Kar, you're so bad," I say with a smile. He stares at me in that way that they always do.

"I do not think it is as bad as perhaps you think," he responds. His brows are furrowed with a look of concern.

Right. Irony. "Kar, it's a joke. I don't actually think it's bad. During my time, we occasionally teased people verbally. When I say something like that in that tone of voice, it implies the opposite. In other words, I don't think it's outrageous."

He stares at me quizzically. "Don't people get confused?"

"No, not really. It's all about the tone of voice."

"But what is the point? What is the benefit?"

"The point is humor. The point is to build rapport. I don't know. I guess it's also to indicate that the other person is someone you like and that they're worth a little joke. We usually befriend those who have similar types of humor."

For Pete's sake, this is tedious.

"But we're not friends," he says, staring at me deadpan.

Ouch. That hurts. That stings way worse than I would have thought. Of everyone, other than Kemi, Kar was the closest thing I considered a friend here.

"Why didn't you laugh?" he asks. "I was being ironic."

Oh, my God.

"Kar! Your tone of voice! I thought you were serious. You have to change your tone of voice."

I chuckle a bit once I recover and he smiles. Then we're quiet for a few moments.

He breaks the silence first. "That blue is very beautiful. Where did you get such an attractive color for your jumpsuit? It is an exact match for your eyes. I have never seen such a color in clothing before."

"Oh, thank you. Luya and her team designed it for me. I asked her for it yesterday."

Kar beams with pride. As much as they can beam, I guess. But then he actually breaks into a grin. What's with that?

"Um, can I have my nutrition please?"

Although I'm not hungry, I do crave the feeling of something in my mouth and stomach. What I wouldn't give for a crunchy carrot.

He hands me a tube. I take it and accidentally brush my fingers against his. I don't even flinch. Our differences don't surprise me so much anymore.

Leaning against the wall, I slide down until I'm sitting cross-legged on the floor. They don't have chairs anywhere. I sip it slowly to prolong the process and watch Kar work.

"When did you and YunJon meet?" I say.

"Why does that matter? Why do you ask?"

"You seem to work really well together," I say.

"We do. But why does it matter?"

"Not everyone works so well together. I thought perhaps you had known each other for many years."

"What would it matter?"

Agh. I'm clenching my jaw. They are so different it's painful at times. The endless explanations of why I ask certain things and say certain things and behave one way over another. It's wearing me down.

And I can't help but feel a nagging sense of inferiority. It's like maybe they have evolved far beyond my understanding. Maybe these mundane details, details like the amount of time you have known someone, are now eclipsed by greater mental pursuits.

"We have known each other for three orbits, ever since we joined this team together," he eventually says very calmly. He isn't moving anymore but staring straight at me.

"Why… Kar, why did you just answer me? Why did you answer a question you didn't think mattered?"

"Because it matters to you."

To my shock, my eyes fill with tears. Clambering to my feet, my arms weave their way around his waist and I hug him hard. With a natural grace that extends well beyond his counterparts, he hugs me back. A warmth permeates the gray cloud of sadness that consumes me and it dissipates a tiny bit more.

I pull back. "Thank you, Kar."

He responds, looking down at me, "I think, Renee, that you have more friends who care about you here than you might think."

A tear rolls down my cheek and, embarrassed, I wipe it away quickly. I nod in thanks and return to my seat. I can't think of anything to say. So I fall back into my normal routine.

He works and I watch. I absorb the way he moves, the way the equipment works and the layout of the room. Everything he does is rapid-fire, precise and with intent. After a while, team members start to enter and exit periodically. I recognize some.

Kemi enters discreetly after a time and walks over to join me. She sits down next to me on the floor and squeezes my hand. Her casual body contact has increased since I've arrived. It's far more natural now than it once was.

"Hello, Renee. The jumpsuit looks so beautiful. You are a walking work of art. It is like you are a piece of the sky."

I'm somewhat startled by the elegance of her words. It's so unusual.

"Hi, Kemi," I manage in response. "What a lovely thing to say.

You are so poetic. Did you rest well?"

"Oh, in fact, I did not. I was… thoughtful about today. But why do you ask?"

"It's a custom. When we care about someone, we ask them if they have slept well. It shows that we are interested in their well-being."

"Oh," she says. I see a little smile light up her face. She has a beautiful smile. The left side rises slightly higher than the right and two adorable dimples appear in her cheeks. I think she is beautiful when she smiles.

YunJon walks in shortly and comes over to join us. He sits down cross-legged in front of us. I can see him staring at my jumpsuit, but he says nothing.

"How did you rest, YunJon?" Kemi asks.

I chuckle and then I swear I can see Kemi blush the tiniest bit. It's hard to tell with their skin tone. YunJon looks confused, but answers as diplomatically as always.

"Thank you for inquiring, Kemi. I rested adequately," he says, carefully modulating his tone of voice.

"You two are something else," I snort. I know they don't get me. I watch them stare at each other, and then at me, and then back at each other.

"Don't ask," I say to preempt their questions. "It's too hard to explain. It's just a cultural difference."

At that, they both smile.

Kar interrupts our moment, and says heatedly, "YunJon! We have received an alert. Command is arriving."

YunJon leaps to his feet. I've never seen him move so hastily. He presses a button on his wristband and murmurs into it. His voice is amplified across the station.

"Unit 32. Assume your posts immediately. Command visit imminent."

Kemi follows suit and rises quickly and athletically. She reaches down to help me stand.

"Come with me," she whispers. She drags me to the back

of the room. We stand obstructed from view behind a piece of machinery. She is clenching my hand hard in hers. God, she's strong. Her grip is like a vice. I don't say anything because I'm suddenly so nervous I might be sick. The tension in the room has ratcheted up considerably. Why is this such a thing? And why are Kemi and I hiding back here?

I'm too jumpy to speak even though I desperately want to hiss at Kemi and demand she explain what we're doing. She still has her hand on my arm while she stares over the top of the machine that is blocking us from sight. With her height, she is just barely able to see over it. My view is entirely obstructed.

There's a shuffle of feet and the murmur of low voices. YunJon's voice rings out in a formal greeting in a completely neutral tone. I hear other voices respond in turn. They are voices I don't recognize.

YunJon thanks them for granting him a 10-orbit delay to solidify his research. His words are brief, perfunctory and straight to the point.

My nervousness mounts as I listen to him talk.

He explains the project and what happened in detail. It's oddly horrible to hear my story told so scientifically. I sound like a lab specimen. It feels grotesque.

"I would like to present to you our guest from the past. Her name is Renee," he concludes.

So far, his voice is the only one that has spoken. When he concludes, you could hear a pin drop. The silence is impossibly tense. We don't move. Kemi keeps a restraining hand on my forearm. She must be waiting for some signal from Kar.

A soft, eerie voice breaks the silence. "Did you say her? You have given this... thing... a name and refer to... it... by a gendered pronoun?"

"Yes, Station Commander. She is a person and similar to us in many regards. She communicates freely in our language," says YunJon, continuing in an impossibly neutral tone of voice.

"I am... shocked, Team Lead YunJon." The voice itself is

almost delicate and the speaker makes long pauses in the middle of his sentences. It's as though he's forcing us to wait upon his words. I instantly dislike him.

"You ought to have reported this immediately. Your lack of judgment will be noted. You have endangered not only your entire team but the whole Research Station with your foolhardy, headstrong desire to handle this yourself. This specimen from the past is highly likely to be at best a destabilizing force to our community. At worst, it is an outright threat. Either of these scenarios is intolerable. I am... extremely displeased."

Kemi's hand is tightening on my shoulder. I cringe slightly. Her jaw is clenched. Her eyes are squinted in anger.

"I understand your response, Station Commander. It is commendable that you have our safety and the station's safety as your foremost concern. I also acknowledge that you will note my leadership choices. However, I ask that before you make any judgments or assessments, you meet Renee in order to understand why I have acted as I have."

YunJon is maintaining an exceptional level of calm. I, however, am not. My heart is pounding. Kemi is still gripping me. I was totally unprepared for this. I thought everyone would be like Unit 32. They've treated me with kindness and empathy, despite our massive cultural divide. Perhaps I was taking them for granted.

"I suspect you have this... thing... contained in quarantine in another chamber?"

I feel a surge of hatred. A light sheen of sweat breaks out on my upper lip and forehead and I dash a hand across it. Kemi looks down at me and pulls me to her. She wraps her arm around me protectively.

"Indeed, we do not. We have run exhaustive tests and are wholly confident that she is not a threat in any way. In fact, if anyone is threatened, I would hazard to say it is her, not us," YunJon says. For the first time, I hear a hint of defiance in his voice.

"This is... unacceptable. We will leave immediately until this area is under quarantine. A squad will be arriving shortly to ensure that everything has been properly contained. We will return only after. Every member of Unit 32 will also be under a temporary, mandatory quarantine to ensure there is no cross contamination."

My God, this is nightmarish.

Is this really happening? Who is this person?

He's smashing to pieces everything I thought I knew about the future. Fear has replaced my nagging sadness. I glance up at Kemi as we hear a shuffle of feet mark the exit of the group. She looks back at me. A wave of anxiety washes across her face. My terror heightens.

"That was far worse than I expected," she exhales. "Renee, I promise I will not leave you."

YunJon rounds the corner where we are standing and grabs us. Putting one hand on my arm and the other on Kemi's, he says, "I will find a way to get us out of this. Do not fight anything for now. The quarantine squad will be here very soon. Just be calm."

We walk around the corner and everyone is looking at us. Anxiety is written on their faces. Even I am able to read their expressions easily. Their normal stoicism and impassivity appear gone. I hone in on Luya because, of all people, she doesn't look afraid. On the contrary, she looks fierce and angry - very, very angry.

I think I'm in shock.

My mind is running at light speed to try and catch up. Unit 32 was my everything until now. They were, unknowingly, representatives of the whole future. I assumed that the rest of the world was just an extension of them.

But not only is the world wholly unlike them, it's threatening. And they think I'm an abomination. They think I'm a thing that will contaminate their society.

They haven't even met me or spoken with me.

Is this how it is everywhere beyond my insular group in Unit

32?

Luya and Kar run over to join us just as the sliding doors hiss open again. That was so fast. I look over and see them.

My fear is visceral. A masked, faceless group of bodies walk through the door. They are covered entirely in thick, white suits that muddy the outline of their form.

Yet their faces themselves are the stuff of nightmares. They are entirely masked in white without any holes, neither for eyes nor mouth. Some of them carry equipment. One walks over to us and addresses YunJon.

"Instruct your team to remain calm while we implement the quarantine process," the disembodied voice says.

Log Entry: R 274 O 3037 ID: Cont 2 YunJon

It took all my willpower not to smash the faceless quarantine specialist into the wall as the door slid shut on Kemi and Renee. With my strength, speed, dexterity and size well above average, I could have done it.

Just as he was typing the lock code into the door I was able to regain control. I utilized the breathing exercises I was taught as a child. I dare not think what would have happened had I failed to suppress such a foolish urge. Violence would have yielded the worst possible outcome for us.

Neither Renee nor Kemi fought the quarantine in the slightest. They walked into the room calmly. Despite my efforts, Kemi would not separate from Renee. She insisted on accompanying her.

I wished to grip her arm and pull her away. Instead, I spoke with as much intensity as I dared allow creep into my tone, "Please, Kemi, reconsider your choice. There could be consequences you are not aware of."

I pulled Luya to the side moments later, but she refused to help dissuade Kemi. She only said, "I respect her decision. I would never wish Kemi to experience the same regret I do now."

Since I could not stop them, I desired to join. But I am the Team Lead and my responsibility is to the team. It is not to my own desires. Being with them would have been both absurd and selfish. No one can manage or lead from the confines of a quarantine chamber. They needed an advocate on the outside, someone to ensure their prompt and safe removal. Accepting this to be true and shouldering my leadership responsibilities has never been harder than on this day.

Once the door was coded shut, the quarantine specialist turned to me brusquely, saying, "Alert your team that each individual will now move to Unit 31 for a quarantine shower while we wash down this unit."

Looking back, I do not know how I managed. Yet I did. I calmly pressed my wrist intercom and asked all team members to please move to Unit 31. I carefully monitored their exit, ensuring that everyone maintained calm. I served as a steadying role model, my face stoic and expressionless. No one spoke. It was eerily silent. Kar stayed with me, at my side, until every single member of our unit filed out. The Quarantine Lead turned his obscured face towards me.

"Team Lead, you and your Science Lead must go."

We did. We left. It felt like the single most cowardly thing I have ever done. Yet it was the only thing we could do. Kar knew it too. If we fought or argued, we lost influence because we lost any semblance of neutrality and rationality. There was no choice but to play along. They must not know we have stakes in this game.

The subsequent passing hours were grim. I was certain the Balance Committee had betrayed my request, ignored my entreaty that they attend and thereby allow Continent 2 SciMed Command to follow their agenda unchecked.

Countless scenarios of what we might do flitted through my mind. I cataloged Kar, Hart, Shee and Luya's skills as my mind played with innumerable developments and possible outcomes. Command did not yet know of Hart and Shee's presence. They were never introduced and were hidden in the rear of the room during the proceedings. Their off-the-grid visits mean that their presence was not registered in our formal personnel database.

With hawkish intensity, I watched for any opportunity to speak with them uncensored. When we were ordered out of Unit 32 for the quarantine, Luya nimbly corralled the two and thrust them into the mix of our personnel as we exited. She then proceeded to rapidly escort them to her personal chambers in Unit 31 before anyone even noticed their presence amidst the clamor of quarantine. In the shuffle, their presence was obscured. The Quarantine Team only tallied registered members of Unit 32 as they conducted the showers, so their presence went undiscovered. I was concerned with their attendance at the proceedings from the beginning, but Kar and Luya both assured me that their presence would be an acceptable risk. We needed outside witnesses. What is more, both Shee and Hart insisted on taking the risk. I elected not to press the issue and am relieved I have no need to regret this.

Yet there was no chance to go speak with either Shee or Hart for counsel. I could not slip away unnoticed. Not only were we being overseen by the Quarantine Team, but several members of Command were lingering in Unit 31, periodically checking their holopads and muttering quietly amongst themselves. This was what they had been waiting for. They could claim that both of our experimental units, Unit 31 last rotation and Unit 32 now, had gone too far and endangered the entire station. The dissolution of our units felt assured.

Our salvation came when I had lost all hope. We completed our quarantine showers and stood together back in Unit 32, wheezing from the overpowering scent of disinfectant. Command was berating me for allowing a team member to sacrifice herself by remaining with the tainted 'creature of the past' and thus ruining her professional chances through willful disobedience and rash extremism. Tuning out the lecture, I could easily overhear the murmurs of disgust from the Command group behind me over Renee's oddly white skin. They were watching her through the viewing panel, commenting on her curvy body and aberrant features.

Then the doors slid open softly and they walked in. Within seconds our entire lab was full of these imposing, silent individuals. They remained still until everyone froze what they were doing and noticed their presence. It was an entire Balance Committee delegation.

No one moved. The Station Commander, at last, broke the icy silence that ran across the room to say, "Greetings, members of the Balance Committee. We welcome you to Continent 2 SciMed Station. I was not aware that you would be visiting us today. To what do we owe this visit?"

His voice was neutral, but pinched. Gone were the pauses he so customarily used to rattle us. A woman stepped forward. She was on the taller side, older and very slim. Her voice rang out with authority.

"Your Unit 32 Team Lead invited us today as he unveils the results of his recent project, Time Window. It would seem, to our displeasure, you were not made aware that this invitation was extended. Indeed, it would appear much has happened already in our absence. You will brief us on what occurred thus far."

She sounded extraordinarily displeased. It did not surprise me. Balance Committee members are chosen for their strong affinity and inclination toward exactly what their name denotes - balance. Anyone, with even the most minute trace of empathy or intuition, could sense the imbalance and lack of harmony pervading the room. I was just not sure upon whom her wrath would fall, Command or me.

While nervous, I was also in awe. They carry an almost ethereal internal calm, and authority radiates from within them. Incredible that a single memo had elicited the presence of five members. The weight of what I had done felt heavy upon my shoulders.

"Speak, Station Commander," said the female. Her tone was

curt. I wondered how harshly she would treat me, a mere Team Lead, given her approach to the highest in command from our station. I summoned my confidence.

"Of course," said the Station Commander. He gave her a painfully one-sided briefing, during which I was forced to harshly clench my jaw to prevent myself from interrupting. His account was so heavily biased it could hardly be called truth.

When he finished speaking, silence imbued the room. She allowed it to drag on for a few moments, before turning to me.

"Team Lead, what do you have to say about this?"

I did not tarry to answer as our Commander had. That was a lesson easily learned.

"The facts, as our Station Commander has presented them, are accurate. However, the lenses through which we interpret them are quite different. Time Window did not succeed as we had designed it. Rather, it exceeded our expectations. We had not even considered the possibility that we might carry a human being through the window we created, and yet we did."

"Why do you call this creature a human being? It is clear from the Station Commander's explanation that it is not."

"I disagree with the Station Commander's assessment. We have spent approximately 25 rotations observing her, interacting with her and studying her physiology in-depth. She is human and poses no observable threat to us. She has certain cultural norms that are different, however, she communicates intelligently and adeptly in our language. She is peaceful and friendly," I paused, catching my breath for a brief moment, and then continued.

"With respect, I ask one thing. Before you make any judgment, please take the time to meet her and converse with her yourself."

It was all I could say. What more could be done?

"I will convene with my colleagues briefly," she said. "Clear the room and return when we call."

We shuffled out quickly. I ignored Command's glares and darted quickly down the hallway and out of sight. I moved straight toward the alternate viewpoint to the room in which Kemi and Renee were being held. Few are aware that there are two points of observation for this room. The second falls on the opposite side of the lab. While there is no door on that side, a viewing window allows one to speak via an audio connection. I selected this option from the display panel and spoke softly and rapidly.

"Renee, Kemi, this is YunJon."

They both jumped at my voice, glancing up from where they were sitting and stopped talking. Kemi nodded. Renee stared wide-eyed around the room.

"The Balance Committee has arrived. It is likely they will be along shortly to observe or speak with Renee. Be peaceful. Minimize facial expressions. And above all, say nothing to compromise us."

I watched Renee's face squint in confusion. I felt a fleeting moment of regret that we had not been more forthcoming about her situation. But before I could say more, my wristband vibrated.

That fast? I thought. They had convened in mere minutes. I dashed back to the lab without another word.

Once more back in Unit 31, without preamble the Balance Committee representative spoke. "Show her to us, but keep her in quarantine. We will speak with her through the audio connection."

We walked past the equipment to the main viewing window in the lab. With a swipe of my hand, I enlarged the transparency space from several square feet to the entire wall. Only a narrow, dark gray outline of the door remained, serving as a reference point for observers.

Several gasps sounded behind me when I activated the screen. Kemi and Renee both stood and faced one another with a respectable distance separating them. They conversed in low tones with little to no facial expression.

"What is that female doing in there?" asked the Balance Committee representative, an edge to her tone. The Station Commander tried to answer, but she shushed him and stared at me.

"That is our assistant, Kemi. She volunteered to stay with our visitor so she would not become alarmed during this precipitous quarantine. We are responsible for her presence here and my team has shouldered this responsibility. We ensure Renee's comfort and facilitate her understanding of who we are. I would like to note that my team has exhibited nothing short of an impeccable performance over the past 25 rotations."

"Interesting," she said. "You do yourself credit by praising your team and taking responsibility for the consequences of your project. However, I do perceive it to be quite rash of you to have allowed one of your subordinates to place herself in such a position."

I did not speak, as she did not ask a question. Little did she know I had very little say in the matter of Kemi's presence in the quarantine chamber. I kept my mouth closed on that topic.

"Activate the speaker but not the microphone. I wish to hear them communicate," she said.

I activated the speaker. My anxiety levels were elevated despite my certainty that I could trust Kemi to do well. Her voice expanded out into the room as though nothing separated us.

"Your governmental system, as I understand it, was based on 50 sub-states under the purview of one larger state."

"Yes, Kemi. That is correct."

"Did this system work efficiently?"

"Regarding some issues, it did. On others, it did not. For instance, there was not a high level of efficiency as many decisions had to be made multiple times."

"What is an example of this?" asked Kemi.

"One matter in which we lacked efficiency was our tax system. The government applied a tax on society in order to provide public goods and services. However, some tax matters were left up to the sub-states, while others were mandated by the state itself." Renee was speaking calmly. Her voice was monotone. She might have been a different person than the one I have come to know. She kept her hands at her side and her face expressionless.

I was quite astonished. She had absorbed far more of our culture than I had realized. Her adaptability was shocking. I felt mildly alarmed. Her speech patterns, vocal intonation and mannerisms were so altered and so reflective of our culture that their precision was uncanny. She had not previously adopted our cultural norms because she was incapable, she had not adopted them because she had selected not to. This distinction carries profound implications in terms of intelligence and strategic decision-making.

I turned off the speaker and looked at them.

"Fascinating," exhaled the female, a look of awe on her face. "This is indeed remarkable. You did right in contacting us."

She tore her eyes away from the screen. With a conscious effort, she cleared her features of emotion. "This is beyond our authority. This type of discovery requires direct guidance of the Regulation Committee before deciding how to proceed. There are multiple angles to be assessed, as we must balance our desire for knowledge with our need to protect our society. As a representative of the Balance Committee, I ordain that this case be brought in front of the Regulation Committee for further contemplation."

A rush of both relief and renewed anxiety swept through me. The Regulation Committee? Not only have I never encountered a member of our highest command, neither has anyone else with whom I am acquainted.

"Prepare the entirety of your data and research, Team Lead. Bring along all integral members of the team. I will send an escort to collect you, which will arrive tomorrow, Orbit 275, in the evening. It will be an Enforcement Detail."

She dismissed me with a single look, making it quite clear our exchange was complete. She turned to our Station Commander and said, "Quarantine remains on Unit 32 as a whole. However, the assistant and this being of the past are allowed to leave the confines of their quarantine chamber so long as they remain in the confines of the unit. Do not interfere on this matter until we have issued a final judgment."

With that, they were gone as swiftly as they had come. They filed out silently, without a parting word. Command followed suit immediately afterward. Everyone on our team remained silent.

I did not walk but rather dashed to the quarantine chamber. I overrode the quarantine code, deactivated the lock and swept open the door. Kemi and Renee's face turned toward mine in surprise and hope. I rushed toward them, placing my left hand on Kemi's shoulder and my right on Renee's, breathing a sigh of relief. As I realized what I was doing, I dropped my arms and stepped backwards quickly.

"I guess they're gone?" said Renee. "Can we stop acting so agonizingly dull?"

"You think we are dull?" said Kemi.

Raising a hand to my brow, I exhaled deeply.

"Yes," I said. "Yes, you may cease being boring."

Renee laughed. "So you actually can make a joke," she said, rather breathlessly.

Of course, I can. What did she think? I understand at least the basic mechanisms of humor, although I do not yet comprehend how she perceives this to be a functional communication method.

EXTERNAL MEMO: ROTATION 274

To:	Enforcement Committee
From:	Balance Committee

We require an escort team and transport for five persons from Cont. 2 SciMed Station to the Regulation Committee tomorrow, Rotation 275, at 17:00 Earth Hours. The nature of this request is highly sensitive and requires heightened security measures. There will be four practitioners of Cont. 2 SciMed:

YunJon, Team Lead, Unit 32
Luya, Team Lead, Unit 31
Kar, Science Lead, Unit 32
Kemi, Assistant, Unit 32

Their profiles are included in this message. The fifth individual does not have identification or a profile. The identity of the fifth individual will be confirmed by Unit 32 Team Lead YunJon. Be on guard for both internal and external threats on this mission.

RENEE

Our departure draws near. The wall display shows 16:42 hours. Only 18 minutes until we are slated to leave. Everyone has assembled in the lab to wait.

My debilitating sadness is gone, replaced by fear. It would seem I have a finite capacity for emotion. Only space for one overwhelming feeling at a time, evidently. My survival instincts and self-preservation have jumped to center stage. They've kicked out grief.

Survival means being present and, God, do I want to live. I had no idea how much.

The sting of broken trust pricks me. My existence in this future world is not even close to as assured as Unit 32 led me to believe. They gave me no preparation, no warning as to what might occur yesterday. They might have forewarned me. I feel hoodwinked somehow.

The door slides open softly. It's barely a hiss, yet the lab is so silent everyone jumps slightly, swiveling their heads toward the entrance. My spine stiffens. I instinctively lean forward on my toes, tensing my muscles.

They pour in with a speed and litheness of motion that simply can't be described as human. Like predator cats, the movements are sleek and supple. They are enormous for such speed, the biggest humans I have seen thus far, taller even than YunJon and Kar. Huge, hulking forms with broad shoulders, they are clothed in black with thick vests and heavy belts. Their eyes are masked.

So these are the Rangers, then. My eyes track them rapidly, following their dispersion around the lab. One is posted in each corner, but I refuse to swivel my head to eye them each in term, so I refocus my eyes back to the door. I don't want to appear nervous or weak, jerking my head around the room. This is only the prelude. Something or someone is yet to come. Everyone can feel it.

Two more enter and flank the door. They aren't holding any weapons that I can see, but their hands are covered in thick, mechanical-looking gloves. I know nothing about futuristic warfare. Perhaps the deadliest of weapons are, in fact, no bigger than a device that can be embedded into a glove?

Somehow, impossibly, I hear his footsteps before I see him. Anticipation mounts and when he turns the corner, I shiver at the sight. The biggest man yet, he doesn't walk but prowls. His eyes are uncovered, the deepest black I've seen, shadowed by fierce, harsh brows. Neither gloves nor vest adorn him. He is clothed only in a thick, black jumpsuit with reinforced joints, a heavily-laden belt and boots.

As our eyes meet, my skin tingles and my senses awaken. I feel an overwhelming magnetic draw. With a rush of realization, I can sense something shockingly different about him. He feels alive. His presence isn't like everyone else's, it isn't muted and dulled and sandpapered down into conformed nothingness. My fear evaporates, replaced with excitement. Something that I was desperately craving, something I couldn't even name, has been found. This is a person who vibrates with life.

I almost take a step forward, but check myself.

He strides toward us, where we are gathered in the center of the lab. Kemi, Kar, YunJon and Luya surround me, but his eyes remain locked on mine. As he draws near, his true physical size becomes evident. He must be a foot and a half taller than I am, at the least, easily breaking seven feet.

I keep my spine locked and rigid, shoving away insecurities. In my time, I was strong and athletic, running long distances, eating healthy, taking care of myself. My body felt strong and fit. Now? I'm nothing but weakness where everyone else is crisp and hard. It's difficult not to let the keen awareness of 'not belonging' eat me alive.

He stops in front of us, with two men to his immediate left and right.

"Stand for identification," he says. His voice is deep, very deep, and although the words are spoken flatly, I can hear hints of depth around the edges.

No one was moving anyway, so we remain as we were. I am fixated on his face.

He removes a small device from his belt, holds it up for a moment and then clips it back.

"Your identifications have been confirmed. Team Lead Yun-Jon, please confirm the identity of the fifth individual," he says. The black of his eyes obscures the exact focus of his gaze. When it rested on me, I could feel the power of it. But now that he's turned his attention elsewhere, it's hard to see where he is concentrated.

A flash of frustration hits me. It's difficult with these modern beings. The whites of the old human eyes served to frame the pupils, making it easy to track where any given person was focusing. Now, I have to squint carefully to distinguish the black pupils from the brown or gold 'whites' these people have. It's a disadvantage I loathe. And, with some people like him, it's nearly impossible to determine.

YunJon speaks in a clear, strong voice, "The fifth individual is Renee." To my shock, YunJon openly breaks social norms and lays a hand on my arm, keeping it there for a good few seconds. Tension ratchets up in the room. So he's trying to prove a point, is he?

"We are prepared to depart," he continues, using such a conclusive and almost rebellious tone, he might as well have just said outright, 'We are not your prisoners.' What's going on with this guy? Has YunJon actually developed an attitude?

All the while, I am feeling increasingly invigorated. The energy and life radiating off this hulking male has flipped a switch.

"Who are you?" I say, shocking even myself with the question. My voice rings out, echoing around the silent lab.

"I am Lead Ranger Striker. You may refer to me simply by Striker, however." He cocks his head slightly as he looks at me. His eyes narrow almost imperceptibly.

"Now we go," he barks abruptly. On a dime, his team is set into motion. Rangers fall into formation around us as we turn to exit the lab.

I'm about to leave the only home I have ever known here, I realize. I have yet to step across the doorway of Unit 32. And without ceremony, without any preparation, I'm suddenly swept out into this big, new foreign world. I have to pump my legs briskly to keep up. My eyes dart left and right. The passageway is large and domed. Everything is a warm, soft white. There are faint outlines of various doors here and there, with the occasional smaller passageway breaking off from ours. I see no one but our own party. The hallways are barren.

In silence, we continue quickly down this corridor for several minutes. I watch the back of Striker in front of me. His footsteps are powerful and intentional. While everyone else I have seen so far moved with smooth, controlled grace, he propels himself forward as though a spiral of energy is coiled within him, waiting to be released. His shoulders, and those of his men, are much wider than the scientists with whom I have become acquainted. I haven't identified a single female in the group of Rangers, which is odd for such a gender neutral society.

The hallway comes to an abrupt end. Striker swipes his gloved hand against the wall and a control panel appears, as if from nowhere. I jump slightly, startled. In response, the two rangers, to my right and left, snap to attention and crouch slightly, eying me and the hallway. Their speed and response is unreal. No person, not even the most athletic of my time, could move at such a pace. My heart pounds.

The fear that left me earlier rushes back. It's as if someone took a pin and popped the balloon of energy that Striker's presence had awoken in me. There is nothing, nothing, I could do if these people turned on me. I couldn't run, fight or escape. Their technology is foreign, their speed and reflexes twice as fast as mine. I am helpless.

Striker turns, sweeping his gaze across the group, and signals his team. On his cue, they relax. He keys something into the pad. The end of the hallway, what I thought was a dead end, is actually a door. It slides open quickly and smoothly to the left. I feel Kemi's gentle hand on my back, propelling me forward. She squeezes my shoulder softly as she guides me through the door frame.

Numbly, I step across the threshold. The world of white ceases, abruptly. It's jarring. Since my arrival, I have lived in hallways, rooms, labs and cafeterias in the same muted white. Even the floors were white. Everything was white. My eyes were, evidently, inured to this sterile environment.

The walls here are a deep gray, with black panels and doors. As the door slides shut behind us, the world dims even further. I blink several times. A headache starts to pound behind my eyes. My stomach turns. Is this color shock? Are my eyes, the eyes that Kar said they fixed, unable to process this? The headache grows more severe. Maybe they didn't fix them properly.

"We have left SciMed Command," Kemi murmurs in my ear. "We have just boarded the vessel that will take us to the Regulation Committee headquarters."

We move forward down a smaller hallway until we reach a mid-sized room with several Rangers operating equipment on the walls. We gather in the center. Striker barks out, "Rangers, confirm vessel security."

"Vessel security confirmed," responds a male voice from behind me.

In pain, and feeling more cautious since the hallway incident burst my confidence, I eye Striker warily. In the dim light, his cheeks appear slightly more angular and hollow now. Thick black hair sweeps across his forehead. His skin is a shade darker than some of the others. It's not as golden as Kemi's, but a slightly darker brown. His neck is thick and muscled. I don't see any hair on his face, apart from his eyebrows and thick lashes.

"My team will escort you to your quarters, within which you are free to move about. One Earth hour ago, a weather alert was issued for the next full rotation. We have been instructed to keep you onboard for the duration. We predict arrival to Regulation Committee headquarters in one and a half rotations. Each of you have been assigned a Ranger as a point of contact. If you need anything, they will assist."

With seamless efficiency, Rangers step forward one by one, each nodding to a separate member of our delegation. I hear murmured introductions around the room. No one approaches me. Lost and confused, I glance around the room nervously.

"I will assist you should you need anything," Striker says, interrupting my thoughts.

"Has no one been assigned to me?" I ask, hesitantly.

"I am. I will be your designated point of contact. You will come directly to me if you need anything or encounter any problems." He pauses, looking at me strangely. "Do you understand?"

"Yes, yes, of course. I understand."

But I don't really understand. Why am I assigned the leader and everyone else gets a lackey? Am I that dangerous? Look at me. I'm the least threatening of the lot.

He swivels a full 180 degrees and beckons me to follow him out of the room. We enter another dark, dimly lit passageway. It winds to the left. There aren't any hard corners, rather everything gently twists and turns like an underground tunnel. I am lost almost immediately, the pressure behind my eyes making it nearly impossible to focus.

I detect a gentle background hum. It's just loud enough to

drown out any minor noises. The further we walk, the more it increases in volume.

As it increases in sound, to my left I see a passageway that leads to a room with a beautiful, soft glow of light radiating from it. Overcome with curiosity, and stunned by the beauty of the gentle rays, I slow my steps. My awe rapidly overcomes the headache.

Looking more carefully, I peer down the hallway and see at the very end, what can't be much more than twenty feet from me, the source of the light and gentle humming. It is a luminous, golden orb. The colors wax and wane slightly, with streaks of darker and lighter gold dancing across the surface. Transfixed, and overwhelmed at the sight of the first truly beautiful thing I have seen since being wrenched out of time, I take a step forward, as if in a trance. My eyes, and brain, have been starved for beauty and art. I didn't consciously recognize it until this very moment.

A profound sadness overwhelms me. How can these people live without beauty? How deeply integrated art and music and expression were in my time, I realize. Tears creep into my eyes, as if in mourning for the barren world in which I now live. How can they exist like this?

I want a closer look, but before I can take another step, Striker's hands close around my waist. One is clamped across my belly, the other on my back, holding me gently but firmly in place. His body is but inches from my side, and he stares down into my eyes.

I gasp involuntarily at his speed and silence. I didn't hear him approach nor did I sense him until the pressure of his hands startled me. Even though I am now still, his hands remain pressed against my stomach and back. The warmth of his palms and fingers make my skin tingle through my jumpsuit.

"What are you doing?" he asks.

"I was wondering what that beautiful light is right there. The one that is making the humming noise?" I answer.

"That is none of your concern," he responds.

His abrupt words, contrasted so starkly to the beauty at which I am staring, and the deep sadness and loss I feel so profoundly, cause me to lash out.

"I don't see why it isn't my concern." Putting my hands on his forearms, I simultaneously twist toward him and shove them away. He doesn't resist my motion, only using the momentum from my push to raise them to the wall behind me, forcing me to stumble backward until I'm braced against it.

He leans down so we are eye to eye. Up this close, so near to his face, I can see, at last, that his eyes aren't all black. There is the slightest of color distinctions, from a deep, deep brown to black. They are strangely profound, his eyes, but also unnerving in such a way that makes me breathless. His skin is flawless and smooth. I can smell him. He smells good.

I inhale deeply. The sensation of aliveness increases. Internal conflict burns me. I want more of it, of this feeling he gives me, this reminder of my humanity and life. But I hate his abruptness and commandeering attitude, and that he manhandles me like a sack of potatoes.

Did... did his eyes flicker down to my mouth?

"You are a guest on my ship only because I allow it," he exhales softly in my face, his voice deep and full of weight and power. "I will tell you what is, and is not, your concern."

"I am not one of your Rangers." I jerk my chin defiantly at the words.

"You are under Enforcement Committee escort. My team has been assigned to this mission. I am the leader. You are the subordinate. It does not matter if you are, or are not, a Ranger."

He inches closer to my face, immune to personal space, appearing unaffected by my physical differences. I sense no revulsion or disgust in his features at being confronted by someone so alien as myself.

"Do you understand?" He breathes. His breath is light and fresh on my face. I inhale deeply.

I part my lips to speak, a quip ready. But then I remember

how fast his Rangers moved in the hallway when I jumped. They were like lightening and they elicited a primal fear in my core. I also remember that I'm going to what might be my death or life-time sentence in someone's cage.

"I understand." My voice is soft and weak. The urge to cry nearly overtakes me, but I hold back. I hate myself, and him, in that moment. I am a coward. But at least I'm not a fool.

He cocks his head, continuing to stare down at me. I wanted to be so close to him just moments ago, and relished his very presence, yet now I wish nothing but space. No matter how alive he makes me feel.

Exhaustion grips me and my headache is revived, in full force. Unexpectedly, he releases me and reaches out a gentle hand to my shoulder. I recoil. He withdraws his hand and turns around, silent, and continues down the hallway as though nothing happened. I follow behind him, praying for privacy and space to myself before I lose myself to the tears of pain, frustration and isolation that threaten to overtake me.

A few moments later, he stops and swipes open a door to my right.

"These are your quarters. If you need anything, I will assist you."

I walk in and before I ask how to contact him, or how to reach my team members, the door slides shut and I am alone. Solitude. Relief washes over me.

The room is not large. The walls slope softly to the ground as in my old room in Unit 32. But here, everything is dark gray, including the floor. For once, though, there are actually small fixtures along the walls. There are several tabs jutting out, one that looks like a resting place for a holopad perhaps. However, there is no bed, shower, desk or even table.

Exhausted, I lie down on the floor. My head is pounding. I'm confused. Alone, on the floor, I try to relax my limbs one by one. With my eyes closed, my headache begins to subside.

The next thing I know, I hear Kemi's voice.

CHAPTER TWENTY-FIVE

"Renee? May we enter your quarters?"

I must have fallen asleep. Her voice is tugging me out of unconsciousness. Although groggy, my headache is now gone. Kemi repeats the question. Where is her voice coming from?

I pick myself up off the floor and walk toward the door. I touch it and a screen pops up. I press the button that says "open." The door slides to the side.

All four of them, Kemi, YunJon, Kar and Luya, are standing there looking at me. They are flanked by four Rangers.

"Oh, hello," I say, my brain still foggy from the nap.

"I have brought your nutrition tube," Kar says.

"And we came to check on you," Kemi tacks on.

I gesture them in. They settle, cross-legged onto the floor. The door slides shut, leaving the Rangers in the passageway. I sit down with them. They look crisp, limber and fresh in their suits. I feel sleepy and disheveled. I run a hand through my short hair. We exchange some greetings, and without further ado, I begin questioning.

"Who are the Rangers? Why didn't you tell me about them?"

"I did not explain this to you yet," says Kemi, "as I had not anticipated it to be a relevant piece of knowledge for you. I did not want to overwhelm you with too much information too fast. Of course, circumstances have proven me wrong. To answer who, exactly, the Rangers are? I suspect YunJon can answer best." She nods at him. He nods in return. They stare at each other for a bit longer than normal. Curious.

"At birth," YunJon answers, "we are all tested for our character traits. These tests largely determine what field we will enter when we get older. From our youngest age, we are aware of our dominant traits and are taught how to use them to our best advantage. We are also taught to control them when they may become detrimental. For example, I have a high empathy trait. This trait is good in a leader, because I can relate to my subordinates and understand what they will need to succeed. Secondly, and more importantly, a high empathy trait in leadership ensures that I will not become distracted by power nor my own interests. My empathy will keep me grounded in the well-being of those I lead. A good leader must sacrifice for his or her team. An individual with high empathy is best suited for this position.

"There are rare individuals who are born with a high risk-taking trait and high aggression levels. They are primarily male, although there are also females, approximately 15 percent. These children, from birth, are guided into the Enforcement Committee. They will become Rangers. This gives them a healthy outlet for their aggression and risk-taking. These traits are tapped into and used for the safety and protection of society, rather than being allowed to manifest in a negative or detrimental way. These individuals are put through intensive training in order to ensure that they channel their dominant character traits for the betterment of society and themselves.

"These males and females, you know them as Rangers, make up slightly less than 1 percent of society. It is a very small minority. They are often admired for their bravery, as they are the ones that lead exploration expeditions as well as performing any tasks that require risk and force. Exploration expeditions make up the majority of their exercises. Use of force is extremely rare in society today."

YunJon stops speaking. I look at him and at Kemi for a few moments. It's so logical, and it sounds so sophisticated a system. But something nags at me.

"What," I pause for a moment, reflecting, "what about people's passions and drives, though? For instance, what if someone isn't born with high aggression but wants to explore? Or what if someone is born, I don't know, with a low academic intelligence? But they still want to be a scientist? Someone who is passionate about something can often work hard enough to overcome their handicap and become, occasionally, better than those who are even naturally gifted in that field."

I can't read their faces. There is a spell of silence. YunJon opens his mouth uncertainly, then closes it. Finally, a look of resolve flashes across his face.

"In certain cases, they are willing to overlook particular character traits if someone can demonstrate a strong interest and willingness to enter a certain field. Also, genetic trait testing has a small rate of error, and knowing this, they do occasionally make exceptions." He pauses, and I see his eyes flash quickly toward Kemi. I'm getting better at tracking some of their eye movements, at least. And eventually I will figure out what's between those two.

"Like me. I was almost denied admission into SciMed. My empathy trait was too high for this field. Empathy is good in moderation, but can be perceived as a definite weakness in Science and Medicine. They say, well, they say it can cloud judgment in a field that requires perfect rationality. However, I was and have always been able to demonstrate an extremely high level of proficiency in the field of Science and Medicine. So they overlooked it."

"I did not know that, YunJon," Kemi says softly. "Kar, did you?"

Matter-of-factly, Kar says, "I knew."

YunJon looks startled. "How did you know, Kar?"

His face deadpan, Kar responds, "I hacked into the system and gained access to our team's private personnel dossiers."

YunJon and Kemi stare at him in shock. I stare at him in shock. We all stare in shock.

"At this point, I believe it is expedient to tell you. It could be beneficial to the team. You may wish to utilize my skills later for the well-being of our unit and Renee."

We continue to stare.

"Does anyone else know you can do this?" YunJon finally gasps.

"Luya does."

"Do not disclose this to anyone else," he finally says.

It's all kind of funny. I can't help but chuckle a little. YunJon actually glares at me, which I find to be downright amazing. I'm almost proud. Look at him showing some emotion.

I also feel slightly less distrustful of them than I did this morning in the lab. Perhaps they really are just bungling along. Maybe they didn't intentionally mislead me. Maybe they're actually just scientists who don't really have a clue.

"So, Kar," I say, tongue-in-cheek, "what else can you do?"

Only Kemi smiles, understanding it as a joke. YunJon clears his throat to speak, taking my words very seriously. "Yes, yes. Kar, this certainly is the time to let us know if you have any other skills of which we should be aware."

"I am a part of a network of scientists around the world who communicate on an off-the-grid server."

"Oh," says YunJon, looking increasingly unsettled. On the flipside, I feel safer already.

I contain my laughter so as not to further upset YunJon, who is looking disconcerted. We sit in silence for a few moments. Eventually, YunJon speaks, "I am very glad you informed us, Kar. You can trust us to keep this in confidence. I understand that it must have taken a high level of trust to disclose this to us."

Ever practical, he turns toward me. "You need to drink that, Renee. It is very important to keep your strength up."

I forgot about my nutrition tube.

"Of course," I say. I chug it. When I'm done, Kar reaches out and takes it from me. He tucks it back into his bag. Kemi scoots a little closer, and pats me on the knee.

Log Entry: R 276 O 3037 ID: Cont 2 YunJon

Despite being a mere five-minute walk from our lab, none of us are permitted to leave the vessel. We are stuck in dock for at least another full rotation until the weather clears. It rankles, being under the thumb of Ranger authority, but not nearly as much as before. My feelings have softened somewhat over the last hour.

An hour ago we left Renee's quarters and I returned to my own. Shortly thereafter, Striker came to me. He recommended we sit together on the floor.

I was thrown off guard. Why would this Ranger, this primal, task-driven male, wish to engage me in dialogue? What could he possibly have to say?

Quite a lot. The entire encounter baffles me. I answered his inquiries as honestly as possible. My hope is that the more allies we garner, the better chance we have of protecting Renee.

But did I share too much?

His voice was relaxed and his hands were resting loosely on his crossed knees as he spoke, saying softly, "I have seen many things in my time as a Ranger. For many orbits, I lead exploration missions and witnessed a great deal. When assigned this particular mission, I expected very little of interest. It appeared a simple escort. However, this is no regular escort mission, is it? There is something different about Renee, something extraordinary."

I stared at him for some moments before proceeding, attempting to discern his motive.

"You are correct," I responded slowly. "We do, indeed, carry someone remarkable with us."

Sensing my reticence, he responded, explaining, "I wish to be clear in my intention. I am asking in part to ensure the safety of our mission, and to understand how best to protect you. However, I can protect you well with what I already know. My primary motivation for engaging in this conversation is curiosity. Renee is not like us. She is different. Are you at liberty to share anything with me? I will not breach your confidence."

He looked at me, his dark eyes fixated on mine. He sat slightly higher, despite my above-average height, and his broad shoulders gave the impression of being bigger still, despite the black of his uniform obscuring his muscles and physique.

"Why were you so aggressive when we first met, and now so peaceful? What is it that you want?"

My blunt questions surprised even me. I have changed, it would seem, in more ways than one since Renee's arrival.

"The memo I received, the one requesting this escort, was obscure and vague," said Striker. "I was anticipating trouble. And given that I was entering an unknown situation, with almost no details, my first priority was to ensure the safety of my own team. That is why I was aggressive. But we are now on the ship and I have had time to assess you personally. There is no risk. You are safe, and my team is safe. I can afford to be peaceful.

"You ask what I want? I want to know what it is about Renee that makes her, quite possibly, the most fascinating individual I have encountered in a lengthy, full career. My motives for asking are personal. You do not have a professional obligation to answer them. However, you may find me to be a useful resource, should you need one."

How could a Ranger see Renee's presence as the marvel that

it is and with a mind more open than a member of the Balance Committee?

I kept my face straight. I needed to buy myself time to think, to feel out this male in front of me. Was he trying to weasel information out of me to feed to the Committee? Or was this a genuinely curious individual? My senses told me his intentions were true. If I were to meet such a being, I would wish to know as much as I could about her in order to sate my personal curiosity as well. I felt a genuine interest from him, and he was candid in his motivation being a personal one, and assured me I did not have to disclose.

But nevertheless, I proceeded cautiously.

"Thank you, Striker. Do you mind if I inquire after your name? It is unusual. From where does it originate?"

"It is common for a Ranger to be given a second name. While I was in training, I had an unusual talent for hitting any target, mental or physical. I was given the name Striker, short for 'to strike,' because I always hit my target."

What an intriguing custom. I enjoy the concept of a name you earn and that describes you, rather than a name assigned by random lottery at birth.

Yet I could not keep stalling. I made a decision.

I had not promised to keep details of her existence confidential. I was breaking no rules in telling Striker. Best case scenario, I win an ally. Worst case scenario, he is suspicious. But I would not tell him anything more than the Balance Committee already knows, so he would have no power over us.

"Renee is unique," I said slowly. "She is not from our time. Our research, a project called Time Window, was intended to create a window into the past. Yet it surpassed our expectations. Instead, it created a door. It is this door from which Renee came. She is not of our time. She hales from the early 21st century. I refer to pre-drought times, before the Last Wars, before so much strife struck our world. When you see her, you are looking at a walking, talking and living piece of our history. In fact, you are likely looking at genetic code that has been wiped from the face of the Earth. You see how physically different she appears to us? Perhaps her particular genetic branch, her unique genetic heritage, was wiped off Earth. She may hale from one of the decimated peoples. We haven't had time yet to explore any of these astonishing possibilities. She nearly died from the time warp, and has spent much time recovering and adjusting to what, as you can imagine, is the most traumatic experience a person could live through. She did not speak our language, so we stimulated the language portion of her brain and implanted our speech, but only several rotations ago. We are only now establishing a deeper connection. You are absolutely right to call her unique. She is!"

The words flowed out of me. I realized, with some surprise, that I wanted someone to know the marvel that is her existence. I wanted to openly and freely share the miracle of her presence. It was stimulating beyond words to be able to, at last, disclose what we have been protecting so vigorously these past rotations to an avid listener.

"Incredible," he exhaled in response, his face registering emotion. It completely altered his visage, rendering him far more appealing. "What is she like? Is she like us? I noticed some differences in her when I escorted her to her room. For instance, she did not seem to understand our societal structure."

"She does not!" I responded, excitedly. "It is every scientist's dream come true. Speaking with her is like viewing our society through a lens with which we could never have conjured on our own. The mere exercise of explaining our society, and listening to accounts of her own, is endlessly fascinating. Anatomically, you may be surprised to find she is actually quite similar to us. She appears more different than she is because of superficial variances, such as being shorter and her hips and breasts being more pronounced. There is also the matter of her skin tone and lighter hair, but these are all matters of pigmentation. Then, of course, her eyes. Her eyes! They are such a blue as I never imagined possible. There must have been so much more diversity than we previously imagined. You know how so many records were destroyed and history lost in the droughts and war. Perhaps we have missed so very much, so very much more than we thought!"

"Have you had the opportunity to study her genes?" he asked, his tone laced with hints of excitement.

"Not in depth. We have had very limited time with her. She has been with us for less than 30 rotations, of which 15 she spent in a coma."

"What?" He exclaimed, shock rippling across his features. "How has she adapted so quickly?"

"That is the most marvelous thing! She adapts so fast. You ought to see her imitations. She can imitate people easily, as naturally as breathing. Her emotions are also remarkable. They run from ecstatic laughter to tears. She must feel so much more than we do. She is clearly physically inferior. She is weaker and more delicate. Her bones do not have the same density as ours. Yet, somehow, she does not give the impression of physical weakness. And she responds remarkably fast to our medical treatments. I would say her response time is twice as fast. Her body thrives on our nutrition, which Kar has tailored to her metabolism and dietary needs."

I stopped speaking at that point, before allowing myself to be entirely carried away, and revealing more than I ought to. But I was just as flush with excitement as he was. He sat leaning forward, absorbing every word I was saying.

"When," he paused, thinking, then went on, "when you say that she is physically weaker, does that mean we will harm her if we touch her?"

"Oh, no. She is not nearly that weak. We just have to be slightly careful. Also, her reflexes are a little slower. And I think, although we have not tested extensively, that she visually processes color differently than we do. Curiously, she also likes physical touch. It is natural to her in ways it is not to us. We have not yet determined if this is a question of nature or nurture."

"Are we biologically incompatible? Could she reproduce with

one of us?"

"What an excellent question! I confess, we have not explored it yet. I do not know if our genes are compatible. I would suspect that they are, as we are direct genetic descendants, however we cannot know yet. From our body scans, her internal sexual organs appear to be the same as our females. You must understand, though, time has not been on our side. There has been so much to learn. Also, how can we know if there has not been permanent damage from the physical trauma wrought by her arrival?"

"Ah," he said, and looked pensive.

After several more minutes of conversation, we concluded our discussion. He nodded deeply before departing, thanking me for my transparency, and assuring me he would maintain my confidence to the extent that he was able.

His questions raise so many more questions of my own about Renee. It is easy to forget how little she knows. For instance, she was shocked to discover that the Regulation Committee headquarters are in orbit and that this is, in fact, where we are going. I had to explain that it is the only way the Committee can ensure they have no preference for one continent over another. To be a truly independent governing body, there must be no conflict of interest or bias due to geographical location.

She was intrigued and excited to learn we were going into space. Does this mean that they did not engage in space travel? Or that it was limited? Surely they must have. In fact, I am quite certain of it. Yet was it so rare? There was no time to ask. We had other more pressing matters to discuss.

And now, I have this Ranger to ponder. Why was he so intrigued? How did he immediately recognize her value, and why would he break professional protocol to inquire for personal purposes? I will not report him. If he is acting as an agent for the Regulation Committee then they will see my negligence in reporting the conversation as suspicious. So be it. I accept the risk.

Because if he is not acting on their behalf, and on his own

initiative as I suspect, might we need him at some point? A fully trained Ranger is a powerful weapon indeed.

Renee

My fingers slide across the walls as I walk around the room counterclockwise. I brace myself to accidentally activate some screen or command station. Yet no panel nor disembodied voice greets me. Feeling a growing sense of frustration, I grab at a couple of the knobs and twist. Yet there's still no response.

I should have asked how to do it while we sat on the floor, cross-legged, like a class of kindergartners during share time. Now, of course, it's too late. They've gone back to their quarters to digest our many revelations, and I'm stuck here with no idea how to get in touch. It's just me and this gray, barren room with its few jutting knobs silently mocking me.

I know there's a bed and a toilet in here somewhere. It can't be that hard to find the activation unit. Why is it, then, so hard?

The creeping sense of frustration bubbles to the surface and morphs into anger. My knees collapse under me and I sink down into an awkward, splayed seated position on the floor. This is all so stupid. My very existence in this future is stupid. This mission to the Regulation Committee is stupid. I can't locate a bed in my own room. I can't find a toilet, for God's sake.

The anger builds inside me until my entire body is engulfed in flames of frustrated rage. It's probably masking sadness and fear, because isn't that what anger always does? But anger is easier. It doesn't care. It's safe. It's strong. Let it grow.

As the rage continues to burn within me, I crawl back up to my feet and prowl the room. My body is veritably brimming with health, stronger than it's ever been, so there's plenty of fuel to feed the fire. The irony of this adds more kindling to the fury. I've never felt stronger, never had better eyesight or such impeccable hearing, never have my muscles vibrated with such health. Yet I have also never been more helpless and dependent upon others.

As my hand skims the wall, my attention is drawn to the skin of my exposed flesh. I slow to a standstill. I despise how it looks, so smooth, white and unmarred. It's as though someone transposed the skin of a baby onto my adult body. I want my old skin with its marks and memories, scars from the time I fell off my bike when I was seven and when I cut my forehead when I was twelve. I had laugh lines to prove my life had joy.

But now? Now I have nothing. My identity and culture erased, buried under centuries of time. And what did all that work come to? All the labor and efforts of my ancestors, family and friends? This. This crappy culture. This dry, sterile, barren and regulated world of semi-humans.

In a fit of rage, I swing my first against the wall. My hand connects with all the strength of my fury and pain pierces my fist and up my arm. I yell and drop back down to the ground, gripping my fist to my chest with my other hand.

Bright, red blood arises from my middle knuckle. It stands starkly on the skin, brilliant on my pale flesh, and rolls ever so slowly down my hand. I watch as the pain washes over me.

The door swooshes open. I jerk my head up. Before I can say a word of protest at the intrusion, a dark form is above me and strong hands, hands like iron, push me onto my back.

"Let me go!" I scream.

"Stop moving!" The male voice grunts.

At his voice, I do. Shocked, I turn to study the face looming above me. Despite the shadows, my suspicion is confirmed. It's Striker. His dark features hover over mine, only mere inches from my face.

"I don't want to hurt you," he says, his tone gentler than I thought even possible. "I want to ensure that you are safe before I release you."

I inhale his scent once again. His features, so close to my own, are alien and different yet powerful and brimming with health and strength.

"Why is your fist bleeding? I am taking you to the medical center."

"No!" I say, with more vehemence than I intended.

He lifts me from the floor. His left hand is cradling my head and neck, as though I am a small child. I feel weightless in his arms. His brow is wrinkled in concern, an unusually human expression for one of them.

"Am I hurting you?"

"No, no you're not," I say, somewhat breathlessly. "I don't want to go the medical center. I'm fine."

"Extend bed," he barks. A flat platform extends from the wall. So that's how you do it.

He gently sets me on the bed. One large, strong arm stays wrapped around my shoulder. With his right hand, he picks up my fist to look at it. Bright red drops of blood well on my knuckle.

He stares at it. I stare at it. Tension ratchets up, making my nerve endings hum. "This will scar if we don't take you to medical." His voice is husky.

"I don't care. I want it to scar."

"Why do you want an imperfection?"

"You wouldn't understand," I say, my voice imbued with bitterness. "We carried our life on our skin. Every imperfection, scar, wrinkle and bruise was a story. Our medicine wasn't advanced in the ways in which yours is, and there was no way to keep our skin looking as smooth as it was on the day we were born. It aged as we did. Only newborn babies had such flawless skin. When I was pulled through time, all my skin was burnt off my body. They regenerated it in this tank. But I didn't get my skin back. I got this. A whole new skin grew back. My entire history was erased off my body. And you know what? I hate this new skin. You would think that this would be every person's dream come true, right? Perfect skin. But it isn't. I want who I was, with all the memories and reminders and proof of my life. Proof that I existed and lived."

His dark eyes stay fixed on mine with an intensity and focus that awakens something inside of me. He is so close I can see his eyelashes. They are startlingly long and curl up to nearly touch the eyebrows that appear permanently fixed in a scowl. They are the only soft feature on his face and, if I weren't so close, they would be obscured by the darkness of his eyes and shadows of his brows. I want to reach out and touch his face, run my fingers along those long eyelashes.

We sit in silence for a moment, until I can bear it no longer.

"What do you want?" I finally say. His body, so close to mine, is making me keenly aware of how much I have missed intimate human touch. Real human touch. The initial attraction I felt to him is back, and stronger.

Rather than speak, he raises a hand gently to my face and runs large fingers softly down my cheek.

"I like your skin," he says.

Shock rattles me. My pupils dilate, heart-rate rises and breath quickens. Confusion and uncertainty rush through me.

He drops his hand and licks his lips.

"Your eyes," he continues, "they are so beautiful. Initially, the white that surrounds the pupils startled me. Yet now I find them endlessly compelling. They showcase the brilliant blue. It is easy to read where you are looking and what you are feeling. Your face is so expressive."

He leans toward my neck and inhales deeply. "Your scent. It is intoxicating. I have never smelled anyone like you before."

The fear and frustration from earlier melt away. I know these waters. This man, this being from the future, may be foreign to me, but intimacy is something I understand. Attraction is something I understand. My natural instincts kick in and I raise my hand to his face and run my fingers softly across his eyelashes. He doesn't flinch.

"What are you doing?" he asks.

"Your body is so different from mine."

"Do I scare you?"

"Not now. You did before."

"I do not want to scare or hurt you. I understand that my large size and features, in comparison to your own, might be repulsive. If you wish me to stop touching you, I will do so immediately. Yet if I am attractive to you, I would like to mate. I am a good partner, and can assure you that it will be a satisfying experience for you."

My eyes widen. Heat rushes to my cheeks. This man has asked my permission to have sex here and now, while in the same breath assuring me he would be a good lover.

My first response isn't repulsion. It's desire. And respect. Takes guts to do that.

I thought I repulsed every person, man or woman, I encountered. But I don't. This man wants me. Could this be a chance at physical intimacy? Something I believed would be denied to me for the rest of my life?

"What were your mating customs like?" he asks, jerking me out of my thoughts. I jump at the chance to pause for a moment, to save myself from saying yes or no right away.

"We never called it mating. Animals mate. Human beings make love, or have sex with one another. When a man or a woman, or two women or two men, care for one another or want to meet their physical needs, they agree to, as you call it, mate. It can happen under very different circumstances, in many different places and as frequently or infrequently as someone wants. Sometimes two people commit to one another and agree to only mate with that other person. It's called being exclusive. Sometimes they don't. It's very complex, I guess. It would take me a long time to explain the nuances."

He looks pensive. "I have many questions. But I will ask a basic one first. Is this a situation in which I could ask you to mate with me? Have I offended you with my question? You were silent for some time."

"Usually there is more seduction or connection before someone asks, but it's not inappropriate. You haven't offended me. We are in private, you are being respectful and we are both adults. How does it happen now? Is this the normal way you do it?"

"We have mating cycles. We are allowed a certain number every orbit and we sign up in advance. We can select someone to mate with from that pool. We can also decide, at a certain age, if we would like to procreate. We are then offered a pool of candidates if we are deemed viable."

"Oh, my God." I speak in English accidentally. First time that's happened since they, I don't know how to describe it, downloaded their language into my brain.

"Is that your language?" He asks, excitedly. "What did you say?"

"There's no translation in yours."

"I would like to hear more later. Yet first, what do you think of our customs and traditions?"

"What if you meet someone and want to mate with them outside of your turn? It seems, well, very controlled for something that is usually very uncontrolled."

"It is frowned upon and cause for sanction. It disrupts the flow of society. Also, it would be difficult to find someone to mate with outside of their cycle."

"Have you ever done it, though?" I ask.

"Yes. I have."

I look at him quizzically. This is the most candid conversation I've had since waking up in 3037. I was starving for this. I needed it. For someone who was as independent as I, it is shocking to me how truly dependent I am on human interaction. Kemi, YunJon and Kar? There has always been a space between us. There is something that blocks this kind of exchange.

Raising my cheek to his face, I softly brush my skin against his. I don't have to explain myself. The contact is warm, gentle and stimulating. My eyelashes flutter against his skin. With my eyes shut, I feel like I am touching a man, not an alien being from the future.

"Why are you asking me, then, if it's against the rules?" I whisper.

"Because I desire you," he said, "and because being with you is more important than social expectations. There is an inexplicable connection I feel between us." His last words came out slowly and almost too quiet to hear.

Thoughts flash through my mind.

My fate will be decided in these next days. The Regulation Committee may condemn me to death at worst, or life in a cage somewhere at best. Unit 32 tries to protect me, but I can feel the truth even if they won't admit it to me out loud. This type of society won't allow me to assimilate. I thought they might before that horrible day when Command came and threw me in quarantine. But I saw the truth on their faces. I saw my destiny.

Up until a month ago, I was an independent person. I fought for what I wanted. I paid my way through school and worked my way around the world. My life was a product of my design. I had a lot to give and a lot to offer. I wasn't always happy, but I was always free. I knew that, no matter the circumstances, I would land on my feet.

That's all gone now.

This man offers me a glimpse of my former self. He offers me a chance to be equal and human and to feel a connection, perhaps for the last time in my life.

He leans down to my neck and inhales deeply. His hair tickles my face. Slowly, with delicate precision, he runs his cheek back up against mine.

"What is your answer, Renee?" he says, his voice deep and gravelly. I can hear his breath. "I want to respect you and your culture. Do you agree to be with me? Are you comfortable?"

This may be my last chance. His enormous black eyes gaze fixedly at me. His large body surrounds me. My heart pounds in my chest at his proximity. Lust and desire ripple through me.

I'm taking the chance.

"Yes," I whisper. "Yes, I want you. I want to be with you."

Suddenly, smoothly, he leaps onto the bed and holds himself carefully over me. His legs straddle my sides and his arms are resting by my head. I reach up my hands to his neck and pull his face toward mine. I breathe in his breath as he exhales, and very gently touch my lips to his. I feel a stab of warmth in my belly. Adrenaline shoots from my stomach down my limbs.

"What are you doing?" he asks, softly, pulling back to look at me.

"I am…" I pause. I realize now there is no word in this modern language they have taught me for kiss.

"You don't have a word for it in your language. In mine, we call it a kiss. We touch our lips together with another person. It is intimate and stimulating. I… we don't have to do it, if you are unfamiliar with it."

I feel unsettled. Can we even do this? Kissing is so natural, how can these people exist without it?

"No, please. I liked it. Let me try again."

He lowers his face back down to mine. I can feel his breath on my lips. He touches them to my own gently. It is such an innocent gesture. My body responds to his and I feel the embarrassment of earlier wash away. I slip my tongue between his lips and I hear a groan deep in his throat. It arouses me.

Eventually, we pull away. I am flushed.

"I like this activity. We will need to do more of it," Striker says. His voice is low and throaty. He is staring at my lips now. They are slightly parted. With one of his fingers, he traces the outline of my mouth.

He's a fast learner, this one.

I raise my hand to the neck of my jumpsuit and pull it down. Before I have a chance to get it past my shoulder, his hands have replaced mine and he gently undresses me.

Gasping, he stares at my body. I want to cover myself, but I don't. This is who I am.

"You are so beautiful. Your body is so different from any female's I have ever seen. It is so different from mine. You are all curves and softness. Everything about me is hard. Do I hurt you?"

His tender words surprise me.

"May I touch you?" he asks.

"Of course," I respond.

He runs his hands up my hips, frames my waist and then runs them along my breasts. It is strange to see his hands, the fingers all the same length and so large, on my body. I feel myself succumbing to desire even while my brain tries to process our physical differences.

Then I stop thinking. My body, never so healthy as it is now, responds quickly and eagerly to his touch. All the pent up pain, sadness, confusion and anger dissolve into lust and nothingness.

I wrap one arm around his neck and push one of my hands on top of his and guide it down my body.

"Are you alright?" he asks.

"Of course," I gasp, wanting to feel more. "I am more than alright. Why do you ask?"

"You made a noise. I was worried that you are in pain."

"Did I moan?"

"Yes," he answers.

"It is with pleasure. We make noises. I don't know if it's something I can really control. Is that a problem?"

"I like it," he says finally. "I can know when I am doing something that you like. Do not try and control yourself. I want to understand everything about you."

His kisses quickly turn from exploratory and tentative to passionate. My body responds to his like a candle wick to fire. He takes his time to learn my body and our differences. I feel unusual but marveled at and appreciated. We learn each other.

There is no rush. No time. Hours slip past. It takes me a while to get used to his size, but soon enough I have adjusted. He comes inside me.

We rest, holding each other, and then make love again. Almost everything I do is new to him, as though he is a virgin. I had no idea that sexual customs could evolve so rapidly over the course of only a thousand years. It seems like some things wouldn't change. I guess they do.

When we are done, I lie on top of his chest. I love the feeling of so much skin contact and the rising and falling of his breath. His heart beats slowly. His hands stroke my short hair. I drift off to sleep, his body heat warming me.

I awaken to his hands gently stroking my back as he whispers my name.

"Renee, please wake up."

I pull myself out of sleep. "Yes, Striker?" I answer sleepily.

"I must go. I need to check on the ship. We depart soon."

I want to fall back asleep with him, but say, "Of course, I understand." In the dim room, we kiss one last time. I wrap my arms around his neck and squeeze, then slide off his chest toward the wall.

Striker slips off the bed, graceful and silent. In my sleepy daze, I can feel him tucking the blanket over me. He whispers to me before he walks away silently.

"Renee, I have never mated with a female like this before. You are very special. I will protect you."

I smile, despite a deep sadness settling on my chest. He can't protect me from an entire society. Will he hide me in his ship's closet?

If things were different, Striker and I could continue to get to know each other. We would answer all those questions at the beginning. Is it a flash of passion? Or a deep connection? We could sleep with each other every night if we wanted.

Yet I let the thoughts go. It isn't possible in this society and I want to treasure this moment without grief and pain. There will be time to be sad later.

I hear the door swish open gently and close behind him.

Log Entry: R 278 O 3037 ID: Cont 2 YunJon

Should I be content with their ruling? It could be worse. Yet I am uneasy.

"The one concern of the Committee is that this person will influence and destabilize our society in some way. As everyone knows our primary concern, above all else, is balance and harmony for the greater good of our community. That said, based on the data in your reports, we have determined she is not a threat to our society if she remains contained to a small unit and does not physically integrate or mate with anyone. It is our verdict that she will remain there to be studied and observed.

"However, if further research indicates that she proves a destabilizing force, we will reevaluate our lenient position. To monitor this, every member of Unit 32 will be tested regularly for physiological and psychological balance. She is to remain, at all times, safely quarantined in Unit 32 and may not, under any circumstances, depart those premises nor interact with members outside of Unit 32 who have not been pre-approved by the Committee."

We made the right choice in keeping the presence of her pheromones suppressed. We did not reveal nor even hint at what we uncovered about them, neither in our first person testimonies nor our reports. As their concluding remarks made clear, had they known, their verdict would have been quite different. I suspect immediate elimination.

After this pronouncement, we were praised for our ingenuity, our ground-breaking experiment and the innovative nature of our work. We have been asked to prepare a detailed account of our scientific findings and observations.

The praise means nothing to me. We omitted the full truth. How long will it go undiscovered? What will happen then? With such rigorous oversights in place, I do not see how we could continuously hoodwink the authorities; not with an entire unit of staff under detailed and constant evaluation.

Renee was present throughout the proceedings. She maintained a look of calm as they issued the verdict. Periodically, her jaw and hands twitched, nearly imperceptibly. I am not sure if anyone noticed apart from myself. I made it a point to monitor her frequently.

The committee members were seated in an elevated semicircle around us. We stood to the right. She was requested to stand slightly apart, to the left, flanked on both sides by Rangers clad in all black with their faces covered. I could see her easily when I glanced to the left.

However, when we left the hearing, she refused to look at us. We walked her to her quarters and she shut the door behind her without a word. I wanted to follow her in and was poised to press the voice com button, but a Ranger appeared. He stared at us and Kar pushed me away. As we rounded the corner, I looked back and saw him standing, arms crossed, guarding Renee's door.

Tomorrow, early morning, another shuttle takes us back to Earth. I will speak with her then. Now, I must go. Kemi pages me.

RENEE

I prowl back and forth in my quarters, my vision narrowed down to a fine point.

They think they are so sophisticated and advanced, their society so balanced, what with their utter fixation on harmony.

God, the future's got overused buzzwords just like we did. So overplayed they're meaningless. Only they don't cry "freedom," they just go on endlessly about "balance" and "harmony" until my ears bleed.

Balance? Harmony? For whom, exactly? And for what?

I know their type. They're the person who is so damned certain they're right that they'll steamroll everyone and anyone who is in their way. They're the smug, self-satisfied idiots who think it's their God-given right to decide exactly who is and isn't fit to be a part of society. They're blind. Blind to their biases, blind to the 'other' and blind to the fact that they are completely and entirely full of shit.

They stifle the best of their people's creativity. Individuality is crushed ruthlessly under the guise of concern for society's welfare. Even those who are born as natural risk-takers are shunted off into the military where they can be played like pawns on a chessboard because God forbid they be allowed to rustle up society or follow any passion they might truly care about.

I was a non-entity to them in that room. They spoke about me as if I were a specimen in a petri dish. I loathed their self-satisfaction. There they sat, content with with their self-perceived leniency.

I can't stomach that this is what humankind has become.

Can it be? That we became so wildly individualistic and greedy we destroyed ourselves through overconsumption of resources and wars?

Rather than find the balance they proclaim, we swung to the opposite extreme. Rather, it is a cold, calculating society with no passion, creativity or personal freedom. The "human" element is lacking in the humanity.

When I first met Kemi, YunJon and Kar, I thought humanity had far surpassed what we had once been. They were so intelligent and sensitive. Even in my confusion and despair, I understood this.

Yet when I saw them standing in front of that committee, with their faces deadpan at the officials descriptions of me, it hurt. Badly. They did nothing to defend me. Not a single word.

Am I fair? Because what could they have done? But it stings. Striker wasn't there.

Why would I expect him to be? They are all just cogs in this great wheel. From birth, they are trained to follow a predetermined path based on Genetic Trait Tests. What would happen if they defied the Committee? Probably their careers and lives would be over.

And why would they do that for me?

I don't want to think about it.

I walk over to the wall. I extend the bed and don't bother to take off my jumpsuit. I just kick off my boots and climb up.

I press the button that deactivates the lights.

The room is bathed in total darkness. It meets me. Despair rises up to keep me company.

I will now live with the knowledge that any day, any week, could be my last. They may determine I am negatively influencing the psychology of Unit 32 and call it the end of their "leniency."

The rest of my life, however long or short it may be, won't even be life - just a half-life. Can a person live with this type of knowledge?

There is no space for me in this world. I don't belong. And I don't even know if I can live with the knowledge that everything we worked so hard for back in my time, all the causes and research and passions we poured ourselves into, all turned into this.

Log Entry: R 279 O 3037 ID: Cont 2 YunJon

Renee avoided us all morning. Her already pale face was paler than I imagined possible. Her features, usually so lively and expressive, were locked. She hunched, with a hand pressed against her lower abdomen.

I was eager to get her alone so we could speak freely, without the watchful eyes of Rangers. At last, when we returned to Unit 32, we had privacy. Escorting her to her quarters, we entered uninvited and sat on the floor. She simply stared blankly into space. Initially, I thought she was ill.

She was not ill.

I spoke to her, trying to coax information out of her about her condition. "Please allow us to give you a medical assessment. We have ways that we can help you if you will come with us to the medical facility on the ship. The sooner these matters are addressed, the faster they are dealt with."

She raised her face at last to look at me. For the first time since yesterday morning, her eyes locked with mine. The warmth in her features was gone. I did not recognize the Renee I had come to know.

"I do not wish treatment."

Her words were sharp. I have become accustomed to Renee's lively moods. I understand now that it is part of her cultural dynamic. I enjoy it. However, I had not foreseen this. And I was not enjoying it.

Kemi was also looking at me. It was an expectant, rather irritated look. I could not pinpoint exactly what emotion she was feeling, but I did not like it either. She and I had not had the opportunity to speak privately since before the hearing yesterday.

All in all, I was feeling very uncomfortable

I glanced at Kar and Luya. They were consulting over a piece of equipment and a medical reading. At Renee's words, both their heads raised and their murmured voices stopped. Neither of them said anything. Their faces gave me no clue.

"Could you please explain why?"

Her irritation turned to indecision, as if she was not sure she wanted to tell me, or perhaps she felt it was not worth it.

She took a deep breath, as if steeling herself. The look of indecision evaporated. She straightened her back.

"Yesterday," she paused, and then continued. "Yesterday, when we stood in front of the Regulation Committee, they spoke about me like I was a non-person, an animal, a… a mere science experiment. None of you defended me. I can only guess that there was nothing you could actually do in the face of the Committee, but I thought that at least someone might have spoken to my humanity. You must know that they have cast me into a prison. Any day, my life may end if I am perceived to be a negative influence upon you. I did not ask for this life. I did not ask to be here. I have lost everything that mattered to me, and now what little reason I might have had for trying to stay alive and forge a life has been taken from me."

She exhaled. A spark of anger lit in her eyes. "You think you are an advanced society that exists in harmony, but I believe you are blind to the reality of your existence. Yesterday, all I saw was a bunch of politicians patting themselves on the back for their open-mindedness when, in reality, I'm here because your science experiment went wrong. Yet I was offered no apology and no guarantee of safety. You meddled in time and I'm the only one to pay the price. You cannot expect me to be grateful for what happened yesterday, and you cannot imagine that things will not be changed with that ruling."

No one spoke. We only looked at her. Her blue eyes were blazing like icy fire in her pale face.

"I thought I could have at least counted on a greater defense from you and your team. But now, it would seem, I am nothing to you but a lab specimen as well. Perhaps this is all I have been to you all along."

She blinked rapidly and turned her face from us. We all sat in shocked silence. Our small, strange, fiery little guest from the past had taken us by surprise once again.

She was not wrong. And she surprised me again with her insight. I was uneasy with their ruling, yet I said nothing. Why? Because I acquiesced to our system as we always do, and as we always have.

As I was thinking, she raised her hand to her face. There was a bright, red gash on the middle knuckle of her hand. It was bright on her pale skin. It must have caused her pain. We easily could fix it, and she knew that. Yet she had requested no aid or treatment.

We are so profoundly different, I realized. And perhaps that lens, the lens through which she sees the world, is what I need to put our world into focus. For I could easily see the truth in her words. And a situation that appeared one way to me was turned on its head when she described it from her perspective.

Kemi put her arm around Renee's shoulder and glared at me. She had not even been allowed into the hearing. She is an assistant. They did not put her on the list of attendees and she watched it on the live-feed from her quarters.

Kar spoke. "Renee, we are sorry."

"No," I interrupted him, my voice laced with tension. A Team Lead always takes responsibility. This is an infallible tenet of leadership.

"Kar owes you no apology. I am the Team Lead. I assume responsibility for what occurred."

My team looked at me expectantly. I felt uneasy once more. I have never experienced that before. A leader is not ever to operate under the emotional pleasure or displeasure of their subordinates.

Yet the weight of their expectations sat heavily on my shoulders.

"I see that I did not respect you and your needs," I said slowly. "This was an ethical failure. For this, I apologize to you. You are a victim of circumstance, and are being treated as the responsible party."

Then I experienced a blinding moment of insight. It was one of those very rare and precious moments when the solution to a difficult problem leaps into stark clarity. I had not seen Renee as a true person. For the first time, in that moment, I chose to see her as such. She was no longer an exciting lab experiment. She was a human like myself. The weight of what we have done to her, and the ramifications it carries in her life, settled upon me. I could suddenly see our society as it appeared through her eyes, and our society suddenly looked very different to me.

It is no wonder I avoided perceiving her as such. We play mind games to avoid pain. And I felt pain in that moment. I feel it now.

Experiencing an unusual sense of claustrophobia, I stood and prepared to leave. The weight of what we had done, and our situation, were suffocating me. I needed time to think.

"Wait!" Renee cried. She ran toward me, and turned me around. The top of her short, light hair barely reached my shoulder.

"YunJon," she said, looking up at me, her strange blue eyes locked on mine. "I accept your apology. Now, you need to go figure out what we are going to do."

She stepped toward me, squeezed my arms and gave me a

small smile. I returned an uncomfortable nod and walked out as quickly as I could, whereupon I went straight to my quarters.

Striker's team did not escort us back, so I did not have an opportunity to speak with him again. I will need to send him a memo.

External Memo: Rotation 280

To:	Team Lead Striker, Enforcement Committee
From:	Team Lead YunJon, Unit 32, Continent 2 SciMed

I hoped you would be our escort back to but regrettably we were assigned a different team. I wish to continue my conversation with you. As you demonstrated a concern and interest in our work, I would keep you apprised.

The Regulation Committee has ordained that Renee may continue to live amongst us while we study and learn from her, secluded in Unit 32, so long as she does not affect anyone, directly integrate or influence society in any way. They will hold periodic assessments of Unit 32 personnel to ensure we remain unaffected. Her presence is to remain confidential.

The response to this verdict has been mixed. There are those who feel they failed to respect her dignity as a human being who was brought to our time against her will.

We, the members of Unit 32, will continue to respond as we deem appropriate for the safety and well-being of those to whom we are responsible.

If you indicate interest, I will continue to keep you posted. This is an offer made in the spirit of cordiality and friendship and not in my official capacity.

EXTERNAL MEMO: ROTATION 280

To: Team Lead YunJon, Unit 32, Continent 2 SciMed

From: Team Lead Striker, Enforcement Committee

I welcome your offer of friendship. Keep me apprised of all developments. I may be able to offer resources you do not have at your disposal.

LOG ENTRY: R 281 O 3037 ID: CONT 2 YUNJON

We snuck Shee and Hart out of our unit this morning. They paid us a great service and, in return, we were forced to smuggle them like thieves off our facilities on outbound vessels.

I expressed my frustration to Kemi that we could not treat our allies with more respect. She hinted that Shee enjoyed the process immensely. Despite her uncanny intuition and ability to read people, I struggle to see what he might have enjoyed in this.

Yet no alternatives were available to us. With the arrival of an external observer sent unannounced from the Regulation Committee, we were left with no choice. Shee and Hart's presence had never been made known to the Regulation Committee, and they would not take kindly to learning our deception.

While we were away at the Regulation Committee, Shee and Hart had returned from Unit 31, where they went to hide from the quarantine, and had reestablished themselves in Unit 32. They spent the three rotations we were away reviewing our research and working with our assistants.

Kar alerted us moments before the external observer's surprise arrival. As such, we were able to ferret Shee and Hart away to my quarters in time. While Kar monitored the observer's movements on his holopad, Kemi intercepted and distracted him so he would remain contained. During that time, Shee and Hart exited the unit.

We walked them down the hallway, instructing them to move silently. Kar disabled the visual sensors, but left the audio sensors online so as not to trigger the system alarm. Shee was particularly exuberant. His walk, or creep, resembled something of a controlled leap, bringing to mind images of a tightly wound spring bouncing uncontrollably down a hallway.

We bid them goodbye at the bay dock, where a vessel was awaiting them. I did not ask for details on who it was or how Kar coordinated it.

It is a pity that their precipitous departure did not allow for our team to bid them farewell. Their exit was necessarily immediate. The team has become attached to them, particularly Shee, whose long-winded ramblings and rather lackadaisical manner proved popular with the unit. I regret that we did not have the opportunity to properly express our gratitude for their solidarity and scholarship.

The observer himself will remain indefinitely. I find his presence and the situation it engenders borderline intolerable. He arrived unannounced. He hovers around our lab and in our public areas. His questions are incessant and irritating. And yet we must answer him, and anything other than a cordial response sounds suspicious. To speak privately, we are now forced to regularly meet in someone's personal quarters.

To make matters worse, Renee is not well. She is in the lab under 24-hour care. Around midday, she began to show signs of nausea and dizziness. I am extremely worried. We all are. There is no evident cause. All her readings are healthy.

Although, certain hormone levels are altered. They are different than what we measured prior to the Regulation Committee visit. Yet it is difficult to see how this can be the cause, or what it may indicate. We do not know what is her "normal," and so attempting to draw conclusions is extremely risky. The hormonal difference from before and after the trip could be attributed to a simple stabilizing of her body post-trauma. Or not. We cannot know.

Luya and Kar are working on it now in Kar's quarters. Kemi is with Renee in the lab. We are attempting to downplay the situation, so it does not appear too alarming to the observer. I believe we should not keep her in the lab under surveillance for too long. We may need to move her back to her quarters.

Everything must appear as normal and tranquil as possible, so that the Regulation Committee has no reason to reinvestigate Renee's presence.

I see the time and must go. I am meeting Kemi in her quarters. I have hoped for a few moments of private discussion with her. There are things I would address, and this observer has a never-ending source of energy, appearing here and there at random and unexpected moments. It is nigh on impossible to ensure a conversation without his prying intrusion.

RENEE

I was getting used to this new body. No aches and pains in my joints. Those irritations that are so ongoing they become simple background buzz? Poof! Gone. No heat or cold sensitivity in my old cavities. No dry eyes after a long day wearing contacts. Nothing. Just limber limbs and perfectly comfortable, extraordinarily odd skin.

Now? It's rebelling against me. Since the day after we returned from the Regulation Committee trip, I've had strong waves of nausea and dizziness. Swallowing my nutrition tubes is like trying to drink cough syrup. I'm exhausted, tired, grumpy and don't feel like eating anything.

Everyone is, of course, freaking out, which doesn't help at all. They've asked me to stay in the lab. They want constant medical attention 'available.' I prefer not to, but they're so damn concerned I veritably crumbled under the pressure. Especially after YunJon's apology.

"Renee, can you drink a bit more?" Kemi asks, interrupting my thoughts. Her giant eyes look like big, shining dark moons.

"If it will make you happy, Kemi. But you know I won't die of malnutrition if I skip one nutrition tube. And you also know it might make me throw up on you, right?"

"It is the role of a medical professional to care for those who are ill, regardless of their physical states," she said, her voice pierced with dignity.

Sometimes their answers sound like direct quotes from a training manual.

"I'm just teasing you. I can avoid throwing up directly on you." This time I wink.

"Your eye!" she exclaims.

It makes me laugh.

"It's called a wink. We do it when we are making a joke, flirting with someone or establishing confidence."

"How do you know which of those three a person is intending?"

"By context, I guess."

"That seems to leave a lot of room for misunderstanding," she replies thoughtfully.

She's right, of course. It really does. I can already think of a couple uncomfortable scenarios involving winks from my past life.

I throw back the nutrition tube and recline once more on the bed. The ceiling, the boring white, domed ceiling, occupies me until my stomach settles. Kemi is playing with her holograph. Despite myself, my thoughts wander to Striker. I wonder why he wasn't our escort back?

Even though it's hopeless, silly and totally pointless, I did wish to see him again. I even dreamed about him last night. His warmth, his acceptance, his laser beam focus.

A hand drifts to my lower abdomen.

Oh, my God.

Wait. No, it really can't be.

The realization makes me gasp out loud. Kemi darts to my side, hovering over me. I stare at her. What were we thinking? Having unprotected sex?

"What?" she asks. "What has happened?"

"I… I think I might know what is wrong."

My arms and legs are tingling in shock. I place both my hands on my belly.

External Memo: Rotation 281

To:	Team Lead Striker, Enforcement Committee
From:	Team Lead YunJon, Unit 32, Continent 2 SciMed

I write with urgency. We need you in Unit 32 immediately. It is an emergency regarding Renee. Exercise extreme caution. There is a Regulation Committee observer embedded in our unit, and what we will discuss must remain confidential - not just for Renee's sake, but for yours.

We will expect you late tonight. Confirm your arrival.

EXTERNAL MEMO: ROTATION 281

To:	Team Lead YunJon, Unit 32, Continent 2 SciMed
From:	Team Lead Striker, Enforcement Committee

I will arrive before the end of Rotation 281.

Renee

My hands fidget awkwardly on my lap. They smooth my already perfectly fitted jumpsuit. Frustrated at my inability to be still, I pinch the material, watching it stretch and shine, trying to distract myself with its fascinating malleability.

I'm really nervous. Everyone is looking at me, and I'm betraying my unease by twitching like a five-year old. Only I guess five-year olds in the super future probably sit still like statues.

YunJon, Kar, Luya and Kemi stand in front of me. I'm sitting on the edge of my bed. Everyone else appears a bit anxious too, except Kar, who is standing really close to Luya, kind of looming behind her like an ominous shadow. Weird.

We're waiting. No one has anything to say. I continue fidgeting. The scrape on my knuckle is almost healed, with only the hint of a light pink mark marring the skin. A flash of a memory surfaces. Striker's intense black eyes locked into mine while he holds my hand with the gentlest of touches despite his strength. The memory of his black eyes is unsettling and alluring. How all these contradictory feelings can exist inside one wretched mind is beyond me.

He should be here by now, right?

It's so mind-bendy, mixing one thousand year old genes with present day genes. Is this some kind of moral abomination?

CHAPTER THIRTY-SEVEN

Will I permanently alter the fate of mankind with my unnatural existence?

Whatever. I don't buy that self-aggrandizing, dogmatic and arbitrary mumbo jumbo. My existence feels way too mundane to mean anything significant.

Anyway, if I did believe that crap? I would have killed myself by now. Or convinced myself I was the second coming.

Bad luck happened. Now life is playing out its course. No big plan. No great moral mandate. I'm just a piece of charred flesh that landed on some random scientist's living room floor and happened to live. Now, like all life, I'm trying to cling to another day, might even procreate and perpetuate my genes. There can't be any more to this, can there?

God, this is depressing. And I am so, so tired. The exhaustion mixed with the nerves makes me feel strung out and brittle.

YunJon's wristband chirps. He glances down and darts from the room. Striker must have arrived. It is very late. Anxiety mounts. Kemi walks over to me. Her golden eyes glow protectively.

"Do not worry, Renee. We are going to figure this out," she says softly. I only hope she is right. My whole world has shifted in the past 24 hours. I am no longer just Renee. I'm Renee and I'm pregnant. It's not just my survival anymore. I have bigger questions to answer. Assuming I don't lose it, I face the most brutal of decisions.

It would be a lab rat. And does love for a child dictate that I end that torture before it begins? A deep, uncontrollable rage bubbles up inside me at the thought. Maybe I should just kill myself and it with me. Save it the pain of being a specimen in some dystopian, futuristic science chamber.

The door swishes open. I feel the soft, comforting hand of Kemi on my lower back. YunJon enters first, his face as serious and implacable as usual. His tan suit crisp and impeccable, he steps to the right and Striker enters. The door swishes shut behind him. Silence reigns.

I feel his presence immediately.

My senses have felt heightened since arriving. Every scent, color and touch is vibrant and strong. What is most distracting now are the sensations within my body. It is as though I can feel the chemicals and hormones shifting. The blood pumping through my veins, the chemicals in my brain, my skin and even my bone structure aching and creaking with exhaustion.

As such I don't just see him. I feel him. Clothed in black from head to toe, his face is masked. He raises black-gloved hands to his face and removes the material masking his features. With slow steps forward, he comes to stand in front of me.

A sudden and unexpected stab of fear strikes the pit of my stomach. It hadn't occurred to me that he might be repulsed by the thought of us creating a cross-millennial child. I become deeply afraid. People betray each other all the time. Sometimes they don't even betray us. We simply create expectations that they don't fulfill. We imagine realities that don't exist. We project feelings and emotions that were never expressed.

Maybe he will be horrified. Maybe he'll betray us all.

"Why do you hold your stomach? Are you ill?" he asks, his voice gravelly. He never breaks eye contact.

"You may tell him," said YunJon. "I think it is your right to do so."

I swallow and nod. The team confirmed my suspicions with specialized testing. Their responses sure were something to behold. I would have laughed under different circumstances.

Apparently, pregnancy testing isn't even a routine part of the most elaborate of medical screenings, because no one 'mates' out of cycle.

"Striker. I am happy to see you. Thank you for coming." I reach out a hand to his arm and touch him gently. He is frozen like ice. I quickly retract my arm.

Better just get it out.

"At the time, when we," I stutter a bit, "when we mated, I didn't think of the repercussions. It didn't even cross my mind."

I pause for a moment, unsure of how to proceed. This is so awkward, telling someone you're pregnant with an audience. I force myself to maintain eye contact. His gaze has intensified, his eyes squinting slightly in concentration.

"Did I hurt you?" he replies softly. "YunJon, did I hurt her?" He turns, his brow creased and his muscles tensed.

"No!" I answer in response. He looks back toward me. "You didn't hurt me at all. Rather the opposite, I guess?" My hand wanders to my stomach, unbidden.

He gasps. Staring at my belly, he looks up at me and then gapes back down again.

"It cannot be," he says, and drops to his knees in front of me. His face is at the level of my belly. He rests his hands gently on my hips and leans forward, inhaling deeply and shutting his eyes. Awe and shock soften his harsh features. He looks up at me from where he kneels, and slowly puts his hand against mine so it rests against my stomach as well.

"You… you are… we created… life?" His voice is deep and husky. He stares at me with such a raw vulnerability that we could be alone, not locked in a room with four observing scientists.

Knock me over with a feather, somebody.

"Yes, Striker. We did. I'm pregnant." The words feel awkward on my lips. I am so stunned by his response, I can't think of anything else to say. He is veritably glowing.

"It is a miracle," he says.

"What?" I say, startled. I am overwhelmed. Tears of relief spring unbidden to my eyes, threatening to overflow, but I aggressively blink them back. The tension in the air and the emotions flooding the room are getting to me. I feel a fresh wave of nausea flood through me. This couldn't happen in a worse possible moment, could it?

"Kemi, I'm going to vomit!"

Quick as lightening, she grabs a bag she's been keeping on hand. I try and turn away for privacy and throw up repeatedly. This is some morning sickness. But isn't it awfully soon for morning sickness? It's only been five days or so. I didn't even know you could test a pregnancy so early. I can't remember what's normal. No one close to me was ever pregnant. None of my friends had gotten there yet.

Striker is demanding an explanation, hovering over me with concern. Kemi snaps at him to get out of the way. I would laugh if I wasn't so miserable. Embarrassed and overwhelmed, I try to tune them out. Feelings, hormones, adrenaline spikes and sensations flood through my body. These are normal pregnancy sensations? Should these changes be happening so rapidly?

A fresh wave of nausea strikes. I try and swallow back the bile. Kemi gently encourages me to lie down on my back. Luya is running a medical scanner over my body. I hear her consulting quietly with Kar, "I think her hormones are adjusting too quickly to the pregnancy. Perhaps her body's attempt to keep the fetus safe? Their genetics might not be as compatible as we thought. We need more information."

I feel a stab of panic, even though I'm not certain keeping the baby is a good idea, anyway.

Kemi looms over me. "Renee, I'm going to give you something to help you rest, okay?"

Log Entry: R 282 O 3037 ID: Cont 2 YunJon

We are in the early hours of Rotation 282, yet I will not sleep for more hours still.

When Renee disclosed her pregnancy to Striker, his response took us by surprise. I have never witnessed such sentiment at the prospect of procreation.

Renee could do little beyond share the news, as she fell ill shortly thereafter. Kemi administered a gentle tranquilizer and she fell into a troubled sleep, her eyes sinking closed as the medication entered her system.

We ought to have taken her to the medical unit for proper, comprehensive tests. It was too risky with the Regulation Committee observer hovering incessantly. Her pregnancy? It is strictly forbidden. And this observer suspects something already. Otherwise, he would not be so diligent, so unwavering and unceasing, in his observations.

Only once Renee sunk into a restless sleep did Striker move. He sat down on the floor and stared into the distance for some while. I watched him process something in his mind, exactly what I did not yet know, with eyes squinted in concentration.

After a few moments, his eyes snapped up to mine. He looked

at me expectantly. There was nothing we could do but lower ourselves to the floor across from him. We cannot refuse an invitation to dialogue. Striker knew that.

Kemi sank down gracefully next to me. She sat immediately to my left, so close that her knee gently brushed my own. We were aligned next to one another, such that we both faced him front on. She did not create a circle as is custom.

Her message was perfectly clear; we are united against you.

I felt a compulsion to reach out to her and feel the warmth of her skin. I wanted her eyes locked on mine, and looking nowhere else. It was such an intense urge it nearly bowled me over, leaving me breathless, my heart-rate elevated and my stomach in knots. It was extremely distracting, and made it challenging to refocus on the important and looming dialogue in which we were about to engage.

Kar and Luya tended to Renee with their mobile units. They nodded politely, indicating to Striker that they were listening. They refused to sit. Although, they changed their minds once his story began to unfold.

This male's life has shaken not just my perception of him but the very foundation of my belief in our society. I record it here with as much detail as I can.

Striker stared at me in the eyes for a long moment. He glanced at Kemi in turn and, just as I was on the brink of snapping at him to speak or allow us to be about our business, he turned back to me and began.

"This revelation requires a reorientation of plans. It also compels me to reveal things to you, things I would never have revealed under any other circumstances. What I will disclose is so highly classified that only a minority of the Regulation Committee itself has access to this knowledge. I tell you now because we face a turning point. We must decide our course of action and determine the extremes to which we will, or will not, go to protect Renee and the child she carries. You cannot do this without the full background.

"I do not know you. I do not know the extent to which I can trust you. My position is not an enviable one, as you will observe as my story unfolds. What I share will provide you with the means to betray me in the most profound of ways should you choose to do so. Yet, you immediately alerted me to Renee's situation. You did not alert the Committee. You have masked her condition from the external observer. These actions signal a certain," he paused in his speech and nodded at me, "proclivity to bend the norms by which we live. And they give me a very keen insight into just where your loyalties lie."

The vulnerability and awe he showed when Renee shared her pregnancy were gone. He looked foreboding and intimidating while he spoke. His voice was a low growl, harsh and abrupt, with a cadence that betrayed nothing but strength and a vague antagonism. His face, darker and harsher than most, had the intense look of a predator strung out on a wire, ready to snap at the slightest provocation. He appeared on guard, as though ready to pounce in defense of Renee or himself at any hint of threat.

Scientists such as ourselves are not used to interacting with Rangers, particularly not the likes of Striker. I can count on one hand the number of encounters I have had with a Ranger, and most certainly never with such a high-ranking one. They say that the higher the ranking, the more vicious the individual.

"At birth, my genetic testing measured my proclivity to aggression, risk-taking and extreme physicality to be off the charts. They were the highest measured in my birth pool and many preceding it. The levels were so high, in fact, that they considered," his face furrowed almost imperceptibly, "eliminating me. Yet due to the slim margin of error of these tests, they allowed me to live under regulated oversight."

"How," I asked, suspicious, "how do you know all this?"

"I acquired a copy of my private records."

"But how?"

We all have records. Everyone knows that. Yet no one ever

sees them. They are the property of the Regulation Committee. They contain our full genetic analysis from birth, as well as subsequent testing over the years. Our full records are never disclosed to us. Only pieces and parts are shared, those which are deemed to be helpful to us in managing our personal conditions.

He stared at me for a moment, then answered slowly, "I had someone acquire them for me."

Two dozen rotations ago, I would have demanded further explanation. Now? The lines are blurring. Black and white has melded into a confounding streak of gray.

I nodded, saying stiffly, "Continue with your narrative."

"I was assigned a monitor. He was extraordinary. He went far above and beyond his assigned duties. Rather than just observe me, he mentored me and guided me. My impulses were so severe as a child that, without his assistance in channeling my emotions, I surely never would have been allowed to live into adolescence. He was, perhaps, the greatest male I have ever known."

Striker paused, and swallowed. His face softened slightly.

"Using the techniques that my mentor taught me, I grew to understand how to mask my differences. I learned to exude a calm and controlled exterior. My abnormalities became an advantage, because he trained me to channel my intense surges of emotion and impulsiveness into the immediate task at hand. If I carefully managed them, the surges in adrenaline were able to enhance my attention far above those of my peers. My promotions were rapid and unprecedented. Within only seven orbits, I was already in the upper echelons of Ranger ranks.

"Several years after reaching the high tiers of Ranger ranks, I developed a desire to produce offspring. What started as a vague interest rapidly evolved into a crushing desire. It consumed me. This is unusual amongst Rangers, but not unheard of. Following standard procedures, I made inquiries into viable mates. Cycle after cycle, there were none. After nearly an orbit of inquiries, they informed me that there was not, and would not be, anyone compatible with my genetic code. I could participate in mating cycles, but never in reproduction. They forbade me further inquiries."

His jaw tightened. The softened look from mention of his mentor was gone.

"I had weathered everything up until that moment. The tests, the surveillance, the constant assessments, the murmurings and half-veiled threats of removal from duty at the slightest hint of a behavioral anomaly. Yet the prohibition of my right to produce an offspring, the right afforded to all citizens, broke something inside me. The system no longer felt controlling but well-intentioned. It felt like a prison.

"This was when I acquired my records. Gaining these records was like gaining the key to unlock all the mysteries of my life. It was marked on my file, from birth, that I was not to be allowed reproductive rights under any circumstances. This was to ensure my genetics would not be passed on into society. They had known all along that I would never be allowed reproductive rights, but did not inform me. Instead, unwittingly, I was allowed to submit application after application over the course of an entire orbit until suddenly, without explanation nor recourse, I was abruptly told to cease all my efforts. They lied to me. There were many viable partners. It was me that was not the viable partner.

"I did the research. There is no proof that my traits are genetic. There is no evidence that it would be passed on to an offspring. But there is also no evidence that it would not be passed on. And the risk was not deemed worthwhile."

"Typical," snapped Luya. She stood over us, her portable medical unit clenched tightly in her fingertips. Her legs were tense and locked, the taut muscles easily visible through her jumpsuit. Our attention jumped like lightening from Striker to her. Anger washed over her features.

Luya has a gentle character. She is prone to mildness and soft reflections. I attributed her leadership skills to her ability to garner the genuine adoration of her team, a wonderful and enviable style of leadership built on mutual respect and trust.

I speak for us all when I say we were somewhat taken aback. Even Kar, who has the most unreadable face of us all, showed some surprise. She went on.

"There is no proof that it is a genetic disorder. I worked on a committee that dealt with similar cases prior to requesting transfer to an experimental unit. We studied whether or not certain medical conditions should be allowed to be passed on to offspring. These were, naturally, always conditions of the brain as everything else is easily fixed. The brain alone remains ever elusive. Proving mental anomalies as genetic is impossible without data. We needed more samples. The only way to get more samples was to allow people with those conditions to procreate. They denied this request.

"No one on my team seemed to mind. They thought it prudent. Yet this is not how you conduct science. You must have a full, robust data set before drawing conclusions. And our policies, particularly on matters with such profound implications, must be made solely on the basis of science. There was not a large enough risk to prohibit us from exploring the matter further. What is more, it has yet to be determined whether it would happen anyway, given that this may very well happen spontaneously in utero."

She ended abruptly, promptly staring down at her feet. She interrupted her own silence before anyone else could. "That is why I came here to experimental."

I looked at Striker.

"That is unjust," Kemi said. Righteous indignation swept across her face.

Striker spoke slowly, his words weighted with a range of emotions that even I, with all my empathy, could not discern. "How interesting to learn that there were, in fact, those in the scientific community who did not condone this approach."

He inhaled and exhaled deeply before continuing, glancing first at Luya. She abruptly sat, leaving Kar to tend to Renee, and broke the confrontational barrier that Kemi and I had presented.

We now formed a circle. He picked up his story where he left off before Luya's interruption.

"I tried to manage the disillusionment and deceit. My mentor had treated me with care. Yet he never shared this information with me. I was plagued with questions. Had he known? Did he know that I was to be cast aside as a viable member of society, unable to contribute to the continuation of our species? I felt that he must have. I felt betrayed. Yet it was too late to ask him, as he had passed on several orbits prior to my discovery.

"I can only describe what happened next as an increasing loss of personal control. I began to steadily push back against the system. I mated outside of cycle. I was successful. One of the females became pregnant. You are likely unaware, but this happens more frequently than the Regulation Committee reports. The official number of off the grid pregnancies is set at 2 percent, but in reality it is somewhere closer to 10 percent. They do not terminate most of these illicit pregnancies. In most cases where two people mate out of cycle and cause an accidental pregnancy, they are sanctioned but the fetus is allowed to come to term and be born. I thought perhaps, given the uncertainties surrounding my condition, that the life of an actual, viable child would outweigh the prohibition on my record. Yet when her pregnancy was reported and the genetic ID of the father identified, they immediately terminated without consent. I had anticipated their actions incorrectly. They showed no leniency. What is more, we were both demoted within our respective fields. I did not even know that the fetus had been aborted until after it happened. They sent me a memo with news of my demotion."

Pain washed over his face. His jaw tensed and it was almost as though his enormous body was vibrating ever so slightly. Kar no longer hovered over his mobile med units. We all just stared, frozen.

"And even still, even still, they did not tell me what was in my files. Of course, I knew at this point. But they did not know that I knew. But what I did learn was the lengths to which they would go to prevent me from procreating. This was two orbits ago. It was this demotion that threw me into your path. Prior to this, I would never have been delegated to a simple escort mission, no matter how high profile. I ran our most advanced exploratory missions.

"It was my experience in advanced exploration that cued me into the nature of your situation. I knew immediately that the implications of your findings, of Renee, were vast. The nature of my preparations, prior to demotion, were cutting-edge and forward-looking. We were trained to look for the impossible. Before you told me that there was something extraordinary about your discovery, about Renee, I already knew.

"YunJon, when I inquired about our mating compatibility, I had no intentions to act upon my impulse to mate. But when I found myself in her quarters, I was so deeply affected by her presence. It was as though my control was wrestled away from me, and all thoughts of consequences slipped away. I asked for her consent and she gave it. Once that was done, I felt as though nothing would stop me. I could not think of the future nor the past, the only thing that mattered was that we were together. I have never experienced such a sensation, not even when mating out of cycle. Yet with her, all thoughts fled my mind. I simply felt as though I must be with her or…" He trailed off. He did not finish the sentence. He continued in a quieted voice.

"To learn now that she is pregnant? You must understand that having been through this once, I cannot allow a forced termination to come to pass. If the pregnancy itself is not viable for medical reasons, or if Renee rejects the child, then I accept it. Yet under no circumstances will I allow a cessation of pregnancy against our will. I will give, and sacrifice, everything to ensure her care. If this requires us to become enemies, then so be it. I will regret it. But I will also act without mercy."

He stopped speaking.

Compassion and fear flashed over Kemi's face. Sweat shone on Kar's forehead, betraying his underlying emotions. My fists clenched tightly at my sides, while my own personal state of mind sunk into a state of confusion so profound I felt a paralysis settle in my limbs.

This was no mere Ranger. He was the best of the best. His size, litheness, demeanor and posture seemed perfectly calibrated to instill fear in those around him. I saw his eyes flit from mine to Kemi and back. I read the meaning. He was aware of my feelings. And he would not hesitate to use them against me if we fought him.

Yet he did not need threats. His story was enough. But his has been a life of force, violence, betrayal and mistrust. I could not blame him for his actions. He was protecting himself in the only way he knew how.

The silence extended for some time as his words sunk in. The only sounds were Renee's soft inhales and exhales. I knew I must speak, though, so I carefully formulated my words.

"You must surely know that experimental units are generally staffed by," I paused for a moment, seeking the right words, "those with atypical aspirations."

It was not exactly what I had meant to say.

"It is unusual to wish to work in this field. And although we are all extremely different in our backgrounds and skills, we share a motive for being in this room today that did not originate with Renee's arrival alone."

I paused.

"You will find that we are not unsympathetic to your plight."

I knew then what he had been so rapidly and intently processing in those short moments before we sat down. Yes, he wanted to explain himself. But he had also decided to place himself in grave risk by disclosing. Additionally, he was forcing our hand. And he knew that. He was acutely aware that in the sharing of his story, not only was he risking himself but he was forcing us to take a stand on one side or the other.

We had been waffling. He knew that. But we could no longer. It was time to make our choice.

It was almost a relief. We had been standing on the fence for so long. We knew this was coming. We could fall to the left or right, but we would fall. And I had a split second to make the decision that would permanently alter the fate of so many.

I made the decision.

"We work with you to ensure Renee's safety, not against you. And a part of her safety, for us, is her autonomy to choose her life's outcome. Yet we will not hesitate to inform her of any risks she may face, nor will we hesitate to give her medical advice. The decision must be, ultimately, her own."

"I can assure you," Striker responded, "that Renee will not be allowed to live if it is known that she can reproduce and has already become pregnant."

The Ranger was pushing his advantage. He wanted to know how far he could take us.

"He is right," said Kar. His voice startled me. He hovers so silently on the outside of conversations and speaks so rarely it always take me by surprise. Lately, he has become practically verbose. I need to reassess him, it would seem.

"I took the liberty of monitoring some of the Regulation Committee's private correspondence while we were at their headquarters. There will be no leeway nor room for uncertainty. None at all."

I ground my teeth. Trust Kar to announce this information when it was only absolutely necessary and pertinent to our immediate conversation.

The time for thinking was over, however. It was time for action, and damned if I will be hung up on breaking regulation. We have gone too far now to think twice. I will need every tool in my arsenal.

"Then we have precious little time," I said. "We need to gather more information before formulating a plan. Kar, hack into every correspondence you can regarding Renee. Pay careful attention to our embedded observer's reports. Reach out to your network of off-the-grid scientists and alert them to our situation as delicately and diplomatically as you can. Luya, you are not my team member... therefore I only request of you that you please help Kemi attend to Renee. I am deeply concerned for her health. I will put her in both of your capable hands should you agree."

"I would be honored," Luya said with a deep nod.

"Striker," I turned toward the forbidding male. "You know better than I what can be done to garner more intel on our situation. I trust you to do so. Let us reconvene in two hours, here in Renee's quarters, to discuss what we have found and establish a plan."

Everyone rose immediately but Striker and me. Our eyes locked one final time. Unspoken words passed between us. Then he reached out a hand and he jerked me up to my feet. I suppose that is some sign of solidarity. Better than a fist to the face.

Kar called clear on the hallway, and we exited the room quickly.

We are coming up on our deadline of two hours. I retired to my quarters to reflect, given that I have no tangible skills to afford the team in this moment. Roaming the hallways would only serve to unsettle our external observer.

I hoped this logging exercise would help me gain clarity. Our situation is so unstable, so muddied and unusual, that despite the reflection herein, clarity eludes.

One thing is clear. If Striker had not forced our hand, we might have otherwise waited too long to pick sides. And here we reveal our nature as scientists. How can we, mere scientists, do this? This is not what we are trained for. This is not who we are.

At least, I had not thought so.

I have been proven wrong many times over these recent rotations.

Renee

"Give me an IV, maybe?"

"What is an IV?" Kemi says, her eyes widening a smidgen.

"Oh, it's… it's when you stick a needle into a vein and put in liquid and nutrition."

A light sheen of sweat covers my forehead as I speak. The sleeve of my suit serves as a handy towel. She stares at me as I dab at my forehead. Her head is tilted and her expression one of curiosity.

"Your stomach and digestive tract are uniquely designed to absorb all the necessary nutrients that your body needs. Why would we try to feed and nourish it any other way?"

"So how did you feed and water me when I was in a coma?"

"The fluid you were suspended in was infused with nutrition and is digestible. It provided you with the hydration and nutrition you needed. It is multipurpose. Kar tailored it slightly as we studied your physiognomy, but only very slightly."

"What about people with stomach problems?"

She exchanges a lighting quick look with Luya. "Well, beyond several rare occurrences in infancy, adults do not expel the contents of their stomach. We have not, well, observed it before. We do not have a standard set of procedures in place should this occur."

A few days ago, I was just a little lightheaded and queasy. But my symptoms have rapidly increased. The heightened senses I have come to enjoy these past few weeks, incredible vision and hearing and sensitivity, are no longer enjoyable whatsoever. They just magnify my nausea. This all means I've been throwing up a lot, way worse even than a 31st century infant, apparently.

My body feels like it's at war with itself. But if the pain stops, will it mean the baby is gone? And would that ultimately be good or bad, in the end? I'm still plagued with fear for its future, for our future.

"Back in my day, we vomited a lot," I explained, forcing my thoughts away from that dark path. "Sometimes we would catch a virus or eat something that didn't settle well in our stomach. People even might throw up if they were really nervous. When a person couldn't keep enough food and liquid in their stomachs, we inserted a needle into their vein and gave it to them intravenously. I can't keep anything down. Maybe I need it."

Kemi looks a bit ill at the thought. Luya is oddly fascinated. Fascinated like watching a train crash. They don't say anything. Even as sick as I am, it's still kinda funny to watch their expressions. The irony does not go unnoticed. All those wasted years of trying to fit in and subtly adjusting my behavior in response to what people 'might' think of me when, apparently, all I needed was to become a real, dyed-in-the-wool freak to get over it. The weight of being different would crush me if I let it. So I don't. I'm over it.

If I could only go back to my old self and my old time now. What a different life I would live.

"Why is it so hard to figure out what's wrong with me?" I say eventually as the silence drags on. Apparently the IV is out.

"We are struggling to pinpoint exactly what is going on. We are unused to what you are experiencing," says Kemi, looking strained.

"What? Pregnancy?"

The door slides open with no announcement and interrupts

us. Kemi and Luya dart around, leaping to their feet like lithe gymnast warriors. YunJon, Kar and Striker enter.

My heart skips a beat at the site of Striker.

"Brief them," says YunJon curtly.

"We do not know how, but the Regulation Committee Observer knows that we are suppressing elements of our research. He sent a memo this evening to the Regulation Committee informing them and requested immediate back-up and authorization to intervene. It is late now, so I doubt there will be response or action until tomorrow morning. But there will be a response." Kar speaks clearly and crisply, his voice emotionless.

We sit in silence. This is terrible news. Yet the dark orbs of his eyes betray nothing. Both YunJon and Striker share his hard look.

"This discovery indicates that we must come to a prompt and immediate decision regarding our course of action," says YunJon. "I estimate we have until early tomorrow morning."

Kar speaks again and, for once, he hesitates slightly, a tiny crack in his stony demeanor. "Given the accelerated time frame and the urgency of situation, I took the extreme liberty of disclosing our situation to my global network of off-the-grid scientists."

Kar glances toward YunJon, as though seeking approval. I didn't think Kar was the type of person to seek approval. He must be under far more strain than he is showing, and it makes my stomach jolt even further.

YunJon pauses thoughtfully, then responds decisively. "Under the circumstances, you did right by taking the initiative. I trust your judgment."

YunJon turns to us now. "Kar is correct. They have forced our hand. We have an extraordinarily limited time frame in which to act. We must come to a decision this night."

My pulse accelerates. I want to reach out a hand to Striker. I imagine him grasping my hand in his, holding it tightly, as the long, wide fingers dwarf my own.

"There have been no responses to my messages yet," says Kar.

"However, the encryption process we use is extremely sophisticated. It can take some time to decode. That is all I have to report." He ceases speaking abruptly.

Fear cuts through my nausea and lightheadedness. Everyone settles down to talk. The conversation begins slowly. It's stilted, but quickly picks up momentum. We discuss and discuss our options, although I say very little. The debate feels endless, yet nothing seems viable. Tensions run high. The questions come rapid-fire. What will happen to Unit 32? What will happen to me? To the pregnancy? To Striker? What will happen to anyone directly involved with me if they discover my pheromones?

Someone raises Continent 7. We circle back to it over and over. It could be our only option for immunity. The "if" we go slowly morphs into "how" we will get there. At first I feel sick in the pit of my stomach, and it's not the nausea. It feels unjust to ask them to give up everything on my behalf. Even if I'm here because of their mistake, it was still just a mistake. But their faces reveal the truth. This isn't a sacrifice for me. Their desire to escape, to free themselves from their constraints, is as evident as anything can ever be on their stoic faces.

This small group of scientists was my entire world when I arrived. They were the whole future. But they aren't the rule that defines this time, they are the exception. I know that now. They are outliers, misfits who don't conform to a mainstream society - a society that has swung so far in their quest for "balance" that they've lost every semblance of it. When does the price of peace become, in fact, a loss of peace itself?

The discussions are dragging on too long. I know it and they know it. The tension is ratcheting up. Every second is precious and every second lost is wasted time.

"The solution is clear," I interrupt, at long last. They've been talking around this course of action for the past hour. They won't own it themselves. I have to say it.

"You have to turn me in. Message them and tell them that I'm a danger. Request they send an escort. Hand me over. Pretend like you're on their side. No one suspects you. With the extra space that gives you, you can all escape with some chance of success. Then you hijack me off the escort ship while it's en route to the Regulation Committee. Take them by surprise. We rendezvous and make our way to Continent 7 together."

I'm tired and scared and I really don't want to do this but I try to keep my voice steady.

"No." Striker's voice cuts like a knife.

"He's right. We won't do it," YunJon says. Kemi nods.

My eyes meet Kar's. He will be my strongest, if only, ally. Together we can convince them. We lock eyes for a moment and confirm our understanding with a near imperceptible nod. I knew he would get it. This is the only plan with even a chance of success.

"You are all responding emotionally to her suggestion," Kar says to them, his voice as steady and straightforward as always. "You cannot allow your emotions to sway your judgment. This is the only course of action that has a chance of success, not just for us but also for her."

A wave of dizziness sweeps through me. I breathe deeply and stiffen my spine.

YunJon's jaw tightens. I don't look at Striker. I can't make myself.

Silence encompasses the room. A part of me wants them to continue to cry "no" with indignation. I am so scared. Putting myself into the hands of the enemy, to whom I am nothing more than an animal, chills me to my very core. Yet what choice do we have?

I steel myself again to speak. The fear cannot win.

"Do not force me to argue this point. I do not have the energy or the resolve. We all know this is the best chance for everyone's survival. You all knew it an hour ago, you just couldn't say it."

My hands clench in my lap. When I look up again, I know I have won the battle and my stomach twists. Their faces reveal the truth. Their acceptance is both a relief and a disappointment.

Chapter thirty-nine

YunJon startles me with his next words.

"Renee, were you normal? Back in your time, I mean. Were you like the mainstream humans of your age?"

"No," I say slowly, "not really, I guess. I never fit in that well." Their eyes are fixed on mine, and I finally say, "I guess we have something in common then, don't we?"

Log Entry: R 283 O 3037 ID: Cont 2 YunJon

We are in the early hours of rotation 283. Kemi is sleeping. A strand of her thick, wavy hair falls onto her face. Her mouth is parted slightly. She gently inhales and exhales, her chest rising and falling softly. Her small, delicate body is curled on her side, facing me as I sit on the floor logging.

Could I sleep on the bed with her?

I did not ask before she fell asleep. That was certainly not a strategic move on my part. I do not see how I can make decisions about the fate of our team if I cannot even discern whether or not a female wishes me to sleep next to her. Indeed, my brain must be addled, because I cannot even determine which of these decisions is the most challenging.

As we departed Renee's quarters, Kemi asked me in a quiet voice if she might sleep with me in my quarters. Her golden eyes were intent and worried.

I hesitated, but only out of shock. I thought I had misheard her. I certainly wanted her in my quarters, there was no doubt. But my hesitation was a source of confusion.

"Oh, of course, I should never have brought it up, forgive me," she mumbled, a flush rising to her golden cheeks. Her eyes were locked on the floor, and she moved to shuffle past me.

"No!" I said, in a voice stronger than intended. Kar glanced at me sharply from across the hall. My hand gripped Kemi's arm, as if of its own accord. She looked up, startled and confused. I ignored Kar.

"Not no, you may come to my quarters. But no, do not go," I mumbled, watching feebly as my wits abandoned me entirely. "I mean, yes, please sleep in my quarters."

Rather than risk speaking anymore, which was proving an absurd venture, I extended my arm to her shoulder and guided her down the hallway. We entered silently. I extended the bed.

We stood. We stared at each another.

"I must send a memo," I said, haltingly. "Please, relax and sleep."

I pretended not to watch as she climbed into my bed. I pretended not to watch as she drifted off to sleep.

Now I have not yet written the memo. And I have not decided to sleep on the floor or next to her. Which did she mean? Did she mean she was nervous and wanted company? Or did she mean that she actually wanted us to be together on the bed?

This is absurd. Kar has probably sent all of his memos already, and his required extensive encryption.

Enough. I will send this memo. And then I will sleep alongside Kemi on the bed. This may be my only chance. We cannot know how the Committee will respond to the memo. We need it to clear the team of suspicion and guilt. Otherwise, our plan will have no chance. And if our plans are dashed, then this may be the last opportunity I ever have to be near her.

EXTERNAL MEMO: ROTATION 283

To: Regulation Committee

From: Team Lead YunJon, Continent 2 SciMed

Subject Renee of Time Window Experiment is exhibiting symptoms of an unknown illness. We spent rotation 282 attempting to discern the cause. No one else in the Unit is exhibiting similar symptoms.

We currently have her under a high level of surveillance and are limiting her exposure to team members.

EXTERNAL MEMO: ROTATION 283

To:	Team Lead YunJon, Continent 2 SciMed
From:	Regulation Committee

A Ranger Escort will collect Subject Renee within 10 Earth Hours. Upon collection, it will become the responsibility of Research and Development High Command.

A separate team will arrive by the end of Rotation 283 to collect all data and research associated with Time Window Project. Prepare for their arrival.

Cont. 2 SciMed Unit 32 has 10 rotations to propose a new research topic for review.

External Memo: Rotation 283

To: 8248hf;9a

From: a74;l;kn99

I was distantly aware of your plight before you sent out the network call. My position grants me access to the matter to which you refer. I have investigated the matter further since receiving your memo.

Your situation and that of your team is grave, far more than you suspect. You must flee, and make haste. Four of the five you identified in the memo, minus the assistant Kemi, are being fully profiled by the Committee.

There is no future for you. Continent 7 is your only option. I urge you again, make haste.

EXTERNAL MEMO: ROTATION 283

To:	8248hf;9a
From:	a333kk6

We received your network call. You need transportation. There are ways to travel off the grid and we are willing to extend our services. Confirm time and place and we will get you there. The fee is a sample of her DNA. Confirm as soon as possible.

External Memo: Rotation 283

To:	8248hf;9a
From:	Continent 7

We guarantee no one entry to Continent 7.

Renee

"What are you doing, Kar?"

I'm sleepy. He woke me up.

"I need a sample of your DNA."

His tone of voice is as monotone as ever, but slightly softer than usual. It feels like the middle of the night.

Anything beyond a raised eyebrow is too much for me.

"Ok, whatever you need."

He takes out a vial, unscrews it and scrapes a small bit of skin off my forearm with a stick protruding from the lid. He screws it back on. I kind of expected something more sophisticated.

He nods, turns and leaves.

I slip back into a restless sleep.

External Memo: Rotation 283

To:	Torsh
From:	Striker

The time has come to collect my debt. What I ask of you is a great favor and with it I release you from all obligations to me.

From the moment this memo arrives, be on standby. Your mission is a simple abduction. An Escort Team of Rangers will be traveling from Cont. 2 SciMed Headquarters to the Regulation Committee today. Your target is their charge, a young, petite female with white skin, light brown hair and blue eyes. She goes by the name of Renee. Handle the target with extreme care. There is to be no damage to the target no matter the circumstances.

This will appear like a routine Escort Team but it is not. They will be highly trained Rangers. Use this knowledge to your advantage.

Do not fail.

RENEE

"Renee! Wake up!"

My mind and stomach roll like a rickety boat in a rocky ocean. My body screams at me to be still. Yet the urgency of her voice jerks me out my stupor.

Swallowing down my queasiness, I pull myself up to a sitting position. My vision slowly comes into focus.

Shit. She's panicking. What's going on?

"They are here. They are already here! We have to get you ready to go."

The door swishes open and Striker runs in with Kar at his heels. Striker moves like a panther, and I jerk back in shock at the speed with which he crosses the room. It feels unnatural, and provokes a primal surge of fear within me.

"Renee," Striker says, his eyes locked on mine. "We only have one minute. Mask your illness at all costs. Assimilate no matter what it takes. If you reveal a single abnormality, just one, they will cut you down without mercy. Do you understand?" His tone is harsh. A sense of dread wells within me.

"When the mercenaries kidnap you off the Ranger's ship, do not fight. Identify yourself as Renee. They will remove you to safety."

His black eyes lock with mine. I nod. He leaps to his feet.

"Stand! Now!" His voice is terrible. The dark features of his face are inscrutable.

A rush of betrayal surges in my gut. Why is he barking orders at me? I'm not his lackey. Doesn't he understand how sick I am?

"Stand!" He yells this time. Tears well in my eyes at the humiliation.

Humiliated and angry, my legs shake as I push myself to a standing position. My knees buckle but I lock them and clench my muscles hard. I will not fall in front of him. The world around me darkens, threatening a blackout. But I force myself to ride it out. Swallowing down bile, I don't dare open my mouth to speak.

I refuse to cry. I would die of the shame.

He grabs my upper arms with his hands. My arms look like toothpicks in his fingers. Leaning down, he stares into my eyes, mere inches from my face.

"Your life, the life of this child and all of our work to keep you safe now depends on you. Show no weakness." He pauses. Then he pronounces each word with a slow, careful and cold intensity that leaves me stunned, "You must not let us down."

Without a word of encouragement, compassion or support, he turns on his heel toward the door. He is gone and I am left shaking but standing, propped up on nothing but an ugly mix of anger, fear, guilt and hatred.

Kemi is frozen. Kar moves forward quickly, grabbing her arm.

"Pull up her sleeve," he snaps at her. Kemi fumbles, the first awkward gesture I've seen, and pulls the sleeve of my jumpsuit up to my shoulder. The fabric stretches easily.

"Hold her arm still."

Kemi holds my arm firmly at the elbow and shoulder. Kar pulls out a small black device. He shoves it up against my arm. Pain pierces my arm as though it's on fire, and I scream involuntarily. Flames lick across my arm to my chest and down my limbs.

It subsides and I find Kar is supporting me. I gasp in and out, as though all the air had been pushed violently from my body.

"What did you do to me?" I ask through gritted teeth.

"It was a shot of the highest dose of adrenaline I thought your body could handle. The pain will recede shortly."

He looks into my eyes briefly and turns to dash out as Striker had. YunJon is nowhere to be seen. Where is he?

Kemi's face flashes with fear and shock. For once, I can easily discern her emotions. I thought Striker had scared me, but seeing her fear is way worse.

"Why?" I whisper softly, as the last vestiges of pain pound their way out of my veins and are replaced by a shaky nervousness. "Why is it so important to hide that I'm sick?"

She embraces me. Pulling back, her eyes startle me once more with their beauty. Odd to notice such a thing in a moment like this. The specks of gold surrounding the black centers appear to vibrate, as though compelled to motion by the intensity of her emotion.

"Kar intercepted a memo with orders to the Escort Team. They have been instructed to kill you if you display even a hint of unusual behavior. They were advised to use discretionary judgment and to err on the side of caution.

"I am sorry but they are right, Striker and Kar. You must not show any behavior that deviates from our societal norms. You know well enough by now what these are. Please, Renee. Do this. I am afraid for you..." Her eyes plead with mine, her voice softened to a whisper. "You will be out of the safety of Unit 32, and they will show no mercy."

Her intercom chimes and I gasp, startled. She pulls away and steps back, clasping her hands loosely in front of her. A look of imperturbable calm settles on her face. I imitate her just as the door slides open. I straighten my back. For God's sake I have never been so afraid in my life.

The tears threaten again. I didn't choose this body. I didn't choose to be here in their space. Humanity hasn't changed in one thousand years. Destroy anything that's different, that doesn't fit our idea of what a perfect society should be? They can go to hell. We should have just killed ourselves out.

It's my last thought before they march in. Four, five, no six hulking men in black suits with their entire faces covered. One shoves Kemi roughly against the wall and her body slams up against it hard. I refuse to look. I stare straight ahead, keeping my face as expressionless as possible.

My nerve endings are on fire from the adrenaline shot. A thousand tiny electrical shocks jangle through my veins. Yet I am still. I ignore the rough hands pushing me forward. I move with them. I don't fight. The sound of Kemi's body striking the wall plays on repeat in my ears.

Every step takes me away from my only allies. Every step carries me into a cold world that sees me as nothing better than an animal. There'll be no benefit of the doubt. No compassion. I'm an antiquated relic from the past that doesn't belong in their present, and they'll be damned if I pollute their freaky little paradise.

Do not betray me, I plead to the fear inside me as we rush down the hallways. The walls are but a blur. Antagonism rolls off the Rangers like a cloud of poison.

Log Entry: R 283 O 3037 ID: Cont 2 YunJon

Our plans are in grave danger. The Escort Team arrived early. They do not trust us. They expected something. They will be watching us carefully, more carefully than perhaps we know.

Worse yet, our plans depended upon a chronological series of events. The Rangers collect Renee. Striker leaves. We escape from Unit 32. The mercenaries kidnap Renee off the Ranger's ship. Striker collects her from the mercenaries at the appropriate rendezvous point. We all meet tomorrow in the early morning hours at a second rendezvous point to travel to Continent 7 together.

Everything hinged on two key points. First, Renee must spend as little time as possible with the Escort Team because of her physical condition. Second, the four of us have to escape from SciMed Command before she is kidnapped. If she is kidnapped and we have not yet left, it will be too late. They will be on us instantly as we will be the primary suspects. Who else would have known of her departure, let alone her existence?

And now? She has already been on their ship for five hours. Shortly her adrenaline shot will be wearing off. Kar estimated it has a life of six hours. When it does, she will be in a worse state than before she got it. And if she shows even the slightest hint of abnormality, such as being ill, they will eliminate her on the spot.

Yet I can do nothing to alter events now and am consigned to waiting. Striker left hours ago. Our transport is not set to arrive for another two. If we leave to the departure bay too soon, we risk discovery while we wait for the vessel. If we wait too long, Renee may be kidnapped off the Ranger escort while we are still here, and we will be subjected to an immediate lockdown and confined to our quarters. It is an uneasy balance. I believe we must yet wait a short while, but depart sooner than is ideal. I have everything prepared and ready. There is nothing to do but endure these last remaining minutes.

The tension is high, yet we must behave normally. We cannot alarm the external observer Rij, who continues to plague us with his presence. This is the cause for my current presence in my quarters. I customarily take several hours each afternoon to work on strategy development from my private office. Kemi is making what appear to be her normal rounds. Kar is with Luya in the lab where they are consulting over a difficult technical problem regarding a piece of equipment. It is a ruse, of course. They could solve it in less than 10 seconds, particularly as they were the ones who caused it last night. They needed an excuse to spend time there as they are attempting to wipe clean the last traces of our research. Last I saw Rij, however, he was hovering over them closely. We have had one boon at least. He has disregarded Kemi entirely as she is only an assistant. Kemi can now discretely prepare a med-pack for Renee based on Luya's research results.

I myself am restless, as I have completed any remaining tasks. It leaves me with nothing to do but think. These are the last moments I will ever spend in this space. I worry for my team. All the records will prove that they knew nothing and were only following orders. Yet will that be enough to protect them? They will undoubtedly undergo a rigorous vetting process, but they ought to be fine. I hope.

I do not worry for them alone. I worry for Renee. Kemi disclosed that she shared with Renee the contents of the intercepted memo. She felt an obligation to be truthful. I disagreed with her decision, but my rebuttal died on my lips. I am frozen in the light of her golden eyes. After last night, the sounds of her gentle inhalations and exhalations still haunt me. Who knew that such exquisite beauty might exist in this world? And that it would be found in something as commonplace as the breath of someone sleeping?

When she awoke this morning, she turned to look into my eyes. The corners of her mouth rose into her slightly uneven smile. My heart-rate accelerated and I remained silent, intent upon memorizing every detail of the moment.

I know that I should reject these feelings. They do not contribute to society's stability. They prompt irrational decisions. Yet I find myself powerless in the face of them. How can I push them away, when I have never had more of a reason to live?

It is right that we leave for Continent 7, and not just for Renee. There is no space for me here any longer. There is no space for us here.

This morning confirmed it, when we knowingly rejected the most basic of social protocol.

A leader has no self-doubt. A leader has no insecurities. Self-doubt and insecurity are extraneous, selfish feelings that impede a leader's capacity to properly direct his or her team. This is the foundational tenet we learn in our training.

And yet, I am now plagued by them. Since Renee's arrival, I have experienced the unsettling sensations of doubt, insecurity and lack of clarity. I have known that this makes me unsuited for leadership. Yet I have also been in a state of denial, refusing to inform my team of my unsuitability to lead. That was until this morning, when I could no longer excuse my egregious lack of disclosure.

Immediately after Renee was taken, we met in my quarters. Her preemptive departure left us in a state of shock. Kemi shook in fear and anger. Kar clasped his holopad with an intensity unusual even for him. Striker paced. Luya looked exhausted and guilt-ridden. She stayed up all night doing research and, thinking she still had more time, had not pulled together a treatment for Renee before she departed. Thus our rushed administration of adrenaline.

"Please sit," I told them. We were in crisis, and it is the gravest of moral offenses to lead a team during a time of crisis when you are incapacitated. They sat. I braced myself.

"I am morally obligated to inform you that I am no longer mentally sound and am not fit to continue to lead the team. I am experiencing doubt and insecurity, which cloud my capacity to make sound decisions. I immediately remove myself from the position of Team Lead, and you may vote amongst yourselves as to who will replace me."

I did not look Kemi in the eye.

Striker said brusquely, "I am not a civil leader. I am a military leader. Military can never lead civil groups."

Luya said, "I have no interest in leading any longer. I want to focus on science again." She shared a quick darting glance with Kar.

"No," said Kar. He said nothing else.

"Your mental state is not so deteriorated that it will impede your capacity to lead," Kemi said. "It is not ideal, but it is still acceptable."

"How do you know?" asked Striker.

"You have been monitoring him, have you not?" queried Luya.

"What are you talking about?" I said.

She did not respond. We sat there for a moment in silence.

"Alright. I will continue to lead," I concluded at last. We were wasting precious time, and if they had no interest in replacing an incompetent leader, then we certainly could not spare the seconds nor energy in a lengthy debate. I had done my part by offering my immediate resignation and keeping them informed. I had certainly not expected Kemi to come to my defense, not after our exchange with Striker before I sat them down to disclose my mental state.

"How could you treat her so disrespectfully?" she had said, marching to Striker and glaring up into his face. I admired her courage in confronting a Ranger, although I had no idea to what she alluded. I had not witnessed the exchange. I was not present. I had to prepare to greet the Ranger team and to manage the external observer Rij.

"I did not enjoy speaking to her in that way. Yet you do not understand how to motivate people in dangerous situations. I do. Renee was exceptionally weak. I leveraged fear to push her further than she thought herself capable," Striker said. His voice was calm but with an underlying tension.

I stepped in immediately after he finished speaking. "You all did the best you could to ensure her survival with the tools you had. I encourage you to stay focused on what we can do going forward, and trust that we did the best we could in the past."

Kemi's eyes sparked at me and she spun about on her heel and walked away. As such, I did not expect her defense. And after they rejected my resignation and I agreed to continue, Luya went on to speak as if nothing had occurred. It was as though they were not concerned in the slightest. Are they unfamiliar with leadership research and standards? Admittedly, it is an enormous relief. I do not wish to resign from my role, but I must always place their wellbeing above my own.

"I now need to share my research results," she said. Her face looked tired and her cheeks wan. But her eyes were burning. With a deep inhale, Luya launched into speech. I record it here with as much detail as I can recall.

"We have been approaching this entirely wrong. We are assessing her based on pre-established parameters. We are comparing Renee to how we exist today, as though we are merely an advanced version of her. For instance, we perceive her to be less-developed. However, we need to study her as though she is a species unto herself, not a poorly-executed version of today's modern human.

"For instance, this female's brain functions in an entirely different manner than ours. She solves problems differently. She adapts differently. To test this premise, I went back and watched our tapes of her when she first arrived. I believed we missed crucial clues. Her movements, mannerisms, hand gestures and motions evolved extremely rapidly to match ours. In fact, it occurred in a matter of days. She does not appear to have some of the higher functioning intellectual capacities, but her assimilation and adaptation is stunning. I compared them to other studies on adaptation, and after a rough calculation, it would appear she can adapt approximately 2.7 times faster than we can.

"What prevents her from developing higher-functioning intellectual capacities appears to be an inability to focus on a single task for prolonged periods. Her time span spent on tasks is exceptionally brief. She concentrates for durations approximately one tenth the average amount of time we do. There have been several separate incidents of what I would call 'hyper focus,' when she appeared to spend what we would consider to be an average period of time on an issue. Yet this appears to require a great deal of energy on her behalf. I measured these by developing software to track the movement of her eyes and ran a comparison to our own.

"With this fresh perspective, I reexamined her vital anatomical information with new eyes. I went into our archives and spent a time weaving my way down a path of obscure publications. I found my way to some interesting, old research pertaining to scent. If I had known how little time I had, I would not have wasted it in this area. Yet now that I have uncovered it, I will share as it does explain a few things and perhaps may carry some implications I overlooked.

"To summarize, in the animal world, odor carries a great deal of information about a potential mate's age, sex, fertility, identity, emotions and health. Judgments of attractiveness are not based only on sight but on smell. In animal populations, these compounds drive behavior almost entirely. This is not present in modern humans. Yet Renee is different.

"All mammals except for humans have a set of genes known as the major histocompatibility complex, or MHC. Mammals select to mate with partners that have dissimilar MHCs. They naturally select to mix up the gene pool in order to keep genetic defects to a minimum and enhance what is known as hybrid vigor. This contributes to the healthy interplay of genes.

"We, humans, have receptors lining our noses to pick up these pheromones, as do other animals. These are known as 'legacy traits' - something that makes up a part of our anatomy which we no longer need. Yet, I asked myself, just how out of use have these receptors truly become? Those of us who have had constant contact with Renee have noticed a heightened awareness of each other as physical beings. We have felt and acted on urges that, if they existed before, were not strong enough to prompt us to break social protocol.

"All of this led me back to a statement that you, Striker, made earlier. You said that you felt an uncontrollable urge to mate with Renee. You could not explain it, but despite your differences, you felt an overwhelming desire to be with her, more so than any other woman you have run across. It is possible that you were able to pick up Renee's MHCs while on the ship. You see, she actually produces these, unlike modern humans. You were in close quarters and she was under stress so she might have been sweating. Perhaps the receptors lining our noses are not inactive as we thought. Perhaps they simply have had nothing to process, as modern humans do not emit these pheromones."

Striker said nothing, he only nodded at her to continue.

"What does this have to do with Renee's current pregnancy and illness? We do not know how much of her particular gene pool survived the drought and wars. As we know, entire traits were wiped out during that time. Additionally, we must not analyze her based on expectations of our own anatomy. She mentioned that it was common for women of her time to suffer from minor illness at the beginning of a pregnancy. Yet, she also noted that her symptoms were far more severe and had a much earlier onset than the norm. Perhaps this has something to do with Striker's genes? We do not know. We only know that we cannot attempt to solve this as we would if it happened to a modern female, as modern females do not experience illness during pregnancy.

"I have entertained several possibilities. One theory is that her body is attempting to reconcile a pregnancy with someone who is genetically different than she is. Her body may be fighting against itself. While it is trying to make the necessary hormonal adjustments to carry the baby and nurture it, her body is also fighting against what could be perceived as an invasive threat, an 'alien invasion' to its system."

Striker spoke, his voice holding a hint of desperation, "What does this mean? Does this mean that the pregnancy… that it must be aborted?"

Luya held out a hand. "Do not jump to conclusions yet. If her body's response is due to what I theorize it is, I believe there are viable medical treatments we could try to stop her body from attacking itself. Auto-immune disorders have long-since been erased from our genetics, but we still studied it in passing during our training as a thought experiment and historical overview of genetic development. There were treatments for them then, and that means we can find them still."

Exhaustion weighed heavy on her features, but she spoke again after taking a breath, "This afternoon as Kar and I work to erase any data trace of our research, I will also try to dig deep into our historical archives for as much information on pre-war and pre-drought human anatomy. I will design a med kit we can take and Kemi can collect the materials for it. While I do not wish to give false hope, I believe that if we approach Renee's medical issues with the mindset I described earlier, then we will have good odds at uncovering the problem. We cannot treat her as though she is a poorly designed version of us. We must treat her as though she is a unique mammal."

Striker leaned forward, looking as though he might say something. But at last, he merely asked, "Is that all?"

"For now," she said.

"Then I must go." He leaped to his feet and was quickly gone.

That concluded our meeting. We had to quickly disperse, as Kar was tracking the external observer's movements and it appeared Rij had finished his report and was on the move again.

Luya's research, while still in its incipient stages, provides a unique platform upon which to approach this problem. I am not certain her theory of an auto-immune attack response is sound, but it is certainly a new line of thinking that does not presuppose anatomical truths.

I will leave it in their hands, however. Our immediate predicament takes priority, and I believe we can wait no longer to depart. The time has come to make a move. If we remain any longer, the risk that Renee is kidnapped while we are still in the unit is simply too high. The time for action has come.

Renee

Inhale. One, two, three, four. Exhale. One, two, three, four. Repeat. Inhale and count. Exhale and count.

Every breath gains me precious seconds of life. Inhale. Exhale. Hours have passed. The adrenaline is seeping out of my system like a slow torture. My joints are on fire. My muscle fibers scream at me. My hands clasp on my lap so no can see them tremble.

One, two, three, four. Exhale.

The suspicion and revulsion of the Rangers surround me like a dark cloud.

Everything depends on me staying strong. Striker said so. He yelled it at me. Stay strong. Inhale. Exhale.

My eyes are locked straight ahead of me. Two Rangers flank me. I don't look at them. I don't look at anyone. I just breathe. Inhale. Exhale.

They aren't coming for me. Striker, Kemi, YunJon, Kar, Luya. They aren't coming. They would have come by now. The fetus can't possibly survive this, can it? There's no way anything could survive the wreck that is my body.

A jolt rocks me to my side. I slip onto the floor and gasp, landing hard on my hands and knees. The jolt of the impact on my wrists and kneecaps brings tears to my eyes. A loud, crashing noise rings out across the ship.

The Rangers yell orders back and forth. Strong, rough hands grab me and pull me to my feet, pushing me back down onto my seat.

People rush into the open space. They are in black but they don't look quite like Rangers. They have strange devices in their hands.

One turns to point his at me.

"Be still!"

I couldn't move if I wanted to. There's another huge blast. I can't help it and again I fall, slamming to the ground once more. This time, I don't just lie there. I force myself to move. I crawl under the bench where I was sitting and curl up in the fetal position.

I can't see what's happening, but there's fighting. Sounds like energy crackling. People yell. There are cries of pain. Pounding feet surround me.

Someone grabs my shoulder and I instinctively kick out before I can stop myself. Striker said not to fight, but I am so afraid. Grabbing the back of my jumpsuit, someone drags me out from under the bench. I'm afraid to look up. I don't want to see a weapon pointed at my face. I don't want to see my death.

They roll me onto my back. I have no choice. The male staring down at me is terrifying. He has a shaved head, black eyes and sharp teeth revealed by a snarl.

"It's me," I gasp. "I'm the one you're looking for. Please, get me out of here."

"No doubting that," his voice cuts sharply like a whip. "Never seen anything like you in my life. Get up."

"Never... seen anything like you... either," I manage to gasp. "Too weak to stand. I'm ill. Please help."

Cocking his head, he scoops me up and throws me over his shoulder. I choke on vomit, swallowing hard and the bile burns my throat.

He runs, a lithe, smooth run, but his shoulder against my

gut and the dizziness from being upside down is too much to take. The blood rushes to my head. My vision tunnels down to darkness and everything goes blank.

Log Entry: R 284 O 3037 ID: Cont 2 YunJon

When we finally arrived at the rendezvous point, Luya could barely walk. Kemi was dazed from her wounds. Both Kar and I had to help them into their tiny quarters.

I do not know how Kar continues to stay alert. But I am not asking any questions at this point. He is at the central work station of our small, dilapidated shelter. He promised to keep watch so I could have a solid rest. He told me, firmly, that we needed a levelheaded and rested leader. I did not argue.

But I cannot rest. I am cramped into the corner of my tiny quarters in the early hours of a new day, my hands shake with exhaustion and a small cot awaits me, yet my body will not relax. My mind does not allow it. Flashes of the day burst bright into my mind, jolting me into nervous awareness every time I try to sleep. Memories. The vision of his crumpled body. The image of Kemi deathlike on the floor.

I could not let harm come to Kemi. His life meant nothing to me in exchange for her safety and that of my team. I could see death in his eyes. He was bigger than her and Luya. They are not large females. Continent 5 breeds them small. He would have destroyed them.

CHAPTER FIFTY-ONE

So I did the unthinkable.

I killed him.

That is really why Kar sent me here. That is why he wanted me to rest. He wanted to make sure I was not going to crumble under the weight of my actions. He wanted to know if I had pushed myself across the brink of insanity. I would do the same in his position. To kill another person? There is no graver offense. There is no coming back from this.

I killed Rij. I can see his lifeless form, bloodied by my hand, as if it were right in front of me. I can see the stunned faces that surrounded me, as though they are in this very room.

It happened so suddenly.

At the end of my last entry, I was prepared to leave to collect the team so we could depart. I went first to the lab to gather Luya and Kar. I turned the corner and my reflexes jerked me back behind the wall.

My heart pounding in my chest, I rebuilt the image in my mind's eye. Rij, the external observer, had his back to the entrance where I stood. He had not seen me. Kar and Luya were up against the wall and were facing me with their hands over their heads. A look of terror spread across Luya's face. Kar's was covered in a chilled rage.

Rij, a tall, looming male, was holding a death gun in his right hand. I could not fathom how he came to be armed. Not even Rangers are allowed to enter civilian territories with weapons.

My stomach twisted. I had obviously miscalculated the timing. Renee must have been kidnapped off the Rangers' ship before we were able to escape ourselves. Because of the Rangers' early arrival to collect Renee, the mercenaries must have had to kidnap her earlier than planned or risk missing their window of opportunity altogether.

It was the worst possible outcome. They knew our intent to escape before we had a chance to do so, and they were locking us down. But like this? With weapons?

"I knew you were hiding things," Rij said, confirming my

conclusions. His voice was laced with disdain and, to my disgust, pleasure. There was an edge of arrogance and cruelty.

"The Committee knew it too. That is why they sent me. I have no empathy trait. I am not weak like others and do not fall prey to emotional traps."

A deep rage stirred within me. In that moment, I hated not just his voice but him and the Committee. I hated the arrogance that drove him to gloat in front of unarmed hostages. I hated that the Committee would wield an E-Absent male as a weapon against people. How could the committee ever entrust such a person with a weapon? I felt as if I were being betrayed by a system I had trusted my entire life.

And empathy is my strongest trait.

I felt an overwhelmingly violent revulsion to Rij.

Adrenaline pumped through my system, sending my body and mind into overdrive. Would he kill them? He would. I was certain. Then he would find Kemi. If they knew we were hiding things, they must surely know of her involvement.

"Get on your knees," he said to them.

My vision tunneled. My mind felt disconnected from my body. He was ordering them into an execution stance. A cold rage took hold of me, overriding rational thought. I would not allow this male to destroy my friends. I acted. I chose to fight.

I test very high on physicality, but under the threat of life or death I was spurred to a new level of speed. I rounded the corner on silent feet, snatching the nearest scanner and sprinted toward him. In the last moment, he sensed my approach and jerked to me. His face twisted in disbelief as a strange sneer pulled at the corners of his lips. I locked my eyes onto his cold, inhuman ones. I did not hesitate. As he twisted toward me and swung his weapon at my body, I leaped and smashed the scanner down on his head with all my force. It connected with a sickening thud and the resonance of the blow jarred my arms.

I knew he was dead before he struck the floor. No one could survive such a blow. I crouched on the balls of my feet, gasping for breath and glanced up at Kar and Luya. They looked down at his body, which was twisted awkwardly on the floor. Blood seeped out of his head. His neck bent at a strange angle. Kar and Luya were frozen on their knees. Their eyes locked on his corpse in stunned shock.

A noise at the entrance to the lab drew my attention. Kemi and several other assistants stood there, staring. I could see horror flash on her face as she processed the scene and locked eyes with me. It was a fleeting look, but it was enough. She could read what had happened. She may have even seen it. Her eyes were momentarily awash with fear not of him, but of me.

Yet despite this, she was the first to jump into motion. Ushering the assistants backward, she guided them around the corner. In the silence of the room, we could hear her every word, urgent but calm, "Go directly to your quarters. Stay there. No harm will come to you. Tell them that we forced you back with the weapon."

In but a moment, she was back. None of us had moved. Running toward me, she looked down at Rij's corpse and leaned over to pick up his weapon. Running to Kar and Luya, she grabbed their arms and jerked them into motion. They stood unsteadily.

"Come on," she hissed, looking at me. "We must go. We have not a moment to lose."

Her words were like a whip, waking me from my stupor. Jumping back into action, I took us down the hallway to the exit of Unit 32. Kar tapped into the building's surveillance from his holopad.

I swiped the door. It did not open.

"They have locked us in. Can you break us out?" I asked. I did not understand how I could so easily speak and move. It was as though someone else was piloting my body.

Tension ratcheted up. Moments passed. The door did not open but turned transparent. The hallways, what I could see, were barren. There was not a single member of another team walking along what was, under normal circumstances, a bustling passageway.

"I have it now. I can open it at your cue," he said, his voice taut.

"Good. Guide us toward the docking bay where we are set to rendezvous," I said to Kar. He nodded in affirmation, sliding in front of me to lead. We had to go now, even if the vessel had yet to arrive.

Staring down at his device, he said quickly, "They are closing in on us fast. We have to run. The second I open the door, stay close and follow my every move. We just may be able to make it. I am overriding the surveillance system right..." his fingers flew over the screen, "now."

He barked out a command and the door rushed open. In a flash we were in the hallway, sprinting behind him on fast feet. Luya and Kemi practically flew. They were as light and quick as the wind. Perhaps this is another Continent 5 trait, because they moved with a grace and speed I have never seen.

We followed Kar along a complex path of twists and turns through the building, past areas and down tunnels and hallways I had never known existed. It took us twenty minutes to weave our way down to the docking bay we had designated as our pick-up point.

Every moment was tense. Every several minutes, we stopped running, as Kar muttered, "They are trying to get past my override, I need a moment." The only sounds beyond Kar's muttered words were the soft tread of our feet as we ran. We saw no one. Not a single assistant nor wandering scientist. Not a single pursuant. The emptiness was eerie and nerve-wracking.

A light sheen of sweat broke out across Kemi's face, making her glow with a beauty that, even in the stress of the moment, caught my breath. Luya stumbled and I caught her. She looked up at me with gratitude and fear mingled. Indecision washed across Kar's face in one terrible moment as we stood at the crossroads of two hallways, a look I have never seen and hope to never see again on his features.

I did not think we would make it. Yet we rounded one last

corner and Kar, without warning, rapidly swiped a pattern onto a small door. We darted through it the second it opened and he quickly closed it behind us. I heard a great exhale of breath from him when the door shut firmly.

The room was a gray, cramped space. The walls of SciMed are smooth, well-designed and functional. But this place was a junkyard. It looked like a storage space for the remnants of times long past. Old shuttles and equipment were cluttered together in no semblance of order. This was no docking bay, at least no docking bay I had seen.

And no one was there. We were not anticipating them for another half an hour. I stared at the piles of junk, desperately wracking my brain for an alternative escape route. We surely could not wait here undiscovered for half an hour. If they did not come now, it was over.

I forced myself to turn toward my team. As I opened my mouth to speak, I was interrupted.

"Looks like you've been doing some exercise," I heard a lazy male voice say. In shock, I spun about. Small and thin, dressed in a rugged, dirty-looking gray jumpsuit, a male leaned against a broken piece of engine. He appeared from nowhere.

"Are you our escort?" I managed to say, my voice incredulous.

"Who else?" he retorted with a glare. "Now why don't we all get moving. I don't like people, 'specially your type of people, and I've a feeling company is right around the corner."

We jolted forward, following him as he deftly wove his way between old parts and broken pieces of equipment. It was difficult to stay with him. He moved quicker than his voice and appearance led me to believe he could. We were also tired from our frantic run.

He stopped at last in front of a piece of junk. It appeared to be a broken shuttle from last century, or perhaps the one before that even. My eyes narrowed in suspicion as he keyed something into the side. The door slid open. A soft engine hum filled the air.

"Stop gawking at this beauty and get on," he snapped.

The entryway was small and cramped. Hunching down, I boarded the vessel first. It was not a ship. At best, it was a small shuttle. It was cramped. My gut wrenched. There was no way we could fit. There were not even seats. There was just one for the pilot, and he had already squeezed past me and was strapping himself in.

"You've got five seconds to get your sorry asses on this shuttle or I'm leaving you behind," he said, his voice lashing out with anger. Gone was the half-joking tone of earlier. Something must have triggered his nerves.

Slamming myself back against the wall, I pulled Kemi forward to me. Kar pushed Luya onboard and crashed into her, knocking her against Kemi. The door slid shut.

"We're moving!" the pilot shouted. He pulled up his screen. "What the hell. They're hot on our tails already. Who have you pissed off so badly?" His voice was laced with tension.

"There are two fold-out chairs. Strap yourselves down. We're in for a rough ride," he snapped, not bothering to wait nor turn around and check on us.

The ship jerked upward. Luya fell against the wall and Kemi slammed into me. I gritted my jaw and braced myself against the ceiling. Turning, I saw the flip down seat behind me. With the turbulence, it kept sliding out of my grasp. With a grunt of effort, I jerked it down and crashed backwards, collapsing into it.

"Kemi!" I yelled. She turned to me and I had almost reached her when the vessel jerked hard. We were thrown across the shuttle. My shoulder hit the door and pain cut through my senses. I heard Kemi cry out. Fear twisted my stomach. I looked to see her holding the side of her face with blood dripping from her fingers. Her head had smashed against the wall and blood was gushing across her features and dripping to the floor. My pain disappeared in a rush of adrenaline and I leaped to my feet, grabbing her before she fell unconscious to the ground. Holding her with one arm, I pulled the chair back down again and, while keeping her steady on my lap, threw myself down in the seat. She kept sliding, so I strapped us both in together. I placed one hand up against her head to brace it on my shoulder, and not a moment too soon.

Our pilot turned a full 360 degrees and the vessel jolted us brutally. I heard Kar cry over the noise, "I could not hold them any longer! They are back online. Full surveillance access!"

Confused, I looked over to him. Shocked, I watched Kar continue to hack on his holopad as the shuttle bounced and spun wildly. Over Kemi's slumped shoulder, I was able to see that Luya had finagled the second seat down, strapped herself in and wrapped her arms and legs around Kar's torso, jerking him down so he sat perched between her legs with her limbs serving as restraints. She was holding him steady through all the turbulence and shocks. Her face was white from the strain. I could see the cords of her muscles through her jumpsuit. Neither of them appeared injured. They must have strapped in before the jolt hit that threw both Kemi and I across the shuttle.

How was she physically capable? As I alluded to earlier, she and Kemi are both from Continent 5 and are small.

But I could not dwell on it at the time. The pilot spoke angrily in a language I did not understand, before yelling, "You didn't pay me for this shit! They've brought in full forces. What the hell have you done?"

The next hour was the most harrowing of my life. Even at the thought of it, my heart-rate increases and my hands shake. I was frantically trying to stop the flow of blood from Kemi's head wound as she slipped in and out of consciousness, but despite my best efforts, it kept pouring from the cut. Yet I could not get up to retrieve a med kit or risk further injury. What was more, I could see the shuttle's screen from my position. It was distressing. It would have been better if I could not see. Our escape should have been impossible.

The shuttle swept across our planet's surface. We were surfing the dirt itself. Miles of scorched land swept in front of us, broken by ruined buildings, boulders, dried copses of withered trees and craters blown deep into the soil. We literally skimmed the earth itself as we flew over the landscape. We were milliseconds and inches from disaster more times than I could count.

The pilot never stopped talking the whole time. He emitted a low stream of angry words, muttered in the same incomprehensible language as earlier. He piloted us as one would if they had absolutely nothing to lose. It was a tactic I have never heard of, nor ever wish to see again.

My eyes bounced between Kemi, Luya, the pilot, the screen and Kar, who was hunched over his hologram, his fingers flying furiously while he shouted at the pilot. Luya turned horribly pale and her jaw clenched shut tightly. She did not speak a single word. I could feel her fear. It must have been her fear, for Kar and for us, that pushed her to do the impossible. For the entire hideous escape, she held him tightly, with her arms and legs wrapped around him, holding him steady so he could work. If not for her, and for Kar's hacking skills, interrupting and disrupting our pursuer's weaponry and monitoring system, we never would have made it. Every time their weapons locked on our shuttle, he somehow managed to bust the connection or scramble our position and break their hold.

And the whole time... the whole, hideous time... I could feel blood from Kemi's head wound oozing through my fingers. I could feel the life seeping from her body, the blood drenching us in wet, sticky, warm liquid. I did not dare move my hand bracing her head and neck, or the other holding her arms and stomach firmly against me. Such a severe head wound could have also meant a spinal injury in her neck. I could not risk her jolting too severely. My arms cramped from the strain of holding her and the wound on my shoulder shot piercing stabs of pain down my arm. Each jolt was a test of my endurance.

After what felt an unbearable eternity, the pilot breathed a sigh of deep relief. Then, without warning, we were shooting out over the ocean and skimming the deep blue water. Our progress was smooth and uninterrupted. Our pursuers lost. We had either shaken them or they had given up their chase.

Pushing back from the controls, the pilot said in a low, furious voice, "I never want to see you people again. I'm gonna drop you and that's it. Don't contact me. Nothing. They told me you were scientists. They don't bust out that shit for no scientists."

"Can we safely move about?" I managed to say, my voice thick. The words were difficult to form. My tongue felt heavy and stiff.

"Yes and I'll get you some first aid for that female. Don't want her to keep bleeding all over my vessel," he muttered, his voice still angry. Unstrapping himself, he set the vessel on autopilot and moved past me towards the back.

"Kar, Luya, please help me with Kemi," I croaked out.

Luya could not move. Kar had to help her. He gently unfolded himself from between her arms and legs. Crouching in front of her, he unsnapped the restraints and slowly eased her out of them. Tears ran down her face. Her muscles had to have cramped into place. The pain must have been excruciating to bring her to tears.

"Go to Kemi," Luya managed to say to Kar, her voice shaking in pain. Kar paused for two seconds, staring into her eyes and then turned to us.

"Let her go gently," he said. Like Luya, I could not release my arms. They had also cramped into position. Very gently, Kar helped me loosen my grip. He inhaled sharply when he saw the wound on her head. "It is very deep, but the blood has clotted somewhat. The pressure of your hand might have been just enough to keep her from bleeding out. She is still breathing, although shallowly. I will lie her down and treat the wound. I need space. I need to move quickly."

Kemi was pale and deathlike on the floor with her body and face covered in blood. Watching her was worse even than the pain in my body. Piercing needles shot through my arms as feeling returned to them. The agony of my shoulder settled into a pounding ache. I sat shaking as I watched Kar minister to her. What little of her body that wasn't covered in blood was deathly white. She remained unconscious.

The moment the pilot handed over the first aid kit, Kar snatched it from him. He sealed her wound and injected her with an emergency blood supplement, then scanned for further injuries.

"No neck or spinal injuries," he said, reading the scanner. I breathed a sigh of relief. "A moderate concussion and severe blood loss."

Shuffling through the med kit, he measured out several doses of medications and quickly applied them to the skin on her neck. Her eyelids fluttered open and she tried to focus her eyes.

"YunJon?" she said, squinting and dazed.

"Yes, Kemi, I am here. You are safe. Do not try to move. You suffered a severe head wound. Kar has tended to you. You must try and rest now and stay still."

I stood to move to her on the floor and felt myself stumble. I must have blacked out, because the next thing I knew I was leaning against the wall on my knees.

"Son of a gun-hopper," I heard the pilot say to Kar. "That is one seriously impressive wound."

"What?" I grunted out.

"YunJon, you are seriously wounded," I heard Kar say in a tight voice. "Why did you not say anything? Lie down on your stomach."

"Wounded?" I asked.

"What do you know," the pilot drawled. "Maybe you folks are as big a deal as they made. Don't know what kind of genetics you all got going but I want some of that."

"Go away," growled Kar to the pilot. Turning to look down at me, he said, "Your left shoulder is severely wounded. You are bleeding profusely. Keep still and do not move. I do not have the proper equipment to anesthetize you. You will feel pain, however you may suffer permanent damage to your tendons if I do not reconnect them properly. I will do the best with what I have."

I will not elaborate on the healing process.

Renee

"What did you do to her?"

The voice is full of anger, like a wire pulled too tight. The words are slow and terrifying.

My eyelids flutter open.

"Striker?" I murmur. He is holding a man by the throat. The man's face is mottled and clenched in terror. He drops the man like a piece of garbage and turns to me in a flash. He crouches next to me.

"Renee? Tell me how you feel."

"I'm thirsty," I manage to croak out.

As far as I can see, I'm on the floor of a small room looking up into Striker's face. I can't seem to orient myself. It's as though the different parts of my brain aren't working together. Striker is ordering the man in the corner to get me a nutrition tube and liquid. Everything feels spacey and disconnected.

Taking advantage of his distraction, I try and remember what's happening. An uncomfortable kind of sticky fear settles in my stomach. Why isn't my brain piecing together the story? I can't seem to remember.

He turns and crouches next to me. His body moves like an oiled machine, heavy and powerful, full of might and strength and controlled violence. Tears well in my eyes. I am really afraid now. I can't remember how I got here. I don't like this. I don't like waking up not knowing where I am or what happened. It's too much. It's like before, when it happened before.

"Striker, what's happening? Where am I?"

He runs his hands gently up and down my arms. The tension slowly eases from his face. My hand raises, shaking, to his cheek. The warmth of his skin, the human contact, comforts me. Some of my fear quiets.

"You are so fragile," he says softly. He doesn't answer my question. "Your bones are slender and porous. This skin, so light and translucent, could suffer only the slightest bits of sun. Your hands," he pauses and exhales deeply while holding my fingers gently in his own, "they are so thin that with the slightest pressure I could crush them into pieces. Everything about you is so delicate. It is as though you are balanced on the knife's edge, just a moment from falling to pieces. I do not understand it. I do not understand you. Your existence."

Our eyes lock. I stare deeply into the black orbs. Heavy brows shield his eyes. It's as though he's in some kind of reverie, and his words wash over me.

A male interrupts us and hands Striker a nutrition tube. Striker doesn't look away from my face, even while speaking to the man.

"Put the med kit in the corner then leave us. Do not interrupt us. I will find you if we need anything. Page me when we hit the rendezvous point tomorrow morning. Otherwise, I do not expect to hear anything from you, do you understand?" His voice is harsh, full of viciousness and anger that is thankfully not directed at me. I have whiplash from his moods, one second he's spouting tender words, the next angry and vicious ones toward the man behind us.

My eyes flicker over Striker's shoulder to the man behind him. His face looks vaguely familiar. The bald head stirs restless, ghostlike memories but nothing concrete surfaces.

"Striker, please accept my apologies for our treatment of

her. We did not understand. You will not be interrupted. I will personally ensure it. Anything we have is at your disposal." The man nods deeply and nervously backs out of the room.

Striker says nothing in response. With gentle hands, he holds the nutrition tube to my lips. I take a small sip and let my stomach adjust to the feeling. Silently, he feeds me the rest of it. I stop trying to think and figure things out for a few minutes. I focus on the sensation of nourishment sliding down my throat and into my belly. For a few instances I fear I might vomit, but my stomach manages to uneasily hold down the liquid. A tingling sensation floods my arms, legs, fingers and toes. It feels like strength. I hold out my hand and the shaking has stopped. I feel a small smile lift the corners of my mouth.

"I want more, Striker." The nutrition tube is finished. He raises an eyebrow, but turns around and digs through the med kit. He pulls out a second tube.

"Come here. Be next to me," I say to him.

He doesn't hesitate and nods at me. Very carefully, he removes the blanket that is covering my body. Yet before lowering himself down to my side, he places a huge, gentle hand on my lower belly.

"Is it… still here?" His face, usually so severe and stoic, carries such a painful vulnerability my heart wrenches. A terrified sliver of hope shines in his black eyes. His mouth is slightly parted and he bites into his bottom lip unconsciously. I suddenly want to take him into my arms and comfort him.

He's talking about the fetus, I realize slowly. He's talking about what we made together, unknowingly and unwittingly, in a moment of desperation and tortured desire. I don't know if it's there. I feel disconnected from my mind and body.

"I don't know," I say at long last. It doesn't feel gone, but then it doesn't feel there either. How can you tell? No one I know has had a baby yet. Everyone was waiting for their careers to settle, for their lives to settle. I hadn't planned on having one yet for years.

Supporting himself by his arms, he lifts himself over my body so he can curl behind me while facing the door. His body radiates heat and he gently slides his arm underneath my head to serve as a pillow.

"Are we safe, Striker?"

"Yes. We are meeting everyone tomorrow at the rendezvous point. Then we will go together to Continent 7."

Meeting everyone. Memories tug at my mind. That's right. We are meeting Kemi, Luya, YunJon and Kar. Then we are going on to Continent 7.

"Striker, I don't remember anything since when we were back on Unit 32." My stomach floods with unease. The unknown void is terrifying. It could be filled with anything.

"You remember nothing?" Concern laces his voice.

I vaguely wonder if I'm getting better at reading their tones or if they're just becoming more expressive. This is the second time I've been able to read his emotions like I would anyone else I used to know.

"No," the word comes out slowly and hesitantly. "I remember being sick back in Unit 32. Tell me how I got here."

"They came earlier than we expected. We did not think the team of Rangers would be there so soon. It was a trick. They suspected we had something planned and wanted to foil it. I should have anticipated that. It is exactly what I would have done. They took you."

He looks at me intently, searching for a hint of recognition. I can offer him nothing.

"You were on their ship for hours before my contact was able to kidnap you. As soon as he picked you up, you passed out. I joined them at a prearranged spot several hours after the kidnapping. I found you lying here on the floor, unconscious. Then you woke up."

"Yeah, when you were choking him."

"I regret nothing," he said darkly, his voice thick with anger. "They endangered you. If you are permanently harmed, I will kill them."

I couldn't even tell him if they had. I have no recollection of any of it.

"Do you... do you remember when I yelled at you, before you left?" He asks softly.

"You yelled at me?" Shock burns through me. "Why?"

"You were weak. They had orders to destroy you at any sign of unusual behavior. They would have killed you at the slightest hint of illness. I know how Rangers think. I am one. We act first, question later. I needed you to understand how serious the threat to your life was. I needed to scare you. It was the only way I knew how. And I am sorry for it."

I don't know if he should apologize or not. I don't know if I should be thanking him for saving my life. I don't remember.

Trauma victims sometimes don't remember what happened to them. It's the mind's mechanism to protect itself against things that it can't handle. I've read popular psychology nonfiction. Haven't we all?

Is my brain protecting me? And from what?

"Striker, in your society today, do people who experience severe trauma suffer from a memory loss of the event?"

"Not that I am aware of. I never have," he answered slowly.

"In my time, it might happen that someone experiencing memory loss could be suppressing a traumatic event. That or they suffered some kind of brain trauma. But my head doesn't hurt. Maybe that's what is happening to me. Anyway, I don't want to think about it right now. I'm going to try and relax."

The world feels slightly dizzy around me. I shut my eyes and practice meditation. With every inhale, warm light enters into my body and muscles, flushing out tension and fear. With every exhale, my breath forces out the darkness and tension. In, and out. In, and out.

With Striker's warm body around me, I start to feel a slow sense of calm enter my being. Strange aches cause my muscles to spasm periodically. I continue to breathe through them. In, out. In, out.

Just as I'm drifting off into a relaxed sleep, I bolt up to a sitting position and shove myself away from Striker.

"Oh, my God. I remember it all now."

"Renee? What happened? What are you saying? I can't understand you." Striker leaps into a crouch, moving like a lithe tiger and his hands settle tightly on my shoulder, supporting me. Steadying me.

"Jesus, it's all coming back."

I'm speaking English, I realize. That's why he doesn't understand me. I switch back into their language.

"I remember it all. Kar gave me a shot of adrenaline. The pain was unbearable. Kemi told me about the memo giving the Rangers the right to kill me. You yelled at me. I felt betrayed. Then they came. They tore me away from Kemi and threw her against the wall. I sat on their ship forever with the adrenaline slowly seeping out of my body. I thought I was going to die, so I counted," I start to cry. I feel sick at the memory. The tears are streaming down my face.

"I counted my breaths over and over. It was the only way I could stay upright. It was torture. I could feel their revulsion. Their hate. Their disgust. They thought I was an animal. I thought you weren't going to come. I felt so sick. I thought you weren't coming. I knew if I showed any weakness they would shoot me down like a dog. I thought I was going to die."

The words rush out of me. I start to shake. My breath is coming in short pants. My heart is squeezing tightly in my chest. I think I am having a heart attack. My chest is on fire.

"Renee? Look at me. Try and relax. You are safe now. Breathe with me. Please? Breathe with me."

I stare into the black orbs of his eyes. His hands run gently up and down my arms. I try and sync my breath with his. The pain pounds horribly in my chest and my fingers tingle. My body is shaking uncontrollably. I slump down on my side and curl in a ball. Striker wraps his body around mine and runs his hands up and down my side, whispering soothing words. But it doesn't help. This is all too much. It's more than a person can survive.

EXTERNAL MEMO: ROTATION 284

To:	Yunjon, Unit 32, Continent 2 SciMed
From:	Regulation Committee

You are charged with the murder of External Observer Rij, theft of Regulation Committee Property Subject Renee, manipulation of Unit Members for unauthorized motives, unauthorized leave from post, damage to state property, destruction of evidence and gross dereliction of duty.

You are being pursued by the Enforcement Committee with orders to retrieve you dead or alive. Should you immediately and voluntarily turn yourself over peacefully to the authorities and disclose the location of Subject Renee, you will be given a fair and impartial trial and will be given the opportunity for rehabilitation, a right afforded to all citizens.

We have evidence to suggest you are intending to escape to Continent 7. Continent 7 is a lawless realm that exists in a state of anarchy. According to Regulation Committee Law, any citizen who enters this continent permanently relinquishes his or her status as Citizen of Earth as recognized by the Regulation Committee. Should you select this course, you and any persons who accompany you will be denied all rights afforded to citizens for the remainder of your lifespan. Should you wish to rejoin society, you will be immediately taken into custody and granted no leniency.

On behalf of the Regulation Committee, we order you to immediately turn yourself over to the authorities.

Public Memo: Rotation 284

To:	Regulation Committee; Balance Committee; Enforcement Committee; Earth Command; Planetary Command; Research and Development
From:	YunJon, Unit 32, Continent 2 SciMed

I write in response to the charges leveled against me by the Regulation Committee.

37 rotations ago, Experimental Unit 32 of SciMed Cont. 2 executed Project Time Window under my command. The project, originally intended to create a window into the past, exceeded our expectations and instead created a door. Through that door, a female from the early 21st century was ripped through time.

The female survived. Her name is Renee. She demonstrates remarkable adaptability and eagerness to adjust to our times.

In response to Renee's presence, the Regulation Committee ordered her containment under fear she would contaminate society in ways they could not or would not define. They further ordered that we hand her over to their command for more rigorous containment and likely elimination.

We refused to comply.

We reject this fear-based approach to scientific discovery.

We accept that Renee did and continues to influence us. We choose to see this not as the contamination of a society that has reached the pinnacle of evolution, but an opportunity to advance our knowledge and open our minds to possible ways in which we may improve our system through understanding our past. She is a wellspring of knowledge into our evolution as a species.

However, Renee is not only an opportunity for the advancement of knowledge, she is also a human being. She is a victim of circumstance and deserves the respect and consideration any other human would warrant. We have done her a great disservice, and as a society we owe her recompense.

Nonetheless, her humanity has not been considered across the course of this case. As such, we now defend her right to an existence as meaningful as she can find in our time.

The research behind Time Window Project has been destroyed. The project will not be replicated. While Renee's presence is a scientific boon, it is also a personal tragedy for the subject at hand. She was torn from her time and forced to undergo a trial of adaptation that no human being should experience. Now that we know the capacity of the technology we unleashed, we cannot repeat it with the knowledge of what it might do. Unintentional harm can be excused once, but it can never be knowingly committed again.

This memo serves as both defense and explanation for our actions. It is also a formal and public objection to the actions of both the Regulation Committee and Balance Committee in handling this discovery.

We herein assert that the justification of 'peace at all costs' is falsely leveraged in this case. We encourage the Committees to examine the difference between maintaining peace versus maintaining the status quo. We encourage you to reflect upon which of these you were promoting in this case. Evidence suggests you were seeking the latter. As such, we were forced to act upon our obligation to the field of science and to humankind at large.

Renee

I open my eyes, roll over and vomit on the floor. Dry heaves wrack my body again and again. My guts are hell-bent on turning themselves inside out.

After an interminable period, it subsides. I want to wipe my mouth on something, but all I have is my jumpsuit. It's the only one I have. I grab the blanket instead, wipe my mouth, throw it over the vomit and collapse back on the mat on the floor. That's the extent of my energy.

No use avoiding the inevitable any longer. I turn my eyes to the looming figure.

"Striker," I manage. He is, as anticipated, crouching and staring at me with a stoic albeit pinched face. I read hints of disgust on his features. For some reason, it breaks me.

"I know you super humans of the future don't vomit beyond infancy," I offer. I look away. I hate him. I hate everyone. I hate this room. I hate this illness. I hate myself.

The smell of bile is starting to spread. Darkness settles over my mind. I roll on my back and try to numb my mind and senses. I don't want to be in this world anymore. The vision of the disgust on Striker's face repeats in my mind and negative thoughts invade my brain like an unstoppable army. I'm an animal. I'm a disgusting, white, pallid, grotesquely curvy, tiny vomiting bar-

barian who should be destroyed. That's what I am. If I were them, I'd be disgusted by me too. I'm stupid. I'm irrational. I'm weak. They'd be better off without me. I should have died in the time warp. I could have blinked out of existence and been spared this torture. Then they wouldn't have to flee their world for some anarchic hinterland and I wouldn't have to suffer this degradation.

I was someone. I had a career. I had a family. I was smart. I understood things. I got people. I could read situations. I didn't fit the stereotypical standard of society, but it didn't bother me that much because no one else really did either, even if they pretended. People were messy but they were people. They were unique. Society was torn and broken in places, but I thought we were working to make it better. How did we mess it up so terribly? We destroyed our own civilization. We wiped ourselves out and turned into a homogeneous society that prizes some sort of warped stability over everything that makes life worth living. Love, art, humor, creativity, passion.

I don't belong here. I shouldn't be here. I'm an interruption and an intrusion and an interference. I shouldn't bring my genes into this time. I shouldn't have some kid here. I'd curse it with outdated genetics that long ago worked their way out of the evolutionary cycle.

I feed these spiraling dark thoughts. They're addictive. They push me away from the pain of living. I turn them into a dampening cloud. I will annihilate all hope and will to live. I force them out of me. With them gone, I will feel no more pain. They should have left me on the ship with the Rangers. The Regulation Committee was right.

Something jolts me. Striker picks me up and steps over the blanket. He walks to the door and it opens automatically. Someone stands outside our door. I watch the world through an apathetic haze. I don't care. I don't care what they do to me. I vaguely observe them speak and we walk to a new room. Striker sets me down against the wall and I slump there. My head tilts to the side. I hear water running. He is pulling off my jumpsuit. I don't stop him, but I don't help. He speaks to me. I see his lips move and hear the words, but I don't process.

Striker squints down at me. Something that might be concern darkens his features. But I don't care. Nothing has to be real anymore. I don't have to be here anymore. I can retreat into the darkness and oblivion where I belong. There is a blessed numbness there. No more pain. No more fear. Just nothing.

Log Entry: R 285 O 3037 ID: Cont 2 YunJon

I am unsure if Striker's solution of transport to Continent 7 is genius or madness. We are on an underwater vessel. It travels in the very ocean itself, submerged below the depths in the deep and dark waters. It is a slow, antiquated vessel. Even at its highest velocity, it will take us three full days to make it to Continent 7.

By that time, Renee will either live or die. She cannot continue in her current state. If we do not determine a cure soon, the situation will be beyond hope. Our medical equipment is extremely limited onboard. However, we cannot know if Continent 7 would afford us better options than what we have now. And at least under these circumstances, we have full control in a contained environment.

I am taking advantage of a lull to write. I feel a compulsion to acknowledge every detail and every piece of our story. Whether for future reflection, for historical purposes or to give those who may obtain this against our will insights into our purposes, I cannot say. But circumstances are simply too extraordinary to go unrecorded.

Last I logged, we had only just made it - barely made it - to the rendezvous point. We were sheltered in an old, dilapidated structure, awaiting our meeting with Striker and Renee so that we could depart together to Continent 7. I was in such a poor state from the events of that day, which I recorded once and shall not revisit, that I neglected to capture the entire day's events.

Our pilot could not have been more eager to dump us at the site. He did not even turn off the engine. He landed, opened the door and pushed us out while yelling something unintelligible and most definitely angry. He immediately shut the door behind us and launched. We could feel the heat of his thrusters nipping at our heels.

It was night when we arrived yesterday. We stood on a barely-visible piece of broken, decimated terrain. It was one of the many and enduring legacies left from centuries of war. I had previously only seen holographic images of these lands. The images themselves were gruesome, but did not convey the smell nor the magnitude of the destruction. They certainly did not capture the sense of pervading horror that seemed to seep into our bones, as though death haunted the barren soil.

We stumbled our way to the structure in front of us. It was eerily silent, but for the sounds of waves crashing in the darkness, somewhere close. However, it was too dark to see the ocean. In a dazed state, we settled into the dirty, rundown quarters. From there, I logged my last entry, attempted to get fitful bits of sleep and sent my last and final memo in my capacity as Team Lead of Experimental Unit 32, Continent 2 SciMed. After that memo was sent, I understood that I am SciMed Team Lead no more. I no longer lead a unit of scientists in their research. I no longer have the assets and resources that this position afforded me. But I also no longer carry the restrictions. I am now the elected leader of a small band of rebels.

It is not as easy as I anticipated to let go of this former identity, one which defined me for the entirety of my adult existence, and confront the uncertainty of the new position that faces me.

As sundown approached today, we gathered together near the exit. Dark was growing rapidly. We looked into one another's faces. We were tired. We were injured. But there was resolution, too. I wished to reach a hand out to Kemi's features, but the memory of the haunted look on her face when she saw that I had killed stopped me. I did not wish to make her uncomfortable. I did not wish her to fear me. I wanted to explain.

"Let us go," I said. Wordlessly, they filed out behind me. I guided them toward the exact point where we were to meet, occasionally glancing down at my holopad to check my coordinates. As we walked, the sounds of the crashing waves grew louder and the darkness stronger. As we neared the point, the sun set its final rays and sank us into a deep gloom.

By the time we reached it, everything was bathed in the all-consuming blackness of night except for a small glow radiating from the building that was our designated meeting point. It was a crumbling, oddly shaped structure. It was small and circular at its base and rose up out of the ground several stories.

We stood under the eerie light of the single source emitter. None of us spoke. The tension slowly mounted. Would they arrive? Had they succeeded? They were a terrible few moments.

"So you made it," said a voice from the darkness. I spun around to see Striker step into the dim light. In his arms, he carried Renee. She was limp and lifeless, dressed in a loose grey jumpsuit. I thought she was dead.

We rushed to him, gathering around them.

"Is she dead?" I asked immediately.

"Of course not," snapped Kemi.

"How do you know?" I said, irritated.

"What is wrong with her?" said Luya.

Kemi gently touched her hand to Renee's forehead. I watched her beautiful fingers settling softly on Renee's skin, light as a feather.

"I do not know," Striker said grimly. "She is alive, but barely. She slipped out of consciousness about one hour ago. We only arrived here ourselves ten minutes ago. We have no time to tend to her, though. Our transport is here now. We are late as it is. If they do not think we will appear, they will depart immediately. We must go."

He turned toward Kar, "Please take her. I must lead the way. Be careful." He emphasized the last two words and seemed loathe to pass her over, but did so nonetheless.

Renee's head rolled loosely as Striker passed her gently over to Kar. Her short, curly gold hair leaped into relief in the dim night, and her pale, delicate, pointed face was momentarily highlighted by the dim light above. Her face, without the vibrant blue eyes darting back and forth, looked waxy and artificial. It was hard to imagine that life still resided in those pale features. I felt a renewed stab of anxiety that she may, despite their assertions to the contrary, be dead.

Striker switched on lights on each of his wristbands, and led the way. We fell in line behind him. I assumed the rear position. He led us closer still to the sound of the crashing waves. The noise grew louder and soon it became hard to hear anything at all but its pounding.

When I could feel a chill mist of water on my face, we stopped walking. Striker pointed his lights towards the water and, for the first time, I saw the vast expanse. The ocean. It was magnificent. I now know that no 3-D image, no matter how advanced, no matter if life-sized nor participatory, could ever capture such a geographical masterpiece.

We stood on the edge of a cliff and stared, mesmerized, at the vast expanse of tumultuous water lit up under the glow of Striker's beams. Waves rushed up to the cliff edge and in a mighty crash broke into an ever-changing explosion of water. I have never seen anything like it in my life. How does no one speak of this? Why are the coasts not colonized? Surely it would be worth rehabilitating the coastal regions for this. I cannot imagine they have all been so thoroughly decimated that they are not worth braving for the magnificence of this natural force and vista.

Striker flashed his beams on and off. Kemi gripped my arm and I gasped. A metallic vessel arose out of the water. It appeared as if a giant, mechanical creature were climbing from the black depths. I stared, my eyes wide, as it rose up and a round door opened on the top.

A large female stuck her head out. She shouted to be heard over the noise of the crashing waves, "You're late! This is gonna cost you extra."

"Let us see if you can even get us there first, eh?" bellowed Striker. "How do you expect us to board in these conditions?"

"Creatively!" She screamed back. Reaching down, she pulled out something in the shape of a half moon. Holding it in her left hand, she extended a wire with her left and in a flash a cord whistled out toward us. It struck the cliff at our feet.

She whistled loudly and threw something hard to Striker. He reached up and caught it deftly. He did not stop to inspect it, only crouched down by the wire and, as we were deprived of the shine of his lights, became consumed again by darkness. Standing, he turned back to us. I squinted in pain as my eyes adjusted to the unexpected brilliance of the beams.

"Here's how this works. You grab the two bars attached to the wire and you slide down to the submarine. The moment you land, you go down and get out of the way. Kar, give me Renee, and you go first."

Efficiently and without another word, Kar passed Renee back to Striker and went to the cliff edge. He rotated the bars so they faced up, gripped them tightly and firmly pushed himself forward. As he fell, he swung down and was carried by the slim rope above him toward the vessel. He landed roughly on its surface. The water made the metal slippery and the choppy waves made the footing unsteady. The female grabbed him with both arms to stabilize him. She pushed him quickly down the hatch and out of sight. She shoved the crossbar hard and it slid back up the wire toward us.

"Luya, you are next. Kemi, you will follow. YunJon, you will help me with Renee and will go last."

They were harrowing moments. I had to squelch an irrational

urge to stop Kemi. I involuntarily looked away when she pushed off, my hands clenched into hard fists at my side. I envisioned her losing her grip and falling into the water below, her small body smashing against the cliff and lost forever in the waves. Only when she landed on the submarine could I feel my heart beat again.

I turned toward Striker. "How are you going to do this?"

"Strap her on to me. Use this." He removed something from his belt and handed it to me. I inspected it closely. It was a coiled wrap of very thin fabric about the width of my forearm. I unrolled with the flick of my wrist. In length, it was approximately twice my height. Quickly, I assessed them and measured their dimensions. He positioned her against him and I secured her to the best of my abilities, making sure to brace her neck and head as carefully as possible. Even so, it appeared precarious. Yet I could think of no better approach.

"Go," I said. There was nothing else for us. He looked at me briefly, turned to the wire and swung down.

I did not have a full appreciation for his physicality and training as a Ranger until that moment. He swung down on only one hand while the other cradled Renee's neck carefully. He landed deftly on the vessel even with her body's weight throwing his off balance.

When they disappeared below, I realized it was, in fact, my turn. The female from the vessel was shining a light at me and yelling at me to hurry up. And I understood then why Kar had moved so quickly. Thinking made it much worse. I tilted up the bars as he had, gripped them firmly, envisioned Kemi's face and pushed myself off the cliff.

It stuns me even now, but I enjoyed it. The falling, the rush, the rapid descent downward, the crashing waves beneath me… it was a thrill that ran across my body from the tips of my toes to fingertips. Before I knew it, my feet were skimming the slippery metallic surface and I collided with the woman. She gripped me firmly with tough, muscled arms.

"Down you go," she said and gave me a rough smile. Speechless from the thrill, I nodded and crawled past her into the strange vessel below.

We congregated in the tiny, dimly-lit passageway. The vessel rocked and swayed in the ocean waves. The walls were metal. Metal! They met in abrupt right angles with the ceiling. Around the walls, at approximately thigh height, were planks extending outward at right angles. They were the length of my forearm.

Kemi, Kar and Luya were very gently unstrapping Renee from Striker's chest. They laid her on her back on one of the planks. Kar grabbed Striker's wrist without asking, flicked on the light and flashed it in Renee's face. Her eyes fluttered but she did not respond to anyone's voice, not mine, not Striker's.

"She is responsive to stimuli. That is as much as we can hope for now. We need more space to properly assess her," said Kar.

Settling in was a rushed blur. The female, the proprietor of the submarine, for this is what they call the vessel, is unlike anyone I have ever encountered. Her language is blunt and bold and exceptionally aggressive. She smiles far more than is appropriate. I continue to struggle to assess her character.

She was also deeply fascinated by Renee, marveling over her skin. She did not appear to be at all disgusted. Indeed, she insisted on carrying her down the hallway to a room that was quickly converted into a makeshift medical unit.

"Fix her right up, won't you?" she barked at Luya, before leaving them behind in the room and guiding us through the rest of the vessel. Luya remained behind with Renee to run preliminary diagnostics with the little medical machinery they had on hand.

Each of us was assigned a room. I sat down on my bed briefly to collect my thoughts. I felt somewhat dizzy so I reclined back on the bed. My body felt unusually heavy. The next thing I recall, Kemi was hovering over me.

"YunJon! Wake up!" I blinked, confused. Her face, frantic, was staring down at me. Dark locks framed her face, so close they nearly brushed my cheek. I inhaled deeply.

"What is wrong? Did something happen?" I asked, my voice thick. I cleared my throat.

A look of relief flitted across her face. "You have been asleep for eight hours! At first we let you sleep uninterrupted, but we have been trying to wake you gently for the last hour or so. Nothing worked. I was concerned. What is wrong? Are you ill?"

"Eight hours?" I stuttered. I was confused. That has never happened to me before. I must have lost consciousness from exhaustion.

"What is wrong? What is going on?" Kemi asked. Her tone was severe.

My brain still foggy from deep sleep, I answered honestly before I could stop myself. "I could not sleep yesterday, what with my injury and everything that had happened. I suppose I simply lost consciousness."

"Lost consciousness? No one simply loses consciousness. What injury?" she exclaimed. Her hands were on my arms.

She did not know my shoulder had been wounded. And she did not mention Rij. Suddenly, I wanted to tell her everything. Just as I opened my mouth to do so, we were interrupted. I almost yelled at Kar and Striker as they swarmed in, invading our moment. The room instantly felt claustrophobic. Kemi snatched her hands away. I struggled to a sitting position.

"You are awake," said Striker.

"He was injured and no one told me. And he did not sleep at all yesterday!" said Kemi.

"Are you upset?" I asked her.

"Why did you not sleep yesterday?" asked Kar.

"How did you hurt yourself? Why was I unaware?" asked Kemi.

"Did it have something to do with the male you killed?" asked Striker.

"How did you hear about that?" I asked.

Silence filled the air at once. We all looked at each other. Any boundaries of propriety and position and accepted standards of privacy were gone. We were four people crammed into a tiny metal room under the ocean. I swallowed down the discomfort of adjusting rapidly to a new social structure.

Adapt or die, I thought in that moment. If Renee can do it, so can I.

"Meet in ten minutes in the central command unit. We can review everything. Kar, can you see if Luya can leave Renee briefly to join us?"

I needed time to clear my head. Everyone nodded and filed out, but not without a last glare from Kemi. Was it fueled by concern? Dare I hope?

By the time we reunited in the galley, I managed to clear my mind. I was feeling more alert and spry than I had in two days. The recuperative power of sleep is still, truly, the best medicine.

We settled in. Renee's health came first.

"I think it is a combination of a backlash from the adrenaline shot, stress and the pregnancy," said Kar.

"Can you elaborate?" I asked.

"I have never injected anyone with adrenaline before and I gave her a very large dose. I do not know how it affects people in the aftermath. I assume there is some kind of down period. We also do not know what is happening to her from the pregnancy and, in addition to all this, she just underwent a massive amount of stress."

"So did we," said Striker tightly, "and we are fine."

"Yes, but we were not born over a thousand years ago, impregnated within our first month in a new millennium and threatened with death for hours on end," snapped Kemi.

Tension spread through the room like wildfire.

"Calm! Please!" I spoke before anyone else erupted. I could see Striker's jaw tensing, Kemi's fists balling and Kar's eyes were shooting daggers.

I tried to even my breaths. I could feel myself absorbing everyone's tension and it was ratcheting up my heart-rate. "We are under immense pressure. We are operating under extreme and uncertain conditions. But we must not lose control or turn on each other. At this point, not just Renee's survival but all of our survivals depends on our ability to work together."

Striker's eyes unfocused for a moment, he took a deep inhale and exhale. Kar continued speaking, his voice wound tightly. "Thank you, YunJon. We are working with almost no medical equipment at all. We have very little access to any medical archives. There is no connectivity because we are underwater. To summarize, we are basically working blind and on sheer conjecture. Kemi and Luya developed a very basic autoimmune treatment to see if it can alleviate some of the symptoms, but since her diagnosis was based on a hypothesis, she is reticent to apply it. We are at an impasse."

Luya spoke. She was nervous. I could hear it. "Can you tell us more about what happened when you found her, Striker? It may help us glean what is wrong."

"When I met with the team that kidnapped her, she was unconscious. When she revived, she had no short term memory. She could not remember anything that had happened that day. It was not until we had been speaking for some time that I said something, I do not know what, that triggered her memory. It came rushing back to her. She responded very violently. She cried, trembled and her heart was racing. Before that she had appeared nervous but fine. Eventually, she fell asleep. When she woke back up again, hours later, she vomited, mumbled a few words and then slipped into the state you saw when we arrived."

By the time he stopped speaking, his brow was furrowed and his arms were crossed tightly over his chest.

Kar looked pensive. Kemi was thoughtful and appeared as though she wished to say something.

"What do you think, Kemi?" I asked.

She looked at us for a moment before speaking. Then she said, "I am trying to imagine this experience from Renee's position. For the first 15 days she was with us, she was in a coma regenerating her skin and recuperating from severe physical trauma.

When she revived, she experienced severe mental trauma. She processed the loss of her family and had to adjust to being an alien species in a world of physically and mentally different people. Then, when she was just beginning to gain an understanding of her immediate environment, she was thrust into danger of severe censorship by the Regulation Committee. Seeking out comfort with Ranger, she was accidentally impregnated. Her pregnancy has been extremely difficult. She has been physically ill from the beginning. Then she had to endure a harrowing escape alone and spend hours in the company of hostile Rangers, unsure of whether she would be eliminated at any moment."

She paused, looked down thoughtfully and then continued, "Perhaps it is not physical trauma. Maybe it is mental trauma. The body and mind are intertwined. Perhaps it is too much for her psyche to handle."

I glanced quickly at Striker. His jaw was tensed, but he was under control.

"It is just a hypothesis," Kemi was quick to say.

Luya looked stunned. "Of course," she murmured, her eyes wide. "Why did I not think of that?"

Wait. Striker is calling. I will be back shortly to continue.

Log Entry: R 285 O 3037 ID: Cont 2 YunJon

It is late. Everything I wanted to record earlier feels obsolete now. My surprise at Striker's confession is almost numbed by my exhaustion. He put us through an extremely rigorous training session this evening. But before that, he pushed his way into the room and sat down abruptly.

"Extreme circumstances such as these, constrained to a small space and with no specific role or duty to aid the mission, bring out the worst in my character," he said abruptly. "My mentor, the one I mentioned earlier, taught me to channel my energy into my mission. I trained my mind to stay rigidly on the task at hand."

He leaned forward, resting his hands on the floor. I could see his arm muscles ripple under his black jumpsuit.

"I am accustomed to being the leader, as you are. The added responsibility heightens my mental control. Yet I am not suited to lead a team of civilians. This should not be a problem most of the time. The moment we step foot on Continent 7, I will be able to take charge of our security. I can hire a team, scout out the area and manage our risk."

"So what is the problem, then?" I asked him warily.

"For the next three days, we will be locked in this underwater box. I have no task nor mission right now. There is nothing to focus on."

Beads of sweat broke out on his forehead. A vein throbbed. It must have cost him a tremendous amount to admit this.

I maintained direct eye contact despite a creeping sense of fear. I could feel the tension, frustration and violence radiating off his body. I was rapidly sweeping through all the psychology of leadership literature I had ever read.

"You are a very valuable member of our team. We are scientists. We have no knowledge of military and security matters. Without you, we stand little to no chance."

I spoke slowly, although I was nervous.

"What does our team need to do to prepare ourselves for our arrival on Continent 7?" I asked.

When he started speaking, his brow was furrowed and his voice tense. "We will be arriving into a truly unknown situation. There is no data on Continent 7. Nothing. None of my contacts could dig up anything for me. Therefore, we must approach this carefully. Rapid adaptability will be our greatest asset and we must be prepared for various outcomes."

His cadence calmed and his face slowly lost some of its grim tension.

"How can you best prepare the team, Striker?" I asked again, this time placing the stress on 'you.'

"I would recommend training sessions morning and evening as a group, plus individual training sessions. Each team member must be assessed for their strengths and assigned to the role in which they will best thrive. Then, when we face unknown situations, we can operate smoothly."

"Right. Please assume total responsibility for our training and preparation for Continent 7 over the next three days. Arrange the schedules. The only consideration is the medical supervision of Renee. We must be allowed ample time to care for her. Is this acceptable?"

Our eyes locked. The dim lighting cast shadows across his

face.

"Good," he grunted. "This is acceptable."

"Excellent," I replied with some relief. Managing people under duress is significantly more challenging than managing people in a controlled environment such as a lab.

"In the higher level ranks of the Rangers," he said, settling back and straightening his spine, "to show respect and honor for a colleague, we clasp each other's forearms. It marks an unbreakable contract of mutual trust and loyalty," said Striker. His eyes were locked on mine.

He extended his arm. I raised my arm to meet his. We gripped one another's forearms.

A smile rose to my lips. "I will keep us from killing each other, and you will keep them from killing us."

He laughed.

I wonder... are these the types of personal ties that Renee mourned when she realized where she was and what had happened? There is a depth here. It also feels dangerous. For how will I prevent it from clouding my rational judgment?

Renee

The room slowly comes into focus. A row of metal rivets run along the ceiling. One, two, three are missing. Sitting up is hard, but I do it. The room is small and shoddy. It's dank and smells like an old rusty car.

Pushing my hands down on the bed, I heave myself upward. Yeah, I don't recognize my surroundings. What's new? There's only so much freaking out I'm willing to participate in.

My left hand anchors me to the wall. The skin doesn't shock me anymore. Memories of what it used to look like are fading. Not even a twinge of sentimentality hits me at the realization. Who cares anymore? It's just a hand, and it works.

A rush of dizziness nearly bowls me over. Looking down at the floor to steady myself, I see my right hand resting on my lower abdomen, unconsciously, in that protective way you see with pregnant women. I'd always thought it was a conscious thing, to draw attention to the baby or to feel good. It's not, I guess? It's a subconscious thing, maybe?

God, but is there even a fetus anymore? Is it gone? Would I know? Would I have put my hand there if it wasn't?

My jumpsuit is in a mess on the floor. I lean over unsteadily and get dressed. Even easy movements like this are exhausting. But I don't feel sick. It's more like that feeling when your fever finally breaks and you're on the mend. Relief mixed with joy at the prospect of living pain-free for the foreseeable future.

The loose gray jumpsuit is an upgrade in every single way. That second-skin, Cirque de Soleil bodysuit did nothing but emphasize how much I don't look like anyone else. It was strangely grotesque, despite their whole asexualized existence.

The looseness of the suit not only downplays my figure, but has pockets scattered in handy places. Nice.

A metallic wrenching jerks my attention upward. There's no soft swooshes of near-invisible, mechanized doors here. But I find the ugly, glaring rub of metal on metal comforting. No one can sneak up on me on lithe, futuristic feet.

Luya walks in. She looks thin, thinner than usual. Her face is pinched and tired. Even her eyes are dulled.

"Luya! Are you ok?" My face pinches in concern. "You look ill."

She stares at me. That expression is new. Incredulity?

Then she laughs, but the exhaustion and weariness behind it is unnerving.

"Hey!" My worry is ratcheting up. Striding toward her, I grasp her shoulders. Her eyes meet mine. The skin around her eyes is tired. Thin wrinkles shoot out from the corners. Her eyelids droop down as if the weight of her thick lashes is too much to carry. To me, this is the first time she has ever looked beautiful. It's as if the emotion and exhaustion humanize her and give her face depth and poeticism. She's not just a mannequin. She's real.

I gently press down on her shoulders and we sit on the floor facing one another cross-legged.

"What's going on?" I query immediately.

"You were the one who was ill," she answers, her voice cracking slightly. "Very, very ill. I thought you were going to die. We all did."

"You don't look so thrilled to see me alive, eh?"

"How can you say such a thing? Of course I am happy to see that you are alive." She looks almost indignant.

Ah yes, irony. It's not a thing.

"Of course you are. It was just dark humor. It was my way of asking why, seeing as I'm alive and kicking, you have such a grim face? You seem upset. Oh! Has something happened to one of the team? Are they okay?" Suddenly, worry sweeps through me.

She inhales deeply. Her hands are clenched on her lap.

"Just tell me."

"Right," she says, blinking hard and fast. "The team is fine, well, more or less fine. It's you. When you were so ill, I tried a course of medicine. It's what we would use to suppress an auto-immune disease. I thought, we thought, your body might be rejecting the pregnancy and fighting against the baby, perceiving it to be an invasion. We thought that, maybe, the pregnancy simply wasn't viable and, in fact, might even kill you.

"The medicine did nothing. I did, much too late, what Kemi had alluded to but I was stupid enough to ignore until after the auto-immune treatment. I measured your brain chemistry, particularly serotonin, dopamine and norepinephrine. I compared the results to when you emerged from your coma and felt healthy. It was radically altered. So I regulated your brain chemicals according to the original measurements. You were so despondent and we could not find any physical reasons and nothing else was working. And you know what? You immediately started to stabilize."

"And my pregnancy?"

"I... I do not know. We do not have the medical equipment onboard to check. We could measure it by hormone levels, but yours are so, so varied at this point that it is impossible to tell. And I have no idea what the treatments I put you through might have done to," she pauses and swallows, "to harm you or the fetus."

"Am I still on medication now?"

"Yes, for your brain chemistry. Although I will taper you off soon. You responded quickly and well. Everything snapped back to their original levels almost immediately and they have stayed there. None of us quite understand why and we have not had time for more in-depth analysis."

"Why don't I remember anything?"

"I do not know."

Are those tears in her eyes? It's so hard to tell because they're dark. A funny feeling settles in my chest as I digest her words. Is it relief? Sadness? Do I want to put a kid through the experience of being a lifelong outsider? Maybe it's good if it doesn't happen.

Too many unanswered questions. I could drown in them.

She still looks really upset.

"Don't stress," I say eventually. I'm startled to find I really mean it. "It's all going to turn out, one way or another. I'm alive. You figured out how to keep me here another day."

"It does not have to turn out." Her face is twisted and anxious, her tone urgent. Emotions I've never seen before are sweeping across her features. Angry words just bubble out of her, exploding around me without warning.

"You almost died and I might have killed your baby with my unnecessary treatment!" she cried.

Where the hell did that come from? It's like a dam of emotion just broke and now that it's broken a whole lake is pouring out. How many years has that been bottled up inside?

"I almost did not save you! I may have killed the fetus! It is hopeless. I am hopeless." Her hands jerk in the air like an angry puppet. I'm basically paralyzed with astonishment at seeing such a display of emotion from one of these people.

Then it dawns on me. In this society, they don't really know or understand uncertainty. Everything is ordered, planned and controlled. They've probably got a protocol for how to go to the bathroom. They've never had to stare insecurity in the face and get on with life anyway.

"You can't be perfect under imperfect circumstances!" The words just roll off my tongue. There's a veritable deluge of emotion rolling around this room now. "What were you supposed to do? You did the best you could, and it was good enough. Not just good enough, I'd say, but phenomenal given the circumstances. I'm here. You're here. Stop feeling sorry for yourself. Life's messy."

Shock washes over her face. My words sound harsh even to my own ears, but I don't care because I know where that path she's walking leads. There's nothing as utterly pointless as self-flagellation.

"The fetus? Maybe I'm still pregnant. Maybe I'm not. I don't even know if I want to have it, anyway. If it doesn't make it, it's definitely not your fault, I can promise you that."

The words dangle in the air between us. She sniffs hard and roughly wipes her hand under her eye. I guess I'm not the only one who cries.

"We did this for you and the fetus. We wanted to save you and the fetus." Her words are weak and desperate. It's like the life has been kicked out of her. Her anger is all fizzled and gone. I guess this was the 31st century's version of an emotional breakdown.

"No, Luya," I say gently. "You didn't do this just for me. Every single one of you did this for yourselves too. Each of you was itching for a reason to get out of that half-life you had back there. I may have been the catalyst, but the desire was already fomenting, simmering under the surface. All you needed was the excuse. Otherwise you would have just turned me in and gotten on with your lives."

A pause extends and extends. It's definitely pregnant. Maybe like me. Maybe not.

"Do you really think so?" she finally says.

"Yes." My voice is softer now. Her gentle tone and question disarm me. Another pause extends across minutes. This time I feel compelled to fill it, somehow and someway, with words of comfort. But I don't. What could I say that I haven't already said?

At long last, she says, "I believe that you are right. Do you want to know where we are?"

Well, hello whiplash. That was one helluva change of subject.

"Uh yeah, that would be nice," I manage.

"We are on a vessel known as a submarine. This is a bullet-shaped, hollow metallic structure that is..."

"Luya. I know what a submarine is." I cut her off. It's rude, but for once I actually know what she's talking about.

"You do?" she exclaims. "Have you been on one before?"

"No. But they were pretty common back in my time. So we're underwater somewhere headed to Continent 7? How close? Who is with us?"

Striker's face flashes in my mind. I can see his dark, black eyes staring at me with an intensity that unnerves me even in memory. Where is he? Why isn't he here?

"We are extremely close to Continent 7. You have been unconscious for several days. Everyone is preparing for our landing. Kemi is recovering from a concussion and YunJon has an injury on his shoulder, but that is healing very quickly. Otherwise everyone is fine."

An urgent voice down the hallway yells out, "Luya! Get over here, now!"

She leaps nimbly to her feet. In a flash, she's at the door. Grasping the handle, she wrenches it open with phenomenal strength. I blink and she's gone.

My movements aren't nearly so spry. And I'm relishing having been left behind and forgotten. Being the center of attention is exhausting. I forgot how refreshing it is to go unnoticed.

RENEE

I make my way slowly to the door. I don't rush. They don't need me.

I'm going to soak it in. It's like home. The walls are made of old, battered metal. My fingers run over the right angle of the doorframe. It's a defined edge. Harsh, bold and recognizable. I love it.

I'm weak but at least I'm clear-headed. I feel like myself. Whatever they did worked. Why am I surprised? If they can regenerate my whole skin, why wouldn't they be able to calibrate brain chemistry?

But they can't erase my memories.

I'm not dwelling on that now. I'm tired of it. Tired of being sad. Tired of being in pain. I'll deal with that later if I have to. I'm alive. And I'm damn glad to be.

The hallway is small and dimly light. My gray boots scuff against the dented metallic floor. I follow the sound of voices and hover behind the corner of the wall. I don't walk into the room. Their words wash over me. That's YunJon. Then Kar. There's a female voice I don't recognize. Is that Luya speaking, now? Their voices rise and fall in cadence and volume. Someone interrupts someone else. Their speech moves naturally. While still muted by my standards, for them their tones are excited and nervous.

I can't eavesdrop forever so I step around the corner. It's clear this is the control room. It's compact and full of unrecognizable mechanical structures. Unlike the walls, these gadgets aren't battered and beaten. Sleek 3-D images project across the room, floating like glowing, semi-transparent lamps. They look so real I jerk in shock as Kar walks through one.

Everyone stops the moment I step into the room. I dreaded that. Their senses are so much keener than mine. For some odd reason, the memory of my first encounter with Kar surfaces, back when I thought he was a mutant Scandinavian. I cringe internally.

But all thoughts dissolve the moment I lock eyes with Striker. His face is bare. In the small room, he appears larger than I remembered. His black eyes flash under heavy, prominent brows. It's a hard face.

I hardly take a single breath and he's at my side. Gently, he settles his hands on my upper arms.

"You are well again. I am relieved. Luya informed us that you had responded to the treatment." His voice is deep and gravelly and steady. The intensity of his gaze burns me.

"Yes, thank you. How are you? It's good to see you all."

"We have been very concerned about your well-being," he says. His pitch black eyes are virtually unreadable to me. Yet memories of us together are still with me.

Unsure of how to respond, I squeeze his forearms in return.

"Luya tells me we are coming up on Continent 7. Don't let me distract you. I know you need to prepare," I say.

They avert their eyes away slowly. Striker is the last one to get back to work. I give him a weak smile. After he returns to his spot, I relax against the entryway's doorframe. They function like a well-oiled machine. There's a woman I don't recognize. She's bulky and bossy, snapping out orders about the submarine left and right. I like her. When she gazes at me, it's frank and open and curious. There's hardly anything in their actions akin to the popular sci-fi films of my time. I feel oddly cheated. There's no huge central screen. There's no clear central command. It's not even obvious who is in charge. Everything centers around 3-D imaging stations. Everyone is running their own piece of the puzzle. If I didn't know YunJon, I doubt I would even notice his subtle authority.

I watch for some time as they dart back and forth to discuss the upcoming timing, landing procedures, communications and contingency plans. I want to help, but I would be in the way. Their speech is quick but muted. It's a soft, flowing back-and-forth banter.

I have a flash to a memory from elementary school. I was working with a boy on a handout. The answers were so obvious to me. But he was struggling. I didn't get how he couldn't get it. It seemed so easy. With frustration, he looked at me and exclaimed, "How do you know the answers so easily?"

I could offer him a helluva lot more empathy now than I could back then.

I turn back to the calm of the hallway.

Don't ruminate.

I know enough about the mind to avoid that trap. Distract yourself. Focus on something else.

I wander down the hall and revel in my aloneness and the fact that, for once, no one cares what I'm doing or what I'm saying. The semi-familiarity of the construction is comforting as well. I could almost be back in my time.

The seclusion of my room beckons. There is nothing in it but a mat on the floor and a small pile of medical devices. I poke around in the pile, looking for a nutrition tube. I find one. I've never even opened one myself, I realize. They've been fed to me on a rigid schedule before now, like you would a small child incapable of even the simplest of tasks.

That's where YunJon finds me.

I'm sitting cross-legged on the floor, staring at the nutrition tube. Wordlessly, he crouches beside me and shows me how to open it. It's tricky. He watches as I drink.

"Renee."

That's all he says. The word is weighted.

I look into his compassionate eyes. They aren't frightening or ominous anymore. He's a kind man and a good leader. I doubted his integrity once but no longer. His actions are nothing short of extraordinary given the culture of the day.

"YunJon, would you have ever found your way here without me?"

I thought I didn't care. I thought I knew.

"I mean, would you have turned your back on everything you know? Left everything to go to Continent 7?" I say quietly.

"I have asked myself that question," he answers slowly. "I believe Kar and Luya might have eventually gone together. Striker probably would have as well. I cannot say with Kemi. Myself? It is doubtful I would have left. I was comfortable. I expect I would still be doing exactly what I was before."

"Are you… do you regret leaving?"

"I do not. I regret your pain and suffering. But I regret nothing else."

The tightness in my chest eases slightly at his words.

"Why are you and your team so different?"

"I would conjecture that only certain character types are driven to Research and Development. These are members of society with a natural tendency to question and a desire to learn and explore limits. Amongst that group, an even smaller minority leans toward Experimental Development. There is a very strong selection bias."

We fall into a silence.

"YunJon," I finally say. "I fear that my intelligence is not sufficient to meet the demands of your time. There will come a day when my novelty has worn off and you may start to see me as a liability."

I stare down at the floor. A long pause extends. My insides crinkle like a deflated balloon.

"Renee, you do not yet understand our society in its entirety. You cannot understand the impact you have or what sets you apart. It may not be immediately evident, but it will manifest with time. You have already proven to be an impetus for change and a stimulus for adaptation. However, you do not need to concern yourself with this. I am the team leader and I will ensure that everyone has a role and a function that is suited to their nature."

I smile apathetically.

"Go take care of the crew," I say, mustering a look of gratitude. "I will come along shortly."

He nods, gently rests a hand on my shoulder and stands to leave.

I was a researcher just like them, and I loved it. I had never been happier than when I was exploring new ideas and concepts.

I can barely remember my research topics now.

Suddenly, I'm furious at my own self-pity. Time to swallow a dose of my own hard medicine, the kind I so easily dished out to Luya earlier, and get the hell over it.

If I do end up being pregnant and having some kid? That poor bastard of a time experiment gone wrong will need every ounce of my strength. There's no space for self-pity.

Suddenly, I lurch forward hard. Gasping in shock, I place both my hands on the floor to brace myself. It feels like something struck the submarine. The floor is vibrating wildly. Crawling to the doorframe, I use it for support as I attempt to stand. The room shakes. Kemi runs down the hallway. She cries my name and grabs me as the submarine lurches hard again. We smash against the wall and pain shoots through my shoulder.

"We are landing!" she cries.

"On Continent 7? Already?" I yell back. It's difficult to hear. The engines are overbearingly loud now.

"Yes! Come with me!" She turns, grabs my hand and we stumble down the hall to central command. The tension is nearly overbearing. This time, no one looks up.

CHAPTER FIFTY-NINE

"Renee's here!" shouts Kemi as soon as we enter.

"Get her buckled in!" Striker commands without even looking up. Kemi pushes me down into a seat to the left of YunJon, who is already seated in the center of the room. She buckles me in. Her hands are quick like lightening. I don't protest or try to do it myself, knowing it will only slow her down. As soon as I'm locked in, she runs to the seat next to me. Everyone is sitting down now, even Striker, and a large 3-D cube blinks to life.

There is total silence now but for the hum of the engine, which is starting to quiet. All our eyes are fixated on the rotating block in front of us. I'm really nervous.

The cube dissolves and an image comes slowly into focus. Three men and one woman appear. They aren't smiling.

"Greetings," says YunJon calmly. "My name is YunJon, formerly a SciMed Team Lead on Continent 2. I am accompanied by former members of my team Kar and Kemi, as well as former SciMed Team Lead Luya. To my right is Striker, formerly of Ranger Command, and to my left is Renee. We request entry to Continent 7."

He doesn't explain anything else. The group on the screen say nothing for a long moment. They are taking us in one by one. Their eyes stay locked on mine for a long, long time. I don't dare turn and look around at my team. I force myself to stare back.

When the woman speaks, her voice is harsh. I jump slightly.

"We are the gatekeepers of Continent 7. We hold absolute control over who does and does not enter. If you are denied entry, you will immediately depart. Failure to comply and you will be eliminated."

Her voice is cold and hard. Like me, she's wearing a similarly nondescript jumpsuit. These gatekeepers are the first humans I have seen who show age. Their faces are lined and beaten. But they don't look weak. No, not weak at all.

"Renee. What is your occupation?"

I nearly jump out of my seat but for my seatbelt. What the hell am I supposed to say? Since arriving here, the only thing I've done is try and stay alive.

"I'm a survivor," I finally say. I'm surprised at how loud and clear my voice sounds.

One of the men on the screen mumbles something I don't understand.

"Survivor of what?" she asks.

"Time. I'm a survivor of time."

The audio goes mute. They're conferring with one another. It blinks back on and the oldest man in the group speaks. His authority is undeniable. His voice is weathered and layered with heaviness, as though burdened with a lifetime of suffering.

"Survivor, you are welcome on Continent 7. Your cohorts, however, are not. Why should we allow four highly-ranked committee members, one no less a Ranger, safe entry to our continent? What need have they? What cause have they for refuge? No. This is yet another infiltration attempt and you are nothing but the bait. It is a clever attempt, I will concede that, but no. They are not welcome."

His eyes burn like fire, even through the 3-D display.

I tilt my head and stare. What? Why would the government try and infiltrate Continent 7? The team told me it was allowed autonomy. It was 'good' for society. Was the team lying? Or were they wrong? Were they tricked? Or is this dude just paranoid?

My brain leaps into overdrive. They can't turn them away. They can't. There's nowhere for them to go. I've got to change their minds. I'm the only one they trust enough to let in. I've got to speak for them. So what type of person would they actually let onto Continent 7? Who needs to escape? Who would they let come in? An honest person? Dishonest? Certainly a person with a compelling enough reason to leave everything known behind. That means someone who is desperate.

I've got to say something. I'm running out of time. This is our only chance. I'm going to make the riskiest gamble of my life. I'm going to tell the bald truth.

"You are wrong," I say loudly. I'm terrified. But I don't let my voice quaver. "Their need is as real as my own. And they are not government spies trying to infiltrate your continent."

I'm wracking my brain, putting together the puzzle pieces of my companions. Nothing like the pressure of imminent death to force a picture into stark clarity.

"Kar is a hacker who uses illegal drugs to enhance his attention. Kemi can read minds and has kept it hidden from everyone, including the Regulation Committee. Luya gambled her career on a risky project and lost. She's the most normal, but she's in love with Kar, which makes her kind of crazy."

I don't dare look around me. My eyes stay locked on the images of the people projected on the screen. My heart is about to beat its way out of my chest.

"Striker, the Ranger? He's a thief and a sexual deviant." Ouch. But that's how his society sees him, which in turn makes me a sexual deviant, too. Moving on. "YunJon, our team lead, is the worst of us all. He hid my presence from the Regulation Committee until he could destroy research and evidence. He defied their commands and organized our escape."

I stop talking. I have ruined everything. I'm sure of it. But now that I'm in it, I've got to finish. Go strong.

"Everyone's need is equal to my own. No one is attempting infiltration, but escape. I won't come if they can't. And if you turn us away, we might as well just stay and let you eliminate us because that fate will be kinder than what awaits us elsewhere. We have nowhere else to go. And I will stay with my team. I will not betray them in our final hour. They didn't betray me, and they had every single reason do so."

The silence is intense.

"Is this true?" asks the older man on the screen, the one who is so clearly in charge. There's something gleaming in his eye. He's looking at YunJon.

"Yes," he chokes out. His voice is funny.

"We will consult."

The screen blinks off. They're gone. Well. That could have

gone worse? Maybe they'll change their minds?

"Renee," Kar's voice sounds pained. I turn toward him, ready for harsh words and chastisement at having thrown the team under the bus.

"How did you know these things?"

I'm so surprised by his question I'm speechless.

"She watched you carefully," said Kemi quietly. "It is the same thing she did with me. Then she just guessed. She played up her suspicions and augmented them here and there for impact. She was trying to prove that we are not infiltrators by highlighting all the reasons we would not be trusted by the Committee."

She turns and looks at me. Her eyes flash gold and her face is more confident and at peace than I have ever seen it. "You can tell them I am right, Renee."

"She's... she's right." My words are stuttered. I want to apologize for what I did, but it was the only gamble I could see playing to our advantage. I think it might have given us a chance. But what if it didn't?

"Well done," says Striker. His voice rings out strongly and confidently. His eyes pierce my own as I twist to see him, frustrated by the constraints of the straps on the chair. I feel, once again, that incredible connection. Butterflies surge in my stomach.

"It was a good gamble," he continues. "Bold and risky, but it may well work."

Apparently he had no qualms about being publicly called out as a sexual deviant.

"Kemi," he went on, his brows furrowed and irritation creeping into his voice. "To what extent was she accurate in her assessment of you? You should have told us about this earlier. It would have come in extremely helpful. We might have planned ways to use it to our advantage."

"Helpful?" she gasped, looking completely aghast. "What do you mean, helpful?"

"Do you understand finally?" said YunJon. His eyes are locked on her. "If we make it, you will no longer need to suppress your nature. You can develop and hone your skills. You no longer have to hide your true identity."

My eyes dart back and forth. Before anything else can be said, Kar interrupts.

"Back online in three, two, one, now."

The image blinks to life. This time seven people face us. My eyes run across the group. Terror clenches my gut. They are rugged and mean-looking. I lock eyes with the man to whom I spoke earlier. I force myself not to look away.

"We patrol Continent 7 mercilessly. Committee spies who are intent on undermining our existence are treated with no clemency. They will face eventual death once we have extracted everything they can offer us."

Chills run down my spine.

"With the new information that has come to light, we have altered our initial judgment. We grant YunJon, Striker, Luya, Kar, Kemi and Renee access to Continent 7. Your submarine will now be allowed docking privileges. You have exactly ten minutes to exit the submarine whereupon the submarine and crew must depart immediately. Failure to do so will result in seizure of your craft and the arrest of the crew. The six of you will be granted temporary housing on the dock where you will be debriefed by our team. When the debriefing is complete, you must ensure your own survival. That is the way of Continent 7. There is no negotiation."

The screen blinks off.

Renee

"I am receiving coordinates for the docking bay," says Kar. He squints at his 3-D display. A look of unusual tension mars his brow before he speaks again, "Seven minutes until arrival."

"You have five minutes to gather essential items and meet at the loading gate," YunJon yells.

Kemi and I dash down the hallway to where I woke. She gestures for me to wait in the room and darts off. Moments later, she returns with a satchel and hands it to me. She thrusts items at me faster than I can stuff them in the pack. Frantically, I rush to shove everything in. The moment it is full, she rips it from my hands and pulls it closed, slinging it over her shoulder. We hurry down the hallway. My God but she is light on her feet. I'm out of breath and gasping in moments, still weak from my illness. By the time we reach the gate, I'm clutching my sides.

Striker is waiting for us. He pulls me to him and wraps an arm around my shoulder, using the other to brace us against the wall. Behind me, his body is rock solid. He holds me in place so firmly I struggle to breathe. YunJon is the last of us to appear from around the corner. He's just in the nick of time. A siren rings. The lights blink. A harsh scraping noise grates loudly and the submarine jolts hard. I don't fall but only for Striker's steadying hold.

CHAPTER SIXTY

"Everyone accounted for," belts out Striker, his voice booming over my shoulder.

"Go! Now!" yells YunJon over the noise of the siren.

"Like we trained," barks Striker.

Kar scrambles up the ladder first. Bright sunlight pierces down the tunnel, causing me to clench my eyes against the light. Luya and Kemi follow quickly after him. Striker grips my shoulders and maneuvers me toward the ladder. He wraps his large hands around my waist and I gasp as he lifts me halfway up the ladder. I grip it tightly with my hands and settle my feet on the rungs, pulling myself up one at a time. He's right below me. I can feel his eyes locked on me.

The higher I get, the more blinding the light. By the time I reach the top, it's so bright I squint my eyes shut. Hands grip my upper arms and lift me. I'm weightless for a moment before feeling solid ground beneath my feet. Voices break out around me. The second my arms are released, I raise my hands to my eyes to block the harsh glare of the sun before opening them.

There's a wooden dock under my feet. It's made of thick, solid slabs of wood. Through the cracks there is dark, murky water visible. The waves slap against the wooden pillars anchoring it to the ocean floor below. I sense Striker behind me, pushing me forward.

My eyes adjust slightly. I squint through the pain of the bright sun to stare at our immediate surroundings. A busy, messy, chaotic dock greets my eyes. Only feet from us, I count at least four unknown armed men and women. I don't recognize the weapons, but they're definitely weapons. Walking toward us up the dock, flanked by six others, is the same man from the 3-D image onboard. Despite the distance, there's no mistaking him. His presence resonates even more powerfully in person.

I spare a moment to glance over his head. A dense forest of green lines the horizon, interrupted here and there with buildings. But my eye is drawn down to a distant bustling dock that lines the shore. Our own thin dock juts out perpendicular from this larger one. Ships line the length as far as I can see. Men and women, similarly dark of hair and skin, but in all manner of clothing, work and shout. Many turn to stare at us. Some hold strange-looking machines in their arms. Most glare in our direction, their black eyes glinting under harsh, furrowed brows.

Striker's hand lightly rests on my back and my team fans out around us. Inhaling deeply, I stiffen my spine and stand tall. The delegation is almost upon us. I meet the eyes of the older man as he closes in. He is enormous, the same size as Striker, and is as thickly muscled. Striker's hand tenses on my back. Kemi takes a subtle step towards me.

Then they are upon us. His voice is deep and booming. The words echo loudly across the dock.

"Welcome to Continent 7."

About the Author

Jessica Eise writes both fiction and nonfiction. When she is not writing, she is researching and studying communication at Purdue University, where she specializes in organizational communication and engaged scholarship. Jessica's former pursuits have carried her across the nation and globe, affording her many unforgettable opportunities such as interviewing two presidents and writing on the former home to the dodo bird, the island of Mauritius. Today, she frequently travels to Colombia to conduct research on climate change and coffee farmers. When not writing or researching, you can find her biking somewhere on the back roads of Indiana or, of course, curled up around a good book!

Visit Jessica's website at www.JessicaEise.com
Follow her on Twitter @JessicaEise

88016998R00192